Bessie
Virtual Sorceress

Her amazing adventures through time and space!

By Gib Check

BESSIE HOWARD, VIRTUAL SORCERESS
HER AMAZING ADVENTURES THROUGH TIME AND
SPACE!

Copyright Gib Check, 2021

Check It Out Publishing
Friendship, Wis.

ISBN 978-0-578-86090-9

Manufactured in the United States of America
First printing February 2021

ACKNOWLEDGEMENTS

Many thanks to Ruthie, my loving and usually understanding spouse for being such a help with this novel – not to also mention the long time support of family and friends, whom I often nagged to read parts of this thing. And a special thanks to editor, Rob Bignell, for working to put another of my books between its covers.

DEDICATION

Dedicated to my loving hardworking spouse, Ruthie.

"Magic is just science we don't know yet."
– Arthur C. Clarke

Prologue

The torrential rain had finally stopped, but another towering mass of thunderheads had moved in. Laced by lightning their blackening undersides promised much more and very soon. During the brief interlude Earth's young sun shot slanted rays onto a Triassic beach. As the sea rolled in on long swells, tall cycads further in stood amid soaked giant-sized coleopterous ferns bent to the ground.

Emerging from the ferns, a small amphibian scuttled toward the sea. High above, a pterosaur instantly spotted it. Parting a long beak of needle-sharp teeth, it spiraled downward. Chancing to glance up, the amphibian saw the huge wings gliding in straight at it. Breaking for the water, it splashed in a split second before the predator's outstretched talons could snatch it up!

Foiled and frustrated, the pterosaur landed on a dune. Darting bird-like glances all around, it caught a glint nearby. Hopping over, it looked down at a small plastic bottle. The label read, "50 coated aspirin/caffeine free/81 mg." Uncaring of that, the pterosaur bent to bite it up when...*Flash! Bang!*

Wings askew, the startled creature skittered away. When safely distant it looked back – uncomprehendingly – at what hovered over the sand. Nothing it saw looked the least bit familiar, neither what sat in the chair, nor the computer monitor in front of it. When whatever this was abruptly sank to the ground, its wary witness backed up even more. But then, when reaching down for the bottle, the strange thing made a pushing motion...*directly toward the reptile!*

The early Triassic had not yet evolved many species who so fiercely guarded their hunting territories as this one.

Amber eyes ablaze and great wings fully spread, the pterosaur screeched furiously at the intruder to chase it off.

In turn, the intruder only stared back for a moment. Then, raising the bottle and wagging a finger, its mouth formed words. But they made no sound, nor could its eyes be seen behind the tinted visor. Quickly facing the monitor again, the strange thing leaned back in the chair, and...*Flash! Bang!* Nothing was there!

All of this soon forgotten, the pterosaur was aloft once more and looking for something, *anything,* to eat!

Chapter 1

Connie Howard poked her head into the computer room. "Ben, honey, in a little while Bessie and I will be star gazing. Like to join us?"

Eyes fixed on the monitor, her seven year old shook his head. "No, Mom, I'm gaming Jeremy from school!"

"OK, dear," she said. For Connie his preoccupation with gaming actually was OK, provided he added in other things besides. Which Ben did, anything from building tree forts with his pals, to bicycling off with them to who knows where, and kicking, batting and tossing around whatever ball they had. Fortunately her combined threats and bribes got him to do schoolwork and to even pick up his room now and then.

As for her disappointment with his lack of interest in her favorite pastime, she smiled to herself that one out of two wasn't bad. Entering the den, she called out, "Bessie, honey, come out, come out wherever you are!"

A squeaky yell came back, "Coming, Mommy, I've got your knapsack!"

Smile spreading, she recalled her five year-old's face lighting up when told that tonight she'd not only be taught how to use Mommy's telescope, but would help with setting it up. Seeing her darting in and out ever since, Connie fig-ured her willful little scamp was talking the sun into setting even sooner!

Connie's old family telescope stood in its accustomed corner in the den. Walking over to it, she patted it like an old friend. Though actually, it was, her great grandmother having bought it when Teddy Roosevelt was President.

Qualifying as an antique, the tube's scroll work included

the constellations, Halley's comet, the best known at the time, and all eight planets, Pluto having to wait for another fifteen years. Built of steel and heavy to move around was a draw-back. But the saving grace were the lenses, these exception-ally ground and polished, and able to magnify distant ob-jects with amazing clarity. The lenses alone had made the scope well worth passing on until it was Connie's.

Fairly young herself when shown how to use it, she easily pictured Bessie as the next owner. Before then Bessie needed to know a lot more than she already did. Luckily, with Wis-consin's clear skies offering excellent viewing, tonight was perfect to get her started.

Hearing some scuffling and grunting behind her, she turned to see her old knapsack being dragged over the carpet by Bessie. Big blue eyes barely seen beneath Bessie's Green Bay Packers cap, she had her long reddish-brown hair, or most of it, scrunched up inside it. Hoisting up the knapsack, she grinned, "Here's our stargazing things, Mommy! Let's go!"

Connie held up a hand. "Whoa, honey, I'll take that. It's too much for you."

More independent with each passing month, Bessie's vigorous headshake dropped the cap down over her eyes. Pushing it back up, she wagged a finger, "No-no, Mommy, I'm fine! I'll hold the door for you!"

Connie laughed, "Okay, little Miss Helper, please do!"

As she did so, Connie squeezed by with the 'scope. Setting it down on the stoop to get a better grip, she saw Bessie already hopping down the steps. Connie started to tell her to slow down, but too late. Feet somehow tangled in the strap, Bessie tumbled head over heels into the grass.

"Oh, honey!" Connie exclaimed. "Are you okay?"

Bessie leaped to her feet. "I'm fine, Mommy! Let's get set up!"

"All right, you find a good open spot, and I'll follow."

Trailing her, Connie smiled ruefully over this latest pratfall. Her youngest was always in a rush to see and do so much. With her little head so abuzz she seldom watched where she was going. The resulting scrapes, cuts and bruises had Connie constantly digging for disinfectant and bandages.

When well away from the big oak, Bessie stopped and looked straight up. Deciding there was enough viewable sky, she stamped her foot. "Right here, Mommy, this is good!"

Obligingly setting down the 'scope, Connie let out a breath. "Whew! Honey, you need to grow bigger to carry this! It's heavy!"

Bessie stretched way up. "No I won't! I'm already taller than my friends!"

For all Connie knew, her daughter's clumsiness might be due to an early and very awkward growth spurt.

Again staring up, Bessie wrinkled her face. "It's still too light to see Mars."

Turning toward the settee beneath the oak, Connie said, "Come along, honey, we will when it's darker." Taking a seat, she patted the cushion next to her. "Sit yourself down and I'll teach you a few things."

Still not seeing a single star showing and somewhat mollified, Bessie plunked down, and so did the cap over her eyes. Turning it backward, she beamed up at Connie. "All right, Mommy, now teach me everything!"

As a parent, and also a first grade teacher, Connie knew how kids her daughter's age needed to know *everything*. She knew, too, that Bessie's curiosity burned more insistently than nearly anyone's. Only last week she'd fired a non-stop barrage of questions as they moon-watched through the 7X50 binoculars. These being too bulky for Bessie's small hands to grip, Connie had propped them up on the picnic table to steady them. Ungainly positioning aside, Bessie's few tantalizing glimpses of the Moon's cratered surface had merely whetted her appetite to see more, much more.

Watching her squirm, Connie smiled bemusedly. "My, my, such an eager beaver tonight! So, let's begin." She pointed to the 'scope. "With nighttime coming on, the air gets cooler, so it has to sit for awhile."

Instantly came, "Why, Mommy?"

Dropped into her teacher mode, and at her best, Connie nodded. "This lets the lenses adapt to the cooler temperature and not fog up." Next she pulled out a penlight from the knapsack. Clicking it on, she aimed it at Bessie. "You've seen me use this out here before to see what we're doing. You've also seen what's different about it, right?"

"I know it shines red. But why?"

"The regular shiny white light causes our irises..." Circling her eyes with her fingers, Connie closed them together. "...to get smaller. This lowers our night vision to where we can't see as well. Red light doesn't do that so much." She next pulled from the knapsack her latest copy of Astronomy Magazine. Placing it on her lap, she spread out the monthly star map. Pointing to one of the constellations, she began, "Remember this one? It's–"

Clapping her hands, Bessie finished, "That's Orion! The easiest to find!" When seeing The Hunter through the binoculars, she'd been fascinated by the star-clustered nebula at his belt.

"Good for you, that's right!" Connie next pointed out the map's plane of the ecliptic designating tonight's most viewable planets. "We'll first see the brightest one low in the western sky. Of course, you already know which one that is."

These days Bessie imitated her. "Of course, Mommy, that's Venus!"

"Correct and next Saturn will appear higher to the

southwest. Tagging along behind will also be–"

"Mars!" Bessie squealed. "The planet I love the most!"

Putting a finger to her lips, Connie laughed, "Shh! I think the neighbors heard you. But honey, I'm curious. What is it that you love about it?" In asking, she doubted that anyone at any age could easily answer that, about anything.

Bessie simply felt that Mars was hers and hers alone. Automatically looking up trying to spot it, she saw instead the first points of light in deepening dark blue. Bessie jump-ed up and pulled Connie toward the telescope. "Come on, Mommy!"

Connie could set it up blindfolded by now. Though it still wasn't fully dark, she handed over her penlight. "Here, sweetie, turn it on and hold it steady for me, all right?"

Suddenly all seriousness, Bessie bobbed her head. "I will!" And again her hat slipped down. Too impatient to fool with it now, she yanked it off and dropped it then dutifully aiming the light at the mount, she held it as steady as she could.

Taking another peek through the eyepiece, Connie made a final focusing adjustment. "There you are, Mars! Just perfect!" She beckoned to Bessie. "Now you look! Quick! Before it drifts out of view!"

Bessie already knew from her mom that Earth's rotation caused this, rather than Mars "drifting" away. Instantly bent to the eyepiece, she shifted around for a moment, Suddenly she froze, "Woo-hoo, Mommy! I see it really clear!"

Knowing something very special was happening, Connie was filled with delight, "Great, sweetie, and you can see why it's called the Red Planet!"

Not budging an inch, Bessie came back, "We should call it the orange one!"

Connie laughed, "You're right, we should! Now can you see the polar cap on top like our own?"

Turning from the eye piece, Bessie excitedly poured it out so fast that Connie could hardly follow. "The big book on the coffee table shows our north one with polar bears and the south one with penguins! But Mars has no air to breath, so none of them live up there, right? Oh! And even for them it's way too cold!"

Again Connie laughed, "Do you know what you are?"

Bessie giggled, "A chatterbox?"

"Yes but I like that!" A top-notch teacher, Connie not only valued her students' questions but prompted them to ask even more. Tonight however with barely keeping up, she missed part of Bessie's next remark. "Slow down, dear! Say again?"

"The book said it's so cold that the gas in the..." First finding the right word, she said it carefully. "...at-mos-phere freezes. But it's not like the gas in your car, right?"

"Right, it's what we call carbon dioxide." Anticipating the next question, Connie headed her off. "When frozen it's the same as that dry ice I showed you."

"You mean the smoky kind?"

"Yes, it was frozen CO_2, and Mars also has that."

Bessie again repeated, "See-oh-two! Brr! That was really cold!"

"And so is Mars. It's cold enough during its winters to freeze the CO_2 into snow. Our image here shows the polar cap as a patch of white on top. The reason we–"

Too quick for her this time, Bessie cut in, "Why can't we see the other one?"

"I was about to explain that. You see, our own planet tilts," Cupping her hands, she angled them. "Like this and so does Mars. That's why we can see one of its snowy polar caps at a time."

"Isn't there any snow in the middle of Mars?"

Connie thought, good question. "The middle of Mars is warmer than its polar caps. We call that part–"

Breaking in again, Bessie pronounced it carefully, "The ee-kway-ter." She raised a finger as if at a lectern. "We have one too but it's very hot!"

Seeing the finger, Connie thought her daughter was more like her with each passing day but smarter probably.

"Yes, dear, and the Martian equator gets warm too during its summer. But even then, the nighttime temperature drops lower than our coldest winters in Wisconsin." As far as she knew, the latest NASA data said the summertime equatorial temperature dropped to over 160 degrees below zero Fahrenheit.

Bessie muttered to herself, "I'll have to dress warm and bring my own air."

Connie wasn't sure she'd heard that right. "I'm sorry, dear, but what do you mean? For when?"

Bessie answered unhesitatingly, "When I go there." She said it as if already aboard a spaceship bound for Mars.

Letting it pass, Connie said, "That's fine, dear. Before we go in take one last look."

The earth's rotation had again shifted the telescope's field of view. Bessie saw only the planet's disappearing edge. "I can't, it's almost gone!"

After readjusting the mount, Connie urged, "Hurry before it moves away!"

As taught, Bessie carefully held her hands away to not accidentally bump the tube out of alignment. Unwilling to risk Mars drifting from sight, she said without looking up, "I wish we could do this all night. When I'm a grown-up astronomer, I will!" After another moment passed, she sighed. "It's nearly gone again." Looking up at the little red dot, she kept looking at it.

Letting her be for a slow count to ten, Connie patted her shoulder. "I'm proud of you dear for doing so well, but that's enough for one night. Now I need you to help me take everything inside."

Still looking up, Bessie nodded absently. "I will."

Another time check made Connie raise her voice. "I mean *now,* dear!"

Spell broken and resigned to her fate, being in bed instead of out here, Bessie sighed again, "All right, Mommy, but someday..." facing Connie, she pointed toward Mars. "...I'm going there!"

None of the determination in those big blue eyes was lost on Connie. "You know, sweetie, it won't surprise me at all if you do!"

Chapter 2

Mid-March had blown in an unseasonable foot and a half of snow on central Wisconsin. Between bad driving condi-tions and people slipping on icy walks, Covington Memorial Hospital's emergency room was having a very busy day.

Bessie lay stretched out on an examining table. On one side Connie anxiously hovered over her. On the other side, Dr. Myers checked the back of her head. Looking up, he said, "This doesn't look serious, Connie. For now just go wait in the reception area, OK? I'll get back with you as soon as I can."

He was not only their family physician but a long-time friend. Taking him at his word, she nodded, "Sure, Tom!"

Hurrying out to the reception room, she keyed Rob's number on her cell. Hating to bother him at work, she knew that he and partner, Marsh Perry, were busier than ever these days. But even so, he'd certainly want to know about Bessie. When he answered, she began filling him in.

Rob interrupted, "She fell off the ladder? Jeez, hon, doing what!?"

"Dear, the wind tore off a big branch and dropped it on the roof in front. We almost had it down when she slipped off the ladder and hit her head."

"OK, but on what? There's nothing out there but snow drifts!"

Connie sighed. "You know her, dear. She managed to find the only solid thing, my big clay planter next to the window."

He sighed right back. "Yeah, with Bess that figures. So how is she?"

"From what Tom Myers told me, he doesn't think that it's serious. But just to make sure, he's giving her a head scan."

Normally a jokester, Rob sounded anything but. "Look, sweetie, they've mostly cleared the roads by now. If you want, I can get over there pretty soon."

"No, there's no point in you coming all the way over from Madison. Except for a bruise and a headache, she's probably fine. Later I'll have her keep ice on it and feed her aspirin. Trust me, dear, our Bessie's a lot tougher than she seems."

Relieved somewhat, he laughed. "I guess, but also the clumsiest! It's a wonder she's survived this long."

"Dear, she's having another of her growth spurts. She's all long arms and legs. And none of them very coordinated." Connie smiled at her cell. "We just need to keep her alive till she outgrows this."

"Well, we are pretty busy with Marsh's latest VR brainchild. So if she's all right I'll stay put. But sweetie, give me a call with any more news."

After telling him she would, Connie either thumbed aimlessly through magazines in the lobby or paced back and forth. Again checking the time, she thought, Come on, Tom!

Annie, the elderly receptionist, knew the Howard's quite well. "Connie, the Doc said to tell you the scan shows Bessie's OK. He'll be out here any minute."

Letting out held breath, Connie waved back. "Thanks, Annie, and sorry for wearing holes in your carpet."

She laughed. "Dear, we need to get rid of that old thing anyway."

A moment later, Myers appeared at the end of the hall. Giving Connie a thumbs up, he motioned for her to join him. Walking her back down the hall, he nodded, "She's good to go after a last set of vitals." He added, while ushering her into a spare examining room, "It's a mild concussion and no fracture, so they'll free her up shortly and then I want to show both of you what I found on her scan."

As they sat down at the examining table, Connie asked, "So what was that?"

Myers shrugged. "It's nothing bad but I'll wait till Bessie's here too,"

Connie knew he wouldn't be doing this if it wasn't important. "You might as well tell me, Tom. You know I won't just sit here and wait."

Knowing her pretty well, he shook his head. "Right, you won't." Instead of bringing up Bessie's chart, he then asked, "How old is she, by the way? Sixteen?"

"No, not till next December."

Myers' eyebrows went up. "She's tall for her age. 'Course, she always has been." He chuckled. "If we wrapped her up with all the bandages we've used since she was little, she'd be a mummy. How does she get so banged up like this?"

Connie pointed to her head. "There's so much buzzing around up here that she's unconscious at times."

"Well, luckily the back of her head was only bruised. Keep ice on it until the swelling goes down and have her take it easy the rest of the day."

"I will. but can't you at least give me a hint about her scan?"

Sighing, Myers relented, "All right but I'll have to repeat this when she's here. The scan's image showed me something that's…"

At the door a nurse practitioner interrupted, "Excuse me, Doctor…and hi Connie!" she added a smiling headshake. "Right now Bessie's the one who's scanning our new scanner to see how it works. She'll be right on my heels as soon as the technician chases her out."

Myers laughed. "Thanks, Joyce, I'll chase her home from here."

A moment after the RNP left, Bessie was at the door. "Hi again, doctor. Mom, they want me out of here, so let's go!" Her wavy reddish brown hair was piled up behind her head by a wrap-around cold pack.

Myers waved her in. "First, take a chair young lady. I want to show you and your mom what I found on your head scan."

When Bessie was seated beside Connie, he turned his laptop to partly face them. Tracing a finger over her skull's image, he inscribed a glowing trace line around part of it. After keying in a four quadrant divider, he pointed to the bottom-left quad. "I've highlighted this lowest part of the temporal lobe that rests atop the cerebellum. It's the inferior temporal cortex, or what we call the ITC." Looking at both of them, he asked, "You with me so far?"

Connie nodded. "I had some of this in college."

Bessie started to say, while shaking her head, "No, it was never...Ouch!" Reaching beneath the cold pack, she gingerly rubbed the base of her skull.

Connie placed a hand on Bessie's shoulder. "You okay, sweetie?"

Bessie winced. "If I keep my head still." She carefully turned it toward Myers. "My Biology class never mentioned this...ITC. What does it do?"

He asked, "Sure you're okay?"

"I'm fine!"

"All right. And so..." Promptly tracing another line dividing her brain's side view from top to bottom, he pointed toward the ITC location. "...we use it to see forms of all types. Both the amygdale and the hippocampus are structured here within the temporal lobe. Crucial for spatial navigation and memories of past experiences, they also decide which route we take from one place to another. In any case, these two parts are linked to the ITC."

And then, more emphatically, "Bessie, it turns out that yours is much, much larger than average. First of all, this condition isn't harmful in any way." As she started to reply, he held up a hand. "You know that I also work over at UW's Computer Research Center, right?"

Literally born into a cyber-linked society, Bessie was an expertly functioning part of it. Interest sparked, she nodded eagerly, or started to. "Ouch!" Rubbing her head again, she muttered, "Sure, I've seen you there during our class tours."

Connie frowned. "Tom, do we really need this? I'd just as soon get her out of here and home."

Bessie motioned to her, "No mom, I'm fine. Besides, I want to hear this."

Myers held up both hands. "It's up to you, ladies. I can either fill you in on my neurology work or let it go, which-ever you want."

Mother and daughter traded glances. Getting a nod from Connie, Bessie replied, "Please do. Doctor. The people at the Center have told us science majors about their work, but I'm clueless about yours."

Myers returned a vigorous nod of his own. "Along with my duties and their own, the Center welcomes participation from *you* young people. Especially those of you with advanced computer skills. But you already know that." He then grinned, "Don't nod, OK?" They all laughed. He went on, "And Bessie this is where you come in."

This surprised her. "Oh? How so?"

He leaned toward her, "Your mom here says you're more talented than anyone with using virtual reality headsets." He paused. "What do you young people call this? Multimedia immersion? Augmented Reality? Or what?"

Though still not quite sure where he was going with this, but beginning to suspect, she answered slowly, "It depends...on which of these...you mean. My dopey brother uses Augmented, or AR, to hand-control his silly games. With total immersion, my friends and I just go with VR, or Virtual."

He nodded more vigorously than before. "Yes and so do my younger assistants! At any rate, your mom and dad say you're exceptional with this!" Eyes fixed intently on hers, he leaned even closer. "So *are* you!?"

Bessie didn't like his sudden closing of their personal space. Liking even less to lie, even by omission, she hedged, "Not...necessarily. My dad's business partner is a genius with designing their headsets. So Dad brings home the latest ones for me and my brother to try. You add in our friends also trying them, we all do pretty well. You know?" Leaving her half truth there, she watched him guardedly.

Myers replied excitedly, "Your dad's units are proving to be an important part of our research with AI! Oh, and by that I mean..."

She cut in, "Doctor, we knew about AI back in third grade."

Oblivious to her dryness he went on, "Your dad's headsets help tremendously too! Which is where you come in!"

Mouth tightening, OK, now I get it! Bessie stayed silent.

As Myers shifted uneasily beneath Bessie' unwavering gaze, Connie noticed this. Having this same routine pulled on her lately, she broke the awkward silence. "Tom, do you AI people really believe you can match what our brains have? We're talking billions of...I forget. Neurons? Or synapses?"

Gratefully turning to Connie, he tapped his skull. "We have over a hundred-billion neurons up here. Both you and Bessie are astronomers so you know the math. By multiplying that many neurons by the 7000 synaptic connections we have a total of ten to the," He trailed off,

"Whatever power it is."

Both women commonly used exponents to express the enormous sizes and distances involved with astronomy. For Bessie's part she sometimes even thought in mathematical terms. She fed him a sideways smile. "It's 7 to the 14th, doctor."

Still missing the dryness, Myers nodded, "Yes, you're right, it's a lot!"

Knowing her daughter almost too well by now, Connie missed none of it. First giving Bessie a look that she too knew very well, *to knock it off*, she went on, "All right, but can you duplicate this? I wonder."

Off the hook for the moment, Myers said, "Frankly, so do I."

Bessie began, "Yes they...Ouch!" Leaving the back of her head alone this time, she asserted, "My friends and I think they will do it and soon!" But she'd had enough. "Anyway, doctor, are you saying you'd like to study my ITC?" She also had her answer ready. "Because if so, then no thanks."

Though never intentionally rude, Bessie's directness was disconcerting to those who didn't know her too well. Myers stammered, "Uh...well actually...er...I am. But can I...uh... at least plead my case?"

Adjusting the cold pack, she returned the barest of smiles. "Sure."

Her attention regained, he counted off on his fingers, "First, by now at fifteen your brain structure is fully developed. Put simply, your expanded ITC has nothing to do with today's injury. You were born with it."

Wanting by now to just get out of here, but interested in spite of herself, she kept it short. "And so?"

Knowing, in turn, she had little or no patience left, he ran through the rest of his fingers. "Second, I've never seen an ITC the size of yours. Third, there aren't many documented studies of this, two in China, and one each in South Africa and Russia. Oh. and one here in the United States "But mostly," He pointedly tapped the little finger. "you all have in common your exceptional skill with VR accessories. We still don't know what correlation exists, but we're sure there is one!"

His ingratiating smile wrapped it up. "So again, how about wearing one of your dad's units for us at the Center? This would greatly benefit our research." He glanced at Connie. "We'd also pay her, of course."

Connie simply shrugged. "It's her decision, Tom."

Bessie smiled politely. "Thanks for offering, Doctor, but my decision still stands. I'd hate being wired up at the Center like a lab rat."

Myers frowned. "I...er...wouldn't put it like that, Bessie. Our research people...um...wouldn't think of such a thing."

Fingertips drumming the tabletop, her smile was tart. "You don't think so?"

Seeing those fingers and hearing her tone, Myers knew that pursuing this any further was no use. He threw up his hands. "I'm sorry you won't. Will you at least think about it?"

Rising from her chair, Bessie said, "Sure but don't count on it."

Connie also stood. "Is there anything else, Tom?"

"No, that's it. Bessie, you're a little banged up, so take it easy today. If you experience any dizzy spells or blurred vision, tell your mom and we'll get you back in here." He could not help adding, "And please let me know if you reconsider my offer. Will you do that?"

Injury notwithstanding, Bessie was caught up with cosmology more than ever. Thoughts already, literally, light years away, she blinked, "Sorry, Doctor, I didn't catch that. To do what?"

Taking an arm, Connie pointed her toward the door.

"Let's head home." Looking back at Myers, she added earnestly, "Thanks, Tom, for giving her such a good going over. I'll get back to you ASAP if she has any problems."

As they left the building she called Rob to tell him the news.

Chapter 3

The last of Covington High School's Friday classes were done. Streaming from the front entrance, the students met yet another unusually warm and sunny mid-autumn day. Any-more it was hardly arguable that Wisconsin's seasonal weather patterns had definitely changed. While cause for deep concern by some, these young people weren't sharing it, not today, anyway. This marked the end of midterm exams. Even better, next week was blessedly shortened by parent-teacher conferences from Wednesday through Friday. Stu-dents and teachers alike hoped the summery weather would stay this way.

Hopping down the front steps between her two best girlfriends, Bessie's grin was bright as the sun, partly for the weather, but mostly due to the posted grades for her Physics midterm exam. "Woo-hoo!" she yelled, "did I nail it or what!?" Throwing a wild air punch, she missed the last step and sprawled full length on the concrete walk.

Helping her back up, Lucy Chen scolded, "I swear, girl, first chance I'm building you a robot seeing-eye dog!" Which she could as the top student with robotics and cybernetic hardware design.

Gripping Bessie's other arm, Nina Manchester declared, "And I'll make you use it! Ah would *sew* hate *foah yew* to kill *yoah* silly self!" One of the school's excellent troupe of stage players, her imitation of a favorite English actress, Helena Bonham Carter, was spot on. Then, seeing Bessie's skinned knee, she dropped the accent. "Whoa, girl, are you OK?"

While rubbing the knee, Bessie saw that others watching nearby were laughing and shaking their heads. Straight-

ening up, she muttered, "I'm more embarrassed than hurt."
To her robotics-genius GF she smiled ruefully, "First
chance, Lu, I'll come over to help you get that doggy
built." *If I have time!* Along with math and science courses,
mom Connie was tutoring her in astronomy.

Still fuming over her exam as they headed to the street
Lucy growled, "Your A+ from Hollingsworth is amazing,
so don't get me wrong."

"About what?"

"After working my butt off for him, I wound up with
only a B, that's what!" She left out the rest – that, though
the best of friends, she and Bessie had competed for high
science grades since middle school.

Luxuriating in the sunshine and having none of this,
Nina stretched out her arms. "Lu, let's talk tanning lotions
and not that awful stuff! Let it go!"

With largess to spare, Bessie lent some to Lucy. "She's
right. And we both know that B's from Hollingsworth are
A's from anyone else."

That drew Lucy's grudging nod. "I suppose. Besides,
other than Ravi and me, nobody else got higher than a C,
poor babies."

Reaching behind Bessie, Nina poked her. "Me for
instance?"

"Oops, my bad. But at least you passed it right?"

Nina waved airily. "Yes and speaking for us mathemat-
ically disadvantaged, my C-minus is fine!" And it was,
Nina hating and fearing math like the plague. She also
knew without these two squeaking her through, she'd not
have survived Physics past day one.

Ever supportive, if overly so, Lucy rejoined, "Come on,
Neen, that's better than fine! His exams are so hard, they're
practically…"

Used to Lucy's mothering ways but in no mood, Nina
cut her off. "Thank you Momma Chen, but…" she tipped

her face to the sun, "...it's summer out here and I couldn't care less!"

"Speak of the devil," Bessie said. "Here he comes."

While conducting classes Mr. Hollingsworth moved in slow motion, when he moved at all. Swinging a briefcase, he was practically running down the front steps. After tossing them a wave in passing, he about-faced and doubled back.

Ignoring Nina, he greeted her friends, "Nice work on the exam, girls, and say the same to your boy friend...um..."

Lucy finished, "Ravi, you mean?"

He nodded, "Right! In fact. After class I meant to tell you three about the scholarship grants the University of Wisconsin is offering to our better science students. Though still only sophomores, you're all eligible." Finally noticing Nina, he added sternly, "And so would you! If you spent half the time on your math that you do with your stage work!"

Nina returned a staged smile, "Mm-hmm."

Hoping to have made his point with her, he went on with the other two, "If you do sign up I've talked your older class-mate, Alex Ricci, into lending you a hand. As my Physics lab adjunct he'd be a big help." Stealing a glance at his watch, he shook his head, "Sorry to be so rushed but we'll pick up on this again on Monday."

Lucy swallowed her grade upset. "Why the hurry, Mr. Hollingsworth?"

That got a grin out of him. "I'm helping to host the Advanced Sciences Symposium at UW!" Sponsored by the University of Wisconsin, Madison, it included top researchers in the U.S. scientific community and also from overseas.

Expression doubly serious, Lucy nodded. "I've been online about it all week. Among other things you're discussing cybernetic systems and robotics for space travel.

Without those, of course, there won't be space *anything* happening." Lately her home projects had her deeply involved with both of these technologies.

"I agree. In fact today's opening speaker, Dr. Rama Desai, will pose one of our biggest questions about that. Namely, how will we humans fit in? And frankly, it'll be to a very limited extent, I'm afraid."

"Who is she?" Lucy asked. "I've never heard of her." Gritting her teeth, Bessie had all she could do not to butt in, "Visiting from India, Dr. Desai is one of our most renowned cosmologists. For the symposium she's also representing the Hundred Year Starship Society." The 100YSS was dedicated to laying the groundwork for a space craft to reach the nearest star system within this century. Considering the countless difficulties, the Society was also the first to admit their studies alone might take that long.

Stealing another glance at his watch, he turned to Bessie. "As much as anyone, you know all about them, right?"

A paid member of the Society since eighth grade, she nodded. "I sure do and I'd go over there with you if students were allowed! Which the site said we're not. Their biggest issue is what you and I have talked about this whole term!"

"Yes, and that those other challenges we've covered like going back to the Moon, landing on Mars, and visiting the asteroids are all doable. We both know that reaching the stars is much, much tougher. So much that star travel might not..." he trailed off, "...even be possible."

Only last week Bessie had shown him an article she'd found online. In this the author showed that traveling at the highest velocity yet achieved, some 200,000 miles per hour, to cross 4.22 light years to the *nearest* star, Proxima Centauri, would take 21,000 years! They'd both agreed the only way was to travel FTL (faster than light), or else to teleport, but that this last was even less possible.

Totally left out, Nina said, "He's in a rush you guys. just save it for next week!"

Ignoring her for once, Bessie's head shake loosened more strands of her hair. Impatiently brushing them back, she frowned, "Of course, it's possible! NASA's New Horizon's Pluto flyby was only last year!"

"True, and your essay about their findings was excellent by the way."

"Thanks, I guess." Again she shook her head. "But we know too that compared to the stars, the distance to Pluto is nothing. Even so, there's got to be..." Her turn to trail off, her eyes searched his, "...some way to reach them."

He returned a tired look. "We'd all like to think so." Yet another time check told him his symposium hosting began in less than an hour. "Nuts, I'm late, late! We'll cover this some more next week. Oh, and again, good work on the exam. Gotta run!"

Watching him dash to the parking lot, Lucy said, "He's not so bad actually. He…"

Nina cut in, "Lu, give me a break! Only a total jerk gives exams like his!"

As they went back and forth whether he was or wasn't, Bessie, their aspiring cosmologist, enjoyed the challenge of his tough exams. She smiled to herself, So I'm a science geek!

The three girls lived just over a mile from school. Last year they began by riding the school bus. After a week of winding around through several neighborhoods until reaching their own, they took to walking home instead.

Today, with curly blonde hair cut short in the latest style, Nina sported a striking aqua-marine Cardin blouse and trim-fit Miss Me designer jeans. Her pretty looks and slim figure were the very picture of what one would see modeling these clothes in a local catalog or newspaper ad.

And which, with her mom's help (once a model herself) she'd been doing these past two years. Originally, in fact, she'd set out to be a high fashion model in topmost venues like Vogue, or Cosmo. This screeched to a rude halt her freshman year on finding she'd topped out at only five-foot, *seven* while in her sneak-ers! Unstoppable, not even by genetics, Nina had thrown her-self into the other thing she'd wanted to be; an actress, and a good one, it turned out, as shown by encores received for roles in the school plays, the second of which, she also pro-duced and directed.

Refusing to let shortness curtail current part-time modeling in Madison, Nina, all grins, had dangled one of her pay stubs in front of Bessie and Lucy only last week "Pretty sweet, right? For just strutting my stuff on their runways?"

Roughly the same height, with ear-length black hair combed sideways, Lucy wore a plain white blouse and knee-length gray shorts. Coupled with being quiet spoken, her conservative hairstyle and attire matched what she was – the top of her class in robotics and also at her very best when exploring the micro-circuitry maze of cyberspace.

Half a head taller than the other two, Bessie was their polar opposite attire-wise with her crumpled cargo pants, loose fitting T-shirt, and worn sneakers. Added to these was her long, reddish brown hair, or most of it, stuffed up beneath an old Green Bay Packers cap. When without it she constant-ly frustrated style-conscious Nina by holding her hair back with whatever was handy, usually a rubber band.

Seldom dressed to attract any guys her age, the reason was not that she wouldn't like to. but with all the schoolwork and stargazing studies at home, how much time did she have left for boys? Even so, Elizabeth Anne Howard really liked who she was and truly loved what she did these days. While bat-ting zero with any girl meets guy pairing, she stayed pretty much stitched together by hanging out with family and friends.

As the threesome started home, Lucy said to Bessie, "Sorry to bug you about it, but this exam was the toughest yet. So I've got to know, how'd you do it?"

Shifting her pack this way and that to make it sit right, Bessie started, "Before taking this one, I…! Nuts!" Halting, she reached back to fumble with the shoulder straps. "Give me a second with this!"

Nina got behind her, "Here, I'll get it." Undoing one of the straps, she shook her head. "How do you always get these so tangled!"

Bessie sighed. "You sound like my mom." As Nina fixed the straps, she told Lucy, "What helped was doing a visit to the LHC in Switzerland."

Knowing about the Large Hadron Collider, Lucy nodded. "I can see where that would."

Nina unravelled a second strap. "Hold still!"

Obeying, Bessie went on, "But this time, Lu, my virtual unit…" Oddly she paused. "…actually did…er…take me there," Quickly she finished, "I mean kind of! Neen, are you finished back there?"

Nina slapped her backpack. "You're fixed! Let's go!"

"Let's!" Bessie said. "If Dad brings home his latest VR, I've got a busy evening ahead."

Co-owning his company, Virtual Scope, Rob Howard always brought home the latest VR headsets created by his cybernetics genius partner, Marsh Perry. Next he liked for Bessie and Ben to try them out. In doing so they saved him lots of time and expense with his testing staff.

Nina's own agenda was calling to her. Tomorrow her mother would take her to model for a teen fashion show in Madison. On returning they'd stop at Covington Mall to peruse the chic autumn wear at Janine's Fashion Boutique. Ever tracking the latest styles, Nina practically lived at Janine's.

As Bessie and Lucy rehashed their exam questions, Nina polished her English accent. Looking over at them, she sniffed haughtily in a falsetto, "*No mo-ah* of that awful stuff *mah deahs!* It's *fah* too *goah*-geous today!"

Lucy asked Bessie, "Who is she again?"

"That British actress, I think. But I can't remember…"

Nina interrupted, "Oh come on! I'm Helena Bonham Car-ter. Her grandma was all Mrs. Ames talked about last week in history class."

Lucy mentally calculated, then corrected, "No, Lady Violet Bonham Carter was her *great great*grandma!"

Bessie added, "Right, and I enjoyed hearing about her."

"Well sure," Nina said, "As best of friends with your beloved Winnie."

Nina meant Winston Churchill, one of the 20th Century's most famous personages, and whom they were studying in Modern World History class. Teaching it, Mrs. Ames, an ardent feminist, pointedly ranked Lady Violet above him for having been more proactive with parliamentary politics than most other women during both world wars.

Admiring Churchill's leadership qualities in history class, Bessie had a photo copy of her Winnie as a young British cavalry officer on her bulletin board, along with role models, Albert Einstein and renown astrophysicist, Steven Hawking.

Chapter 4

As the girls again started for home a voice rang out, "Hey ladies, wait up!" Hurrying toward them, Ravi Gavaskar's bright grin beamed strobe-like from his dark brown face. On joining them, though, his mouth bent down beneath a frown.

Knowing him best, Lucy never saw Ravi wearing one. "What's wrong, Wiz, did you just get hacked?"

Tagged Cyber Wizard, or Wiz, Ravi's uncanny ability to burrow past any security barriers, while keeping his own impenetrable to others, was legendary throughout the school. Erasing the frown, he laughed. "With me that'll never happen. Nah, I just saw our physics grades, and I totally blew it!"

His cyber soulmate with their shared math and physics courses, Lucy fully understood. Again donning her mothering hat, she patted his shoulder. "I'd have blown it myself if Alex hadn't helped."

Whistling through his teeth, he nodded. "Yeah, I should've listened to him. You girls did great but I got a lousy B-minus. Man, I wanted that A!"

Considering her own grade, Nina was not at all sympathetic, "Stop whining, Wiz! Less gaming and hacking, and more booking would've gotten you one!"

Agreeing, Lucy switched to chastising. "She's right, especially with your cute little stunt last week."

"What's that?" he asked.

"The one you've bragged about ever since!"

Not to be left out, Bessie wagged a finger. "She means hacking the Pentagon! Mi-god, you could've set off World War III!"

He held up his hands. "I can't hold back! It's such a charge getting past all those firewalls and snooper shields!" He went slump shouldered. "Anyway, I should've listened to Alex's warnings about Hollingsworth's exam."

A deeper voice broke in. "Are you dumb sophomores using my name in vain?" Alex Ricci had snuck up from behind. Tall and heavily built, he placed his large hands on Ravi's shoulders. Easily rocking him from side to side, Alex looked down at him in mock sorrow. "I really grieve for your stupid B." Then he snorted, "Not! I warned he'd ambush you guys with quantum mechanics! That's why I kept after you with that!" Facing Bessie and Lulu, he gave both a thumbs up. "The same with you two, and nice going!" Lucy returned a smile, but Bessie's was wider.

Having moved here two years ago, Alex and his widowed mom lived just down the street from her. The parental mix of Italian on his mom's side and full-blooded Hawaiian on his dad's had bequeathed to Alex a head of curly black hair, high cheek bones and a complexion only somewhat lighter than Ravi's.

When approached earlier this year by Hollingsworth, Alex had readily accepted the offer to be his adjunct student instructor for lab work. Quickly drawn to the more promising students, he'd not only made friends with Bessie, Ravi and Lulu, but with Nina, too, who was barely hanging on.

But she knew right now that so much as another word about Physics and she would puke. Pointing toward home, Nina nodded to her girlfriends. "Great, you're heroes, but we've got to go!"

Again ignoring her, Bessie told Alex. "Well, Brain Boy, coming from you that's a lot! So thanks!"

He reiterated with another thumbs up but higher than before. "You're always great on these exams," he laughed, "but this time, Bean, you outdid yourself!"

Bessie's smile faded. Tall and skinny as a freshman, she'd right away been tagged String Bean, soon shortened to Bean. Her slender figure now somewhat curvier, this was no longer apt but, most annoyingly, her tag had stayed stuck. Biting off a heated reply, she thought it too nice a day to be upset over something so stupid as that.

As Alex resumed ragging Ravi, his victim shrugged it off. "Hey, I got what I got, and cramming for that mess is history. Now let's check out those new games from England at Video-Plus!"

Interest rekindled in both world wars, the British exported video games featuring their major battles. Forever fascinated by war games, the local youth, mostly the guys, snapped up whatever the Mall's video store had in stock.

Alex nodded. "Yeah, Ben said he's after those too!"

Bessie's brother, Ben, owned gamer skills nearly unbeatable by anyone. This included his sister and her group, no matter their own smarts with cybernetics. Although a top athlete, but loving video games as much as sports, he always found the time to play Alex and Ravi. If they weren't available he sometimes lowered himself to play his kid sister. All three guys were right away comparing and contrasting England's games with those of the United States.

Even more bored by this kind of talk than with physics, Nina pointedly stared at two other boys passing by. The one sitting behind her in history class promptly got her widest on stage smile. Returning one nearly as wide, he made Nina's day. Turning to Lucy, her smile grew sly. "I'll start working on Owen right away. He doesn't know it yet, but he'll be taking me to a movie I'm dying to see!"

Lucy laughed, "Girl, you really are something else! So if he does?"

Nina grinned back, "If he passes that test, he's my co-star in the next school play I direct!"

Overhearing this, Bessie kept her eyes on Alex. Whether or not he would like to ask her out was still an open question. She suspected they both felt the same; that by doing so they might screw up what had gone so well so far, the warmly solid comfort of keeping it as it is.

Not buying her girlfriend's reticence with this, Nina had tutored her with the wiles of attracting men, or tried to. Invariably her balky student always groaned, "I don't have time for that!" or whatever other nonsense she thought up.

Taking her aside yesterday, Nina had told her, "All right, you like Alex and he likes you...a lot! So if you want him to ask you out, then start by making him jealous. Trust me, you do it right, this works better than anything!"

To get Nina off her back, and also, admittedly, to see if she could attract him, Bessie waited for her first chance. Looking over at her, he gave her that chance this very instant. "So, Bean, how come you're not into these World War games? Your main guy, Churchill, was in both of 'em, y'know?"

Seeing Nina give her *that* look, Bessie drew in a deep breath and gave him her best imitation of being love-struck. "Oh yes! After studying what he did in World War I, I'm...! I mean, I feel like...!"

Alex motioned, "Say it! Like what!?"

A total idiot, she thought. But aloud she gushed, "I'm head over heels for him! So brave and brilliant as a leader! "If I could go back there in time (no comma) I'd...?" Do what, she wondered, marry him? She finished lamely, "I don't know, something I guess." Suddenly wishing to be some-place else, preferably on Mars, she eyed Alex to see how he took it.

He didn't even blink. "Yeah, he was pretty cool."

Ploy falling with a thud, she dropped back to poking him. "Oh? And what do you know about him? Nothing but what you guys see in your silly war games!"

Shrugging, "Whatever," he turned back to Ravi.

Facing Nina with palms up, Bessie mouthed silently, Now what?

After shaking her head, Nina stage whispered, "Don't quit! You just need more rehearsals!" As she said it, a car exited the student parking lot. When it turned toward them, she recognized the three boys in front. "Ah-ha! Here comes your brother and two other guys. If they stop, watch what I do."

Sure enough, the car pulled over to the curb. Seated on the passenger side, Ben lowered the window and called to Bessie, "Yo Bean! We're going to Markham's car lot so I can check out some wheels! After that we're heading to Julio's! So tell mom I won't be home for dinner!" Julio's Pizzeria was the favorite local hangout.

Bessie knew he liked aggravating her by shouting this Bean thing at her. Usually she ignored it, but hearing it yelled in public got on her nerves. She yelled back, "Fine, Butt Brain, but buy something I can drive! Not some dumb over-sized pickup truck!"

Ben laughed. "You won't be driving anything until you're licensed! No, Bean, you just keep pedaling your bike!" He beckoned to Alex and Ravi. "How about coming with? We've already had a short football practice! So after Julio's we're off to Video Plus. You guys can help me pick out some games and then we'll play 'em at my place."

Dad, Rob, and partner Marsh Perry started their computer accessories business five years ago. Rob's first rate man-agement skills, combined with Perry's inventive genius with engineering innovative VR units had made their company, Virtual Scope, a success. As a result VR headgear and computer ware was scattered from one end of the Howard household to the other. This also made their place perfect for both Ben's and Bessie's pals to play video games to their hearts content.

Ravi shook his head. "Thanks, but I've already bought into a challenge by this big deal gamer guy in Madison. The stuff I need to kill him with is at home, so that's where I'm headed!" His motor scooter was parked near the school's bike racks. Before walking toward it, he gave Lucy a hopeful look. "Need a ride? Your place is pretty close to mine." It actually wasn't, not by several blocks.

For the few times she'd done it Lucy enjoyed sitting behind Ravi on his powered-up motor scooter. But this week she was caught up at home with her own hardware design project, Besides, she, Bessie, and Nina set aside walking home together as their all important girl time.

Sincerely, Lucy smiled back, "Not today, Wiz, but thanks."

Ravi's face fell for the second time, but then, tossing a careless wave like no big deal, "Whatever, catch you later," he sauntered to his scooter.

Alex nodded to Ben, "I'm in, long as we hurry it up at the car place and get to Julio's. I'm starved!" He turned to Bessie. "See you later at your place, OK?" Then with a poking grin, "Unless you're falling in love with Mars out back!" Before she could answer, he hurried to the car and climbed in back.

The boy who passed by was one thing but Nina had drooled over Ben since middle school. Seizing her own chance, she nudged Bessie, "Now watch!" She called, "Oh Ben dear!" When he looked at her from in front, she flashed him a dazzling smile, "Once you do have that car I'm first in line for a ride!"

Though looking back appreciatively at Nina, Ben stopped with that. The last thing he wanted was getting up tangled up between Bessie and her best girlfriend. Keeping it strictly friendly, he laughed, "Since you're joined to Bean's hip, you'll both get to go!" He pointed at Bessie. "And don't wander off with her and get lost! Did you see what Dad texted about his latest VR units?"

"Yes, and he's bringing them home!"

"Yeah, he's hotter than ever for us to try these out! Catch you later!" With that the car pulled out.

Watching it drive away, Nina said, "I know you think your brother's a total pain, but he is one hot item."

Rolling her eyes, Bessie smirked. "You didn't lure him in very well."

British again, she arched an eyebrow. "Not this time. my *deah*, but like you I must simply rehearse some *mo-ah!*"

"Uh-huh! Too bad he's too dumb to pick up on your performances."

A few other girls were heading in the opposite direction. One of them waved to these three, "We're going to Julio's! Are you guys?"

Nina yelled back, "No, we've got too much other stuff!"

That said, they started home for the third time.

Chapter 5

Great-sized maples and oaks lined the street in sun dappled oranges, yellows, and flaming reds. Unusually warm and sunny weather had home gardens displaying flowers still fully in bloom.

Inhaling the fresh-cut fragrance of mowed green lawns, Nina threw out her arms. "Don't you just love it? I wish it would stay this way!" She asked Bessie, "So you're tied up tonight with your Dad's VR thingy?"

Already thinking of little else, she nodded, "I hope so."

"I'm not surprised," Lucy said. "Mom says upgrading your dad's latest one has her research team going 24/7." Her mother, Kathy Chen, a reputable engineer, headed Virtual Scope's technical research and development section. Quite the developing engineer in her own right, Lucy fed Nina a disgusted look, "And they're not thingies, but full immersion virtual reality units."

Unfazed at being corrected, Nina smiled pleasantly, "Uh-huh, and I'm no smarter than a carrot with that. So, keeping it simple, I call my own a thingy."

"You do that just to annoy me, right?"

"Exactly," Nina smiled again.

Bessie told Lucy, "Dad says the neural sensors on his new ones are vastly upgraded. He'll have us using them until they're ready for production."

Lucy said. "Soon as she can, so will my mom."

Nina asked Bessie, "Remember what you told us about those odd sensations you get? This has gone on now since when? Middle school?"

"Ever since virtual units were the helmet kind when I was ten, Dad's original one fit like a bushel basket."

"Speaking of heads, how's yours, when using your thingy since the injury?"

Usually talkative, Bessie's reply was oddly short. "Some aches is all,"

Nina persisted, "You said they found something strange with your head scan, but you never said what it is."

Bessie had disclosed only the sketchiest details as to what Dr. Myers discovered, nor had she mentioned him asking her to participate in his work at the University of Wisconsin's research center. Not inclined to talk about it before, she was less so today. "Let's drop it, you guys!"

Surprised by her uncharacteristic brusqueness, they did so while walking on.

Chapter 6

When starting Virtual Scope five years ago, Rob Howard and partner Marsh Perry had answered to a growing public demand for virtual reality accessories. Along with the VR gadgetry were the hand-controlled augmented reality systems for the video games. Knowing the competition they faced with other companies producing both AR and VR accessories, and focussing on one of these, they set out to upgrade their own VRs to be even more advanced. Fortunately Rob's management and marketing skills combined with Marsh's inventive genius to make their company a profitable success from the start – so much so, they now needed to expand their facility to twice its size. Yet, Rob felt this would shut down their money making operations for too long. For Marsh's part, he was hard pressed as it was to just keep up with the rapidly evolving cyber technology. By now for both men and all their employees, working 24/7 was standard procedure.

Standing beside his desk in their second floor office and holding his phone, Rob anxiously waited for a follow-up call from their downstairs R&D section. Seated at his desk, Marsh was busily working his PC. Nearing the end of another long and tiring day, Rob began to say as much to Marsh when his phone chimed. Usual sense of humor fairly worn out, he growled his answer, "Yeah, Kathy, now what!?" Then his face lit up, "Great, so bring one up! Or no, my kids'll just fight over it, so bring up two of 'em!"

Taking this in, Marsh smiled and nodded, "Ah!" So reserved compared to Rob, this could mean anything from mild amusement to all-out glee.

Clicking the phone off, Rob let loose months of

frustration with a yell, "Yahoo!" All grins, he turned to Marsh, "You heard it, good buddy, she's on her way up! Kathy says your new sensors work slicker than sliced bread!"

Peering owlishly back through wide frame reading glasses, Marsh merely nodded, "That's fine, I guess. But Rob, we still have to do more..."

Cutting him off, Rob nodded back, "Testing? Sure but not today. No, we'll close shop and get out of here early for once. I can even take Connie and the kids to Green Bay this Saturday to see our Packers for the first time this year!"

"Don't they play on Sunday?"

Already excited just thinking about it, Rob said it too fast for Marsh to keep up. "Yeah-yeah, but I've done this before with Connie and the kids to stay there Saturday night. Next we're at Lambeau Field's parking lot early on Sunday to save a spot for our tailgate party with the grill and brats and stuff. And half of Wisconsin all around us doing theirs. Oh, and I've got extra season's tickets I never use. So you and Louise could come too!" Rob was so worked up he'd all but for-gotten the new headsets.

But not Marsh. "Thanks, but I'll stay here this weekend. I'm still not happy with our unit's response time." A consum-mate perfectionist, he was never totally satisfied with any of his hardware constructs. "I'm convinced we can speed it up even more."

"Aw come on! You've put in so much time already that Louise is ready to move your bed over here. Kathy's already told us that your newest brainchild reacts faster to user commands than any others on the market. Besides. we won't turn these units over to production before Kathy adds her finishing touches. Then my two cyber monsters will test 'em better than we can!"

Before Marsh could reply, Kathy Chen, still in her lab coat, rushed in with the two units. Beaming proudly she handed them over to Rob. "Here they are! Our trials show that visual clarity, response time, and sensory capabilities are fantastic! Counting in the additional apps, our clients will love them!"

Before hiring on at the company's start up, Kathy Chen's reputation as a top-ranked cybernetics technician was already established in the Madison area. A firm believer in her ever since, Rob grinned, "We've gotta give you another raise! 'Course you'll be awhile with fine tuning them, right?"

She nodded. "I accept the raise. And yes to the other, but not for long. A process of elimination has us down to two types of units. Our virtual sunglasses still need miniaturizing, and we're still coding their apps into the frames, but these headbands are good to go." She hurried on, "Designing their apps into the band itself, instead of the visor, was easier. With either type you summon them up by voice command, as long as you eee-nun-ci-ate!"

Marsh frowned. "Kathy, that's all well and good, but my neural sensors still have trouble picking up mental commands." His frown deepened. "I'll improve this later but I'm not at all happy about the users now having to do the best they can."

"Mental commands with both types works best when users have WI-FI hand controls. Otherwise, when mousing this still needs work, and also with beefing up the power source. But a user wearing this headband can do it if they really concentrate." She looked over at Rob. "You said Bessie can with our older models, right?"

"Yeah, but she says vocals are easier. As for thought com-mands, I'm not sure how she does with those. You think she'll do better with these?"

"She probably will at your place. Your PC has enough band width to handle the power load. If out and around, her laptop and headband combined might not. This partly also depends on the strength of her GPS system. Of course, if our headband...er...knows where it's at, then maybe so."

Marsh chimed in, "Yes, Bessie can get up and move away from your PC with the headset on."

"OK, but how far?"

"If cabled to the PC it would depend on the cable length. When wireless it depends on the battery charge. If fully charged she could go quite a ways, maybe to the other end of the house. Being so satellite dependent, that's not as far as I'd like. To extend the range I'm miniaturizing a device to transmit and receive its signals for no less than 100 meters in every direction."

Rob laughed. "Come on, metric guy, what's that in feet? No wait, in other words Bessie could walk the whole length of Lambeau Field, right?"

Marsh being Marsh, he nodded seriously, "Yes, something like that."

Kathy added, "With Bessie so up and around, she'd find one big advantage of the headband over the glasses."

"What's that?" Rob asked.

"It will not accidentally come off...unless she falls out of a tree or something. With neural sensors and power pack stitched into the liner, and visor added in, the headband is clunky, I'll admit, compared to the glasses. But we also beat our competitors with our polarized visors that never fog up. Overall, I prefer the headbands myself."

"Why is that, Kathy?" Marsh asked.

"They stay tight when I'm tread milling or even bent over backward with yoga. The sunglasses with flex bands keep sliding around."

Rob said, "I showed prototypes of both kinds to one of our clients, and he said the same. He treadmills every day by the way."

"The only thing left with the headbands is to spruce up the cosmetics with different fabrics and colors," Kathy said.

"They are wireless of course." Pulling two recharge coils from her pocket, she set them on his desk. "Except for these. Mainly, Rob, your kids will have a real eye opener with the upgraded sensors."

"They'll definitely give these babies a good workout."

Marsh asked, "Rob, would you ask Bessie to take some notes? I'm interested in anything she might jot down." He quickly added, "Not that Ben couldn't."

Rob snorted. "As a world-class gamer, Ben's no dummy with VR units, but if he did take notes, you couldn't read his scribbles."

Kathy asked, "Does Bessie do much gaming? My Lucy's not much into it."

"No but she's better than Ben with the VR stuff. She's always been pretty amazing with them."

"You and Connie do have a very special girl there."

"True, when wearing our VR units she has an uncanny ability to integrate with software." His precise way of stating practically anything drew smiles from the other two. Rob simply nodded, "She's shown us that ever since I began bringing these home. Even back then she said they took her to places where she was..." He touched his thumb and fingertip nearly together. "...that close to really being there." He added with a laugh, "There's also her magic staff thing."

Marsh frowned, "Her what?" Childless, he neither knew nor cared about kids playing video games as witches and wizards, or any of that.

Rob shook his head. "It's this so-called sorcoress staff Bess keeps right next to her while doing virtual. She claims that old stick helps her focus better on all the people, places, and things that show up in the programmed environment."

Marsh skeptically raised an eyebrow. "Oh come on, Rob, I know your Bessie pretty well. She doesn't believe in that sorcery nonsense any more than I do!"

"Right, she laughs it off herself as kid stuff. Even so, her friends still rag her about keeping that thing handy when using virtual. Bess couldn't care less and that's because of the fantastic results she gets. It's probably another of those go figure things you get with all these kids."

Busy as she was these days in Video Scope's R & D section, Kathy was the same as her bosses in that she, too, hadn't the time to waste with all this wizardry stuff. "Whatever, but soon as your two and my Lucy try these, they'll flip over them just as we did downstairs." Back to business again, she went on, "And speaking of which, when one of my testers returned from her virtual trip to Paris, she practically spoke French. She swore too that she practically felt the handrail atop the Eiffel Tower!" Something else just now occurred to her. Dead serious, Kathy went on, "There is one problem you both need to know, and it's really important!"

"Like what?" Rob asked.

"It's what happened when Franny finished her trip to France. I'm sure we'll correct this glitch pretty soon. Rob, if for some reason we can't, you need to have this red lettered in our instruction manual. Our user clients would definitely need to be warned about it"

Marsh frowned. "Kathy, could you be more specific?"

"We'd have to caution buyers not to simply yank off these headbands soon as they're ready to exit their virtual environments. The same applies to not just flipping up the visor."

Rob frowned, "After all these months of working on this thing and we've still got problems? Like what!?"

"When Franny finished her trip, she did what I just told you she shouldn't. She right away flipped up the visor and then, oh boy!"

From Rob, "She what?"

"Without leaving it down to first reorient to her

surroundings, she lost it for a few minutes."

Together both men asked, "Is she OK?"

"She is now but at first she just sat there babbling an old nursery rhyme she learned as a kid. Afterward she said it was like she'd truly lost her mind. So naturally I went virtual next to see if the same happened with me."

Rob growled, "Jeez, Kathy, you shouldn't have! And so?"

"So cancel my raise," she laughed. "But yes, after purposely skipping getting reoriented, I also needed a moment or two to settle down."

Marsh said, "This sort of reaction obviously varies with each user." Already typing this on his Word, he gave Kathy an apologetic look. "I should have said something to you before. During my own prelim testing I made the same mistake with the visor. I hadn't realized how deeply my unit entwines users with their environments."

Kathy said, "Speaking of deep immersion, Rob, you've said that Bessie does this with her VR use."

"Yep, she really dives in, especially with Marsh's units. Is this a stopper?"

She waved dismissively, "Along with any user, she'll be perfectly okay if leaving the visor down and first looking around to get her bearings. Once we *do* market these, we need to be doubly sure to include cautionary remarks with the packaging. And bosses, these also need to be worded so people can understand them. Of course, it's the same with any of the older units we've sold so far. So long as users follow the instructions, they're fine!"

Holding up one of the headsets, Rob asked, "What about your kid? You bringing one home for her?"

She shook her head. "Lucy has to wait. Along with these two units, we do have a few others ready, but I'd like to keep those here. During the coming week some of our special clients might want to try them out. Besides, Rob,

Lucy is busy enough as it is with designing her own hardware."

Rob said, "Uh-huh, and so is mine with all her researching." Shaking his head, he laughed, "That whole bunch is something else, aren't they? But it's better than running around hog wild and getting into trouble."

Before long, Rob was carrying the two headsets through the lobby. Seated at her desk, their receptionist hailed him. "Rob, Carmen Ricci just called from the Center. She wants to know if our new headsets are ready yet."

He slapped the side of his head. "Sorry Marilyn, I meant to tell her before I left. Get back to Carmen and tell her we'll deliver a couple tomorrow first thing. They've been after us about these new ones all month!"

"I will! Is Marsh staying awhile?"

"He might camp out up there all night for all I know!" Remembering Kathy's warning about yanking them off, he told Marilyn about that, and then, "Whatever you do, make absolutely sure their people understand this!"

She was already keying her phone. "I'm on it!"

Moments later, Rob was circling Madison's beltway to reach outlying Covington. Normally leaving later, he was unaccustomed to the heavy rush hour traffic. On the other hand, having to slowly wind through it gave him a chance for once to more calmly reflect on the current situations with the business.

As an owner nothing pleased him more than offering a high quality product, except, of course, for clients beating down the doors to buy it. At the same time all the going at it so hard lately had him tempted to chuck the Packers game and fly his family to Florida for a few sunny days on the beach. The headsets wouldn't be ready to market anyway for at least another month. The parent-teacher conferences would free up his kids for a long weekend, and Connie too if she took vacation time to skip her middle school conferences. But nah, she'd never do that.

Besides, if they did sell any headsets ahead of time to preferred clients, like the UW Center, he needed to reword the instructions to include Kathy's warning. There was also the chance she'd finish the headset's cosmetics sooner than expected, in which case he'd jump start them into production. No, vacations had to wait for December's holiday season, if even then. In the meantime they could go to Green Bay on Saturday, spend the night, and catch Sunday's game against the hated Minnesota Vikings. What would tell the tale with this was how well his two teenagers did tonight with these new headsets. Hopefully the only surprises would be good ones.

Chapter 7

Entering his office, Dr. Myron Paul shed his heavy sports-coat. Hanging it on the tree hook, he knew that Millie, his loving spouse of many years, combed countless stores for X-Long sportscoat and matching pants to fit his lanky six-foot-seven frame. His more practical other half had joshed him this morning for wearing anything but a bathing suit on a day starting out so warm as this one.

Between heading the week long symposium and his research department's hectic schedule he'd had more on his mind this morning besides getting dressed. Pulling from the closet the first suitcoat he touched, he later found Mil was right. While still in the lecture hall, he'd felt the confounded coat clinging like an electric blanket on HIGH.

Thinning gray hair combed over his high domed forehead, Dr. Paul's distinguished features matched his position. His prestigious accomplishments as Director of the University of Wisconsin-Madison's Cybernetics Research Center were nationally acclaimed. Ranked among the world's best, in-cluding the University of California's Advanced Computing Research Department, this said a lot for his own efforts. Working with data sets and data streams of enormous complexity to create his own modeling tools, he was currently raising them to higher functionality by using both virtual and augmented reality environments.

Seated at his desk, he loosened the tie. Leaning back, he began recalling what all had transpired at the lecture hall. Realizing it was simpler to just watch it, he summoned up on his laptop the transcript of the proceedings. Pressing FOR-WARD, he skipped Hollingsworth introducing him. Though knowing and liking him well enough, he couldn't help smiling at his junior colleague's nervousness. He'd done just fine with presenting the various speakers, includeing their main one. For this, Paul pressed PLAY.

Wearing an attractive floral motif sari for the occasion, Dr. Rama Desai placed her hands together, she bowed her head. "Namaste! Greetings and good fortunes to you all!" Arranged behind her on a dais were himself and several others. Seated before her in tiered rows was the audience. After the applause she pointed back at him. "Both I and my dear friend and colleague have often spoken of our symposium's major challenge. Put simply, it asks how can we advance any further in our important sciences without first solving certain riddles about them? Many of which, I might add, none of us have been able to do until now. This, my fellow scientists, is why we are here, for if we cannot find answers for these riddles, who will?"

Paul's dear friend and esteemed colleague was as firmly established in math and physics as he was. They were coequals too with applying cybernetics to aid their studies. Especially noted for her brilliant cosmological research, she was also an attending member of the 100 Year Starship Society.

Smiling expectantly, Paul raised the audio as she went on, "In order to move any farther technologically we must now address these troubling issues. Indeed, Dr. Paul, and I firmly agree that putting this off any longer..." Making a small fist, she shook it. "...simply won't do!" Turning toward Paul, she said, "Myron, as one of the guiding lights with creating AI, you are facing one of our largest issues. Most of us know that your current generation of cybersystems is closer to achieving AI than the prior one. Yet you recently said you're blocked from getting any closer. Isn't this so?"

Paul watched himself nodding slowly, "I haven't and, to the best of my knowledge neither has anyone else. No, I claim we must first combine the organic workings of our *human* minds," he drew a long breath, "with mechanical workings of machines." He finished with a headshake.

Desai replied with her own head shake. "Unfortunately, AI is a main curative which we in the 100YSS need for our own biggest headache." She pointed to another of its members in the audience, a young man from NASA's Jet Propulsion Laboratory in Pasadena. "Carl, you have mentioned this quite a lot lately. Would you care to share it with us?"

He said, "Doctor, it's the same one that's driven us physicists crazy since Einstein dropped it on us over a century ago, that nothing can travel at the speed of light." Rising to unfold an article, he held it up for all to see. "I copied this from a well-known science fiction magazine, Analog."

A woman behind him scathingly retorted, "From a sci-fi magazine? You must be kidding!" Wearing a charcoal gray pants suit, she had her black hair pulled back past reading glasses into a bun. Her fine boned features were attractive enough, but she lent the impression of a youngish but spinsterish librarian, and a tightly wound one at that.

The rudeness drew a tight smile from Carl as he looked back at her. "For your information, Miss ..."

She finished, "It's Manley. *Doctor* Manley!"

Apparently unimpressed he simply nodded, "Uh-huh," and turned back to Desai. "As I started to say, this was written by an eminently qualified physicist and computer scientist, E.M. Lerner." There were knowing nods at the name. "It says, and I quote, 'The most obvious difficulty of interstellar travel is that other stars are so remote. Proxima Centauri, our Sun's nearest neighbor, lies 4.22 light years – that's less than 25 trillion miles away.'" He looked around. "For those unfamiliar with interstellar distances, that's just a short hop by the way." He read on. "Humanity's farthest ranging spacecraft, the Voyager I probe – after 37 years of flight, but still just *barely* into interstellar space – remains within one light *day* of the Sun. That's merely a fraction of 1% of the distance from our Sun to Proxima Centauri."

An elderly woman professor from Princeton was seated next to Carl. Also a friend of Desai's, she added with a weary smile, "Rama, as 100YSS members, you and I are in such denial about it that we hate even saying it. But what Carl read makes it painfully obvious that, like it or not, the only practical way we humans, and not just robotic probes, can visit other star systems is by traveling FTL." She too looked around. "By that I mean faster than light."

Again Manley spoke, "First, Doctor, we hear science fiction tales and now this? We all have busy enough sched-ules as it is!" Seemingly oblivious to the groans at her rude-ness, Manley's dark eyes stayed fixed on Desai.

Pressing PAUSE, Paul grimaced. *I'm sure you do, Veronica. While you were here that schedule of yours had the rest of us jumping through hoops!*

Two years ago, he'd sorely needed an assistant director to help oversee his numerous research projects. His most prom-ising interviewee, it turned out, was Veronica Manley. As associate professor of Electrical Engineering at the University of Illinois, Champaign-Urbana, her work background with double-E cybernetics was deemed "Very respectable." Along with a PhD, she held a Bachelor's of Arts in Business Administration. The impressive credentials alone decided Paul to give her a trial period. Unfortunately, she didn't interact very well with others and also assumed too much total authority over the workings of Paul's de-partment.

When he confronted her over this, Manley, to her credit, admitted to wanting from the start to gain greater authority. Paul's heavy work load quickly forced the decision; that Manley's day to day abrasiveness caused him to hire his best researcher, Ms. Carmen Ricci, to permanently fill his A.D. position.

He thought, What a day that was! Its domino effect, in fact, had those little black rectangles still falling to this very day. This began when he told Manley that Ricci would be his AD. Having the sense to not storm out of the building then and there, she'd given a two-week notice, only to then stick around as a royal pain the whole time. The day she left she was employed at Ultra Tech's Madison complex nearby, where her notable credentials instantly had her heading none other than Ultra's own R & D section. Paul could not have cared less, had it not been what happened several years ago when Ultra had donated large sums for the Center to expand its facilities. Kowtowing to their corporate benefactor, the university had quickly given Ultra's R & D people free rein to observe Paul's research projects whenever they chose. To his dismay, he'd wound up still stuck with Veronica, the one big headache he'd thought to be well rid of. Another of his somewhat nagging headaches, Roger Moorland, accompanied Manley today. Her immediate superior over her R & D section, he too occasionally observed Paul's research. Patience often tested by these two, he sighed to himself, Well, what can you do?...and pressed PLAY.

Rama calmly replied to Manley's remark. "'Hocus pocus' you say? That depends on one's cultural perceptions. Ac-cording to my own, it is predicted that at the end of what we call the Kali Yuga, Lord Shiva will destroy the universe and that all the physical bodies within it will undergo a great transformation. By his reckoning this happens over a period of many millions of years. Taken in the context of several thousand years ago, this is close enough to our modern concept of billions of years. So, in a sense, the dissolution of Lord Shiva's then known universe is the same as ours many billions of years from now. But the good news…" She laughed. "…the universe will then be recreated!"

Again Manley raised a hand. Getting a nod from Desai, she sneered her reply. "Doctor, aren't you again just talking magic?"

As others groaned at this rudeness, Paul saw even Moorland arch a disapproving eyebrow.

Desai simply smiled. "Yes, you could say that, Seeing as how so many of us do exactly the same." As Manley started to speak, Desai held up a hand. "If you please! You see, in looking at so called mystical or magical events, we find them occurring throughout recorded human history. Even pre-historic cave paintings, such as those discovered in Lascaux, France, are attributed to our ancient ancestors representing mystical rituals to improve their hunting. Reputable anthropologists say their evidence shows that some of the time these rituals actually worked!"

A local Wisconsinite shot up his hand.

She pointed to him. "Yes?"

He grinned. "My brother up in Mercer thinks they still do! The night before opening day, he salutes a photo of the deer he bagged last year with a can of beer. Then he prays to get another one the next morning!"

"And does he?"

He made a thumbs up. "Each and every time!" The other Wisconsinites in attendance clapped and laughed.

An elderly gentleman from Berkeley U., and an old friend of both Desai and Paul, called out, "Rama, and you too, Myron, if you'll pardon me for saying so…" He pointed to Manley. "…she's right! We're bogging down here with little more than magical concepts, rather than what's real! Wouldn't you say?"

Paul heard himself laugh. "It's funny you say that, Jonas. My assistant director says her son has a young woman friend who kiddingly practices magic while using her VR unit. My point is, people, that while doing so, this young woman achieves amazing results with her VR unit."

Someone else spoke up. "Fine, Myron, but so what? These days so can both of my grandkids!"

"Very true," Paul answered, "But according to Carmen, no one can match this girl. Not even any of us here at the Center."

"As far as what?" someone else asked.

He replied, "That when using virtual this girl, in a sense, actually does go to these places she visits."

There came a rush of responses – "She what?" "Teleportation, no way!" "The poor girl is probably deranged!"

He held up both hands. "I said 'in a sense,' people! In any case, my A.D. herself has seen this girl using her VR headset, and that her descriptions of these places afterward are vivid enough to be real. Carmen can also vouch for her, that she's not the slightest bit deranged."

Sitting straight up, Manley's dark eyes suddenly glittered. "How very interesting, Myron! Could you tell us some more about her?"

Paul sounded more patient than what he recalled at the time. "Dr. Manley, later this week we'll cover topics such as this, along with what Rama mentioned."

Rama Desai nodded. "We shall see that even though seemingly so at odds, both quantum mechanics and magical rituals can say the very same thing. That certain events and even physical objects are much affected by human observation. And yes, even by what they deeply desire to happen." Everyone present knew this was precisely what sub atomic quantum particles had done ever since first discovered by Albert Einstein and Niels Bohr over a century ago.

Paul's final glimpse of Manley showed her gripping Moorland's arm and saying something. His high gain audio dimly picking it up, he heard something like, "...need to get right on it!" whatever *it* was. Moorland's weary expression matched Paul's own whenever she observed his projects.

The transcript had more, but enough for now. Leaving his office, he ambled in a loose, lanky gait down the hall. Poking his head into Ricci's office, he asked, "Carmen, have you heard anything from Rob Howard about his latest units?"

Just then clicking off her phone, she nodded. "That was Marilyn. She said they're sending us a couple tomorrow first thing!"

Straightening from the customary slouch, he nodded back, "Dr. Ricci, you've just made my day."

A tall and attractive brunette in her early forties, Carmen Ricci was currently completing her PhD thesis. "Thanks for the post-doc," she grinned, "but I'm still earning it. Anyway, Myron, it means paying overtime but I'd like our testing people to be here through the weekend. After we get those headsets tomorrow, we can fit in a full weekend of testing. Can I have them come in?"

"Please do! I'd like a head start before Ultra's people get wind of these new headsets. If we also stall with calling them until Monday, that should give us plenty of time to ourselves."

She asked hopefully, "Could we stall Ultra the rest of next week?"

"They'd resent it and make life miserable for us. We'll just do as much quality testing as we can through this weekend."

"All right, and I'll tell our testers before they escape for the weekend."

When back in his office Paul folded up his laptop. Turning off the lights, he smiled about what a gem Carmen Ricci was as his A.D. In another odd way it was too bad his original choice was no longer here. When she was, Manley was at least manageable under his supervision, whereas, her current visits were infernally disruptive. In any case, he'd be free of her interfering nonsense with these new headsets till next Monday.

Chapter 8

Situated in downtown Madison, Ultra Tech's business complex took up half a city block. Aside from the spacious parking lot, the rest of the property comprised the production facilities. Dominating these on one side, stood a starkly modernistic five-story building with sides of dark tinted glass. Less intimidating to first time visitors, the spacious interior was lit by shaded lights suspended from great oaken beams. Pleasantly light toned wood paneling stretched up five floors to the atrium's glass ceiling, allowing daylight to brighten the lobby even more.

Promptly greeted by a cordial, well-groomed receptionist, visitors would sign in at the desk an next be directed to wherever they wished to go. Most commonly the general public was led to the adjoining hall of exhibits where guides displayed Ultra Tech's latest cybernetics paraphernalia. Visitors with special permission were allowed limited access to the second, third and fourth floors. The fifth level was off limits to anyone, including Ultra's own people, without high security ID's and pass cards. The floor consisted of a large work area for clerics and cybertechs, and the offices of the R & D administrators.

Setting beneath clear skies, the sun's yellow orb painted the building's glass sides glowing gold. Unmindful of this, her back to the window, Dr. Veronica Manley jabbed a finger at Roger Moorland standing before her desk. "Crazy as it sounds, Roger, these so-called abilities of Rob Howard's daughter must be checked out! If they are as amazing as others claim, they could seriously impact our own research! Surely you can see this!"

Of average height, slimly built, and sharply dressed,

Moorland was, at times, all about image. Indeed, momentarily striking a pose in his blue dress shirt, pressed tan slacks with matching sport coat, and burgundy tie, he nodded toward the outer office area. "Come on, I bet some of our own people can do just as well." That said, he suavely brush-ed a hand back past his hair. Though barely forty, his hair was whiter than his bright, even teeth.

Manley shook her head, "I know what every one of my testers can do! And no they can't, not like that girl Myron Paul mentioned! In fact, I've heard his assistant, Ms....what's her name, say even more about her."

Letting her zinger about Ricci sail by, Moorland was at least interested enough to ask, "Ricci's son? How would he know?"

"She's his girlfriend, I suppose. At any rate Ricci claims her son has even seen this girl's amazing skills...with her father's units, not ours."

Neither did Moorland miss Manley's emphasis on that. Mostly unfazed by such small competing companies, he shrugged, "Veronica, even if *your* units don't yet outperform his, I'm sure they soon will."

She replied testily, "Not mine, Roger, ours!"

Seeing how upset she was, he had sense enough to reiterate, "I know *ours* will work just as well or even better, provided we hire additional people to cover my own administrative tasks. I'm spread out too thin as it is!"

Driven to not only outperform Ultra's competitors and, for that matter, Moorland himself, Manley wanted none of his whining about being overworked and understaffed. She slapped the desktop. "You're spread thin? Roger, you've twice the people you need for all your fetching and carrying!" Her voice rose. "I've begged you all year for more qualified people for my research! And how many have you given me? Two!"

Still smiling, he admonished smoothly, "Now tone it

down." Nodding toward the outer office again, he even winked. "Can't have them hearing you yell at your boss like that, can we?"

Though oozing bachelor charm and fancying himself quite the ladies man, Roger Randolf Moorland was a top notch administrator. Ultra's growing corporate success in the Midwest was proof positive that it never hired incompetents.

Knowing this, Manley backed off, "You're right and I shouldn't have." More calmly she said, "First, this Howard girl isn't the only one with these abilities. That neuro-specialist who sometimes works with Paul's people, Dr. ..? What's his name?"

"Myers."

"Yes, and both he and Paul think there might even be other virtual users like her who are...close to truly being within the environments displayed on their monitors!"

He barely suppressed a yawn. "Interesting, I guess, but so what?"

"Roger, my research with nuclear fusion at Fermi Lab and also at U. of I. had us very close to finding an adequate energy source to translate sub-atomic particles from one location to another! Instantaneously!" Though functional fusion reactors were still out of reach, Manley believed they soon would be.

Knowing some physics himself, Moorland skeptically cocked his head. "If you mean teleportation, then uh-uh! We both know there might not be enough energy on our whole planet to teleport even a grain of sand." He ended with a superior little smile.

Reigning in her anger over that smile, she held it to a head shake. "I know that. But I'm not sure that this...this ability of the Howard girl depends on that. Or, if it does, we're talking a type of energy we know nothing about. For instance, the *dark* kind we've all been babbling about for ages. But let's say that it is, all right? That, for all we know, this girl might be able to tap into it somehow."

Glancing at his Rolex, he frowned. "Not that I don't care but it's late and I've got a dinner date. Besides, we're at the top with our own VR units and to stay there I'd hate to squander our precious time over some kid who's pretty good with her dad's." Again he pointedly checked his watch.

Seeing that, Manley narrowed her eyes at him over her glasses. "This is a lot more important than chasing after your little cuties. We are *possibly* talking *teleportation* here, and if there are people who can do that by using a VR headset, we have to find them!"

Edging toward the door, he partially agreed. "If you think this Howard girl is one of those, then fine. But to me it all sounds far-fetched."

"Even so we need to at least see what this girl can do, either at the Center or here at our own facilities. Oh, but we need to first scout her out of course." Much as she hated the thought, she also had to butter him up. Flashing her prettiest smile, "Roger, I need you in on it with me..." She drew it out with a feline purr. "...will you please?"

Her wiles working well enough, he threw up his hands. "I'll fit it into your R&D budget." Unable to resist, he added, "Somehow! Now I do need to shove off. Are you coming in tomorrow?"

"For something as important as this, count on it!" Smile morphing into one of disgust, she motioned toward the door. "We don't your little cutie kept waiting, do we?" The sarcasm either lost on him, or he really didn't care, Moorland was quickly gone.

After a moment she pressed her intercom's red key. Instantly a man's voice answered, "Security here, Dr. Manley. Do you need something?"

"Yes I do, Mr. Trainer. Would you please come to my

office? And you might as well bring what's his name, your assistant."

"It's Girardi, ma'am, and we'll be there in a second."

Heading Ultra's security staff, Carl Trainer and assistant Charley Girardi shared an office on the same floor. Shortly standing before Manley's desk, both wore gray jackets with high security IDs clipped to the lapels. As with all Ultra's security people, neither wore sidearms, but these two and several others at the highest level kept them available at need. During Ultra's entire time here, however, none of them had ever drawn one.

Thirtysomething with dark hair cut short, Trainer was taller and more slimly built than his partner. Narrow features broken by a slanted smile, his intelligent eyes missed absolutely nothing. The same age and equally alert, with thinning blond hair and rounded face, Girardi was stout and heavily muscled. While serving together in a U.S. Army intelligence unit in the Mideast, the two became fast friends. Sticking together after being honorably discharged, each had also married, After five years with Madison's Police Department, and each with two kids, they'd switched to a less risky career on the security staff for Ultra. Their duties had since been mostly within the company complex, with occasional field work in and around Madison's metro area.

Frowning up at Trainer, Manley skipped the amenities. "Whatever is on your schedule, set it aside." Before he could utter word one, she went on, "You and your partner are to start keeping track of someone." She tore off her legal pad's top sheet. Handing it over, she again said before he could answer, "Here is what I do know so far, that she's a Ms. Elizabeth Howard. Aged fifteen, her dad co-owns Virtual Scope. Both this and the home address are in our data base."

His iPad in one hand, Trainer thumbed this in. "Starting

when, Doctor?"

"I know you're both off duty by now but I'd like you to start tonight."

Both had made evening family plans, but they knew that when Ultra says jump you only ask how high? They both nodded.

"Good," Manley nodded back, "but don't follow her too closely just yet. Not before I have more of my own information about her. Simply scout out her home, the neighborhood, and friends she hangs out with. Our long range listening devices will let you track their chatty little..."

Trainer did squeeze it in this time. "Doctor, we do know our jobs, OK?"

Either missing his irritated tone or uncaring, Manley moved on, "Meantime I'll have my other people searching her high school records and other places."

Silent till now, but of like mind as his pal with surveillance work, Girardi remarked dryly, "We can also do most of that, Doctor."

Looking closely at Manley, Trainer asked, "Why are we doing this? Is she some sort of security threat to us?" He followed this with the slanted smile.

Totally unsmiling, Manley said, "I don't know yet. Mr. Trainer, but it might turn out that she is."

Chapter 9

After parting with Lucy at her place, Bessie and Nina, who were next door to each other, headed on home. As Nina went on and on about the boys she liked, her modeling and acting, and the latest fashions. Only half listening, Bessie could not stop thinking about the head injury her girlfriends had brought up. Stopping in front of Nina's house, they agreed to meet up later.

Once inside, Bessie knew the rest of her family would be home late today. These quiet alone times let her busy mind relax and wander off to wherever it pleased. Lately, this was usually millions of miles away.

Today her mind kept rehashing what she wished it would not, last April's brain scan. She had brought home a copy of the diagrammed cross sections. This, along with a website about the human brain, had allowed her to more fully understand Dr. Myers remarks about her ITC. Her main understanding when pinning the copy on her bulletin board had been...she was born with it!

Since then she'd realized it actually was possible that she was a mutation of some sort. Wedged in on her crowded book shelves, her well thumbed copy of Darwin's "Origin of Species" explained how genetic mutations had regularly occurred ever since the earliest and simplest DNA strands appeared billions of years ago. So was there any reason that she couldn't be one?

She recalled mom mentioning any number of times that Bessie's great-great grandmother, Lorraine, was a young laboratory assistant for none other than Madame Marie Curie during her research with radioactive elements in Paris. Mom's own grandmother, Michelle, had worked at Los

Alamos, New Mexico, while they built the atomic bomb. The line of daughters working with radioactivity was kept intact by Connie Howard's own mom, Annette. Currently a retired chemistry professor from UCLA, Berkeley, she too had worked with radioactive rare earths in materials used for nuclear reactors. Bessie smiled about the women in her family being drawn to whatever was as hot as it gets.

As a result, was her anomalously large ITC the mutational result of radioactive particles striking all of these women during their working lives? Genetic mutations up until now with bio-engineered food crops of course could certainly include her. As far as her staff also fitting into all this, she still refused to believe that it did.

The staff was where she always left it, leaned against the wall next to the computer monitor. These past five years Bessie had kept this old keepsake nearby when online and also while going virtual. With the staff right next to her, it gave her a reassuring sense of confidence, along with something else she still couldn't clearly describe – an overall feeling of oneness with everything – the space around her, the physical presence of others nearby, the leaves on the trees outside, and with other things much, much farther off. She knew from past experience, though, that trying to explain this to anyone else had only drawn funny looks.

Eyeing the staff from top to bottom, she thought the first and topmost part the prettiest, a deep purple amethyst crystal encased in a small brass holder. Enthralled by witches and wizards and given this by mom, she had christened the crystal her "sorceress stone." The next one down, a wrist-band of brightly colored beads and silver charms, was from great grandma Michelle. Still alive and well, and keeping in touch with the family, she enjoyed spooking Bessie with tales of the "strange goings on" at Los Alamos. Though no believer in magic herself, she related how the local Native Americans attached their own ancient mysticism to the mysterious, highly secret project. One had handed her the wristband, claiming it would protect her from the evil spirits at that place.

Last was a shiny little globe of gold filigree. The instant she'd spotted it at a rummage sale with Nina and Lucy, she'd pulled from her pocket a month's worth of allowance and grabbed it. Curious if the filigree was worth anything, they'd taken it to an antique shop nearby. To their surprise the old owner-appraiser had exclaimed, "This really is pure gold!" And then, "In all my years I've come across only a few gold filigrees designed like yours."

Holding the staff at arm's length, she smiled wryly to herself, Magic *is* as magic *does,* I guess! As for the efficacy of this, she'd long since stopped thinking of it as anything other than pretty silly, and yet? Having it next to her while going virtual made her much more aware of the simulated virtual environment. If not magic, was the staff like a lucky charm helping her to better focus with her headset?

She was convinced it had more to do with what she and Alex debated about during Physics labs, between relativity and quantum mechanics. Saying a little to him about her overly large ITC might also be all right. On the other hand, talking about something so far fetched as a sorceress staff would leave him falling down laughing. Feeling the back of her head, she thought, If I am a mutation, I'll be good at it! And who knows, this could help beat her snotty brother for a change at his stupid war games.

Chapter 10

Soon after Connie came home, Rob burst through the door. Holding up the headsets, he crowed, "We did it, sweetheart! These are slicker than sliced bread!" Along with Bessie and Connie, Ben and Alex were here by now, and all wanted to be filled in. Eager to do that, Rob pointed toward the compu-ter room. "Come on, everyone, let's try 'em out!"

Once everyone was congregated in the computer room, Ben and Bessie agreed (for a change) that she had first crack at using the headset and that Alex could take his turn after her. As she and Ben took their seats at the computer console, the rest pulled up chairs and sat facing them. Atop the console the large flat screen monitor's translucent glassine lit the room a luminescent blue.

As Rob held up one of his headsets, the others were im-pressed that it looked to be little more than a headband with shades attached. He stretched the white elastic fabric a few times. "The design work is Kathy Chen's. She's got these showing only a slight bulge in back from the rechargeable power pack. She's also kept Marsh's neural sensor wafers hidden in the liner."

As he began to go on, Bessie looked toward the doorway. "Hey, just in time!"

Entering, Nina did a modeling pirouette. Bewitching them all with a haute look over one shoulder, she crooned, "*I'm* here, my dears, so *now* we can start!"

Rob and Connie greeted La Manchester's wondrous presence with bemused smiles, the rest feeding her horse laughs.

When everyone settled back down, Rob told them,

"Except for recharging, they're wireless, and the power packs are good for twelve hours. The main thing are the sensors, which Marsh has upgraded like you wouldn't believe. They allow transmitting voice commands more clearly and they now respond to...whatever they are." He said to Bessie, "You know this stuff. What do they call thought sig-nals?"

She smiled. "Since they're electronic, Dad, your partner Marsh would call them mental impulses."

Ben shook his head, "Come on, Pops, are you saying they can read our minds? No way!"

"Not exactly, but they...sort of can if you concentrate and keep your commands really simple," Not quite understanding this himself, Rob quoted what Marsh and Kathy had said. "They translate them enough for the computer to understand. "Of course. this depends on the user. Bessie, you've done this a little with our old type, right?"

She muttered, "Mm-hm."

Rob looked around, "Everyone with me so far?"

Connie patted his shoulder. "Dear, you're excited about them and so are we. But now just hand them over so our kids can get started. They'll figure them out."

He shrugged. "Right, a few minutes with these and they'll know more than I do."

Ben said, "We will after a game or two..." He added a sideways smile toward Bessie. "...between Alex and me."

There'd be no waiting in line for her, not tonight. She returned her own sideways smile. "Sure, Butt Brain, after *I've* challenged you."

Alex said to Ben, "We did agree to that, remember? Since these units are yours and hers, Bean should use it before me."

Ben admitted, "Yeah, yeah, we did," and held out his hand. "Let me have one, Dad." Taking the headset, he eyed it appreciatively. "Cleaner and simpler than your old ones.

But the helmet type had me kinda racing the Indy 500, you know?"

Taking hers, Bessie wrinkled her face at him. "You guys with your hot cars!" Tapping the visor, she smiled, "Just like my headband when skiing. I like it, Dad."

Waving, "Have fun kids!" Connie left the room. Rob heaved his large frame up from the chair. "Give 'em a good run through, you guys. And Bess, you find any glitches, Marsh wants you to note them down. Oh, and listen up! When you're done, don't go yanking off the headband before getting reoriented to where you are. One of our testers didn't and..." he tapped his forehead, "she pretty much lost it for a bit. Anyway, you need me for anything, I'll be watching the sports channel." With that he also left.

Itching to start, Ben nudged Bessie, "OK Bean, put it on and let's play!"

She held up her headset. "No, wait. I need to find a name for this." Like many, she personalized fondest possessions by naming them after favorite people. But only Bessie Howard could be so enamored with Albert Einstein as to name it after him. As Ben went into his groaning act, she hissed, "Oh, shush!" Trying the name, she began slowly, "Al...bert! Al...bie! No, those don't sound so great. Hmm, let me think."

Alex ventured, "What about the famous physicist from way back, James Clerk Maxwell? You just now studied him, remember?"

"I'll try him. Max...well! Maxwell! Ah, that's good!"

Nina nodded approvingly, "That works!"

Ben let out an aggrieved sigh. "Now are you ready?"

"No, there's one more thing." To her right the new staff leaned beside the doorway. Standing it up, she stared at it for a long moment.

Always itching to gain gaming wins, especially against his sis, Ben wanted none of this Harry Potter stuff. "Come on, quit wasting time with that dumb stick!"

Still in a vengeful mood for being ignored earlier, Nina fed him a look of utter disdain. "It's magic, dimwit! FYI, she's a sorceress, and they do that!" Turning to Bessie, she urged, "You go, girl! Beat his socks off!"

Standing behind Bessie, Alex put a hand on her shoulder. Unconsciously placing hers atop his, she glanced up at him. "What?"

Honestly puzzled with no clowning around, he frowned, "I don't get it."

Leaving her hand where it was, she frowned back, "Don't get what?"

"Why you keep doing this sorcery thing. Science can't possibly mix with magic, can it?"

Ben growled, "You two gonna just hold hands or what?"

Seeing their joined hands, both drew them back. Ignoring Ben and still looking up at Alex, Bessie's own expression was just as puzzled. "It's not magic, really, not how most think of it." Looking away, she added, "Or maybe it is, I don't know."

Ben snorted to the other two, "My sis is a whack job, what can I say?"

Ignoring his heckling, Bessie gripped her staff in both hands for a moment, then leaned it back against the wall. She next held up the headband, "So, Maxwell, feel like winning a battle?" Pressing it to her ear as if listening, she grinned at Ben. "He says we'll kick your butt!" Snugging the headband down over her head, she gripped the handholds.

Doing the same, Ben gave her a nasty grin. "Ready for a whipping?"

Releasing the left handhold, she whacked his shoulder. "This time you're getting whipped! Let's go!"

Chapter 11

Headsets energized, brother and sister prepared for battle. Reserving his newer

Wi-Fi games for worthier opponents like Alex and Ravi, Ben had set up an older one, "The Battle of Gettysburg," with Bessie, As both lowered their visors, Alex and Nina moved closer behind to watch.

Her full attention on the monitor, Bessie automatically reached out her right hand and brushed it against the staff. Both hands back to the controls again, she began humming an odd sounding little tune.

Alex nudged Nina. "What's that, the latest top 40's hit?"

She nudged him back. "Shh! It's her spell song!"

Rolling his eyes, he turned back to the monitor.

The game opened showing all four of them a map overview of Gettysburg, Pennsylvania, and the surrounding area in July 1863. The various battles fought from July 1-3 were noted in boxes at the bottom. Once the players chose which army to lead and which battle to fight, their play began.

Ben's game, his pick, he said, "I'm Lee, so I'm attacking you," and moused to Picket's Charge. "We'll fight this famous one! Go on, pick your guys!"

For some reason, he sounded far off to Bessie. "Louder! I can hardly hear you!"

"Clean the junk out of your ears! I said I'll be General Lee!"

She laughed. "Well lots of luck! If you studied your history, you'd know Lee lost at Gettysburg!"

He chortled, "I've studied it, all right, but I won't blow it like Lee did!"

"We'll see about that." She clicked the only other choice, General Gordon H. Meade. "OK, I'm in!" Choices made, the battle scene automatically maximized to the next highest level.

Usually Mr. Cool when starting, Ben jerked up. "Whoa! See how clear it is? Way more than before, right?"

Likewise impressed but fully focused on the monitor, she flicked him a shooing motion. "I see that! Now shush and let me think!"

What all four saw, but far more distinctly by the two with their visors, was a much closer foreground view of tree-lined Cemetery Ridge above a broad valley. The icons along the ridge were the Union forces and those of the Confederacy were spread across the valley floor.

Far beyond rose another tree covered ridge. But for Bessie, as in real life, it looked hazy due to the greater distance. Blinking to clear her vision, she felt a sensation of not just seeing a place but truly being there. Not quite but almost. Thinking, I'm just being silly, she shook it off.

Behind her, Alex said, "Bean, tell me if you want anything recorded."

She answered loudly, "Alex, you also sound faint! Say again?"

Ben said, "Jeez, Bean, I hear him perfectly! What's with you?"

Louder Alex repeated, "I'll record whatever you need me to! How's that?"

Back to fully absorbed with the monitor she nodded absently, "That's better."

Saying, "OK, here's level three," Ben clicked it in and then, "Totally amazing!" Marsh Perry's units upgraded beyond those of anyone else, his highest level rendered people, places, and things very close to the real thing.

As they organized their strategies, Bessie added a technique borrowed from a sci-fi movie, "Galactic Warrior." In this, the superhero outwitted the Dark Power by hurtling through time and space on self-generated laser beams. Imaging up her own, a narrow, glowing golden one, she aimed it at her Union forces on the ridge. Again humming her tune, she rode the beam down closer to the scene.

Suddenly everything around her and the beam went black! She saw rising from the darkness a swirl of freeze framed images; her parents and friends, trees in the yard, Saturn's rings, her physics lab, and more, blooming up like flowers in fast motion, only to separate and fly out of sight. Then all of this stopped!

Glancing around, Bessie was even more astonished to see what occupied her immediate personal space, only her and her chair, a small circle of carpet beneath it, and the front part of the console. The monitor still displayed the game but behind it and all around, the computer room was gone!

Gasping, "What on earth?" she found herself suspended in midair above a grove of trees. Positioned along the ridge just beyond were blue-clad soldiers, thousands of them. Bearing rifles, they were arranged in long lines in trenches, or standing and kneeling behind wooden fences. Arrayed in the valley below, flag-bearing brigades of soldiers in gray and mixed other colors were marching steadily up toward the ridge. In the center of her nearer ridge were blue clad officers on horseback. One of these was handing out messages and sending them off. Incredibly, everyone and everything, including the horses, was moving down there without her voice commands, the controller, or even the mouse. With a heart pounding jolt, it struck her – These aren't CGIs, they're real!

Unable see it, she also felt an amorphous something close around her. She'd sensed it before with the old headset but never so strong as this. Reflexively reaching out, her hands met a slight yielding. With a harder push it went rock solid. Putting her hands to the sides of her headpiece, she called out plaintively, "Can you guys hear me? Or even see me? Neen, are you there?"

Nina squeezed her shoulder. "I'm right here! What's wrong?"

Before Nina could remove her hand, Bessie reached back and grabbed it. "I don't know but whatever it is, it's totally crazy! I need a second to figure this out!"

Busily positioning his forces, what Ben saw through his visor was more vividly enhanced than what Alex and Nina saw. All three still saw the battlefield scene exactly as shown on the monitor.

Ben groused, "Quit messing around, Bean! You ready to play or what?"

From Alex, "Right, you're squirming like your butt's burning! What's up?"

Though both sounded far off, she mostly heard what Alex said. "Never mind my butt! You better start taking those notes!" Fired up a moment ago to beat Ben at his own game, she had all she could do to take in what was happening below.

Cannons and firing crews were moving up to the left side of the ridge. Lined up along the rest of it, blue-coated troops were aiming their rifles. Tearing her eyes away, Bessie looked behind her. Down there in a trampled, muddy cornfield stood a white clapboard farm house. With other blue-coated soldiers entering and leaving, this, she assumed, was her own General Meade's headquarters.

It dawned on her – *I was in that house! Or its replica when her family toured Gettysburg National Park last year. They were also up on this very ridge.* With a heart leap, she suddenly knew that in some unimaginable way she had truly transported back to Gettysburg over one hundred fifty years ago!

Seeing Bessie turning and glancing this way and that,

Nina asked, "Hey girl, are you all right? Talk to me!"

Alex echoed, "Yeah, what's going on?"

Faced forward again and barely hearing them, Bessie saw a mounted officer part from the others and ride toward her. Heading for Meade's HQ, no doubt. From among her scat-tered thoughts, one said that even behind the handlebar mustache he looked Ben's age. Just then she saw the trooper glance up...at her! His legs shot forward into the stirrups. Pulling back hard on the reins, he reared the horse to a halt. Yanking off the hat to shield his eyes, the young officer stared up at her for several seconds. Lowering the hat, he cupped his mouth and called up to her.

All that Bessie heard was her pounding heart. Worse, she hadn't a clue as what to do next. So, simply raising her hand, she waved back to him.

The young officer's jaw dropped but not for long. First shaking his head to clear it, he clamped the hat back on. To Bessie's disbelief, he then tipped it to her! With that he jerked the head of his horse around, dug in his spurs, and sped off at a full gallop toward the farmhouse. Giving Bessie a last look over his shoulder, he crouched lower and spurred the horse even faster!

Everything she had seen and done so far had happened in the space of little more than one minute. What registered next were distant sounding voices, "Earth calling Bessie!" and "Come on, Bean, what's up!?"

All of this suddenly too much, she sprang from the chair and tore off the headband. Looking around wildly, Bessie reached out for something, anything!

The nearest, Nina, grabbed her shoulders. "Come on, girl, are you all right!?"

"Yes! No! I don't know! Give me a second!" Bessie gasp-ed. As everything began coming back into focus, she blurted out, "Am I glad to see you guys!" Reoriented, she looked at the monitor. Doing a double take, she saw it was still just showing the game. For once in her fifteen years, Ms. Elizabeth Ann Howard was totally speechless.

Chapter 12

Heeding Rob's warning about the headset, Ben was oriented to his surroundings. Seeing how shaken Bessie was, he skipped the Bean tag. "Jeez sis, what happened!?"

Gripping Bessie' shoulders even harder, Nina shook her. "Snap out of it, girl! Talk to us!"

Blinking and senses regained, Bessie began "Give me a second to...Ouch!" Wincing, she put her hands to her head. Having never had headaches till the injury, she found this one head splitting. A moment of rubbing her temples made the ache recede. Finally more alert she sounded out of breath, "You guys won't believe what happened! It was so crazy that..." she looked over at her staff, "...no, that's even crazier." Raising the headband, she asked it, "What did you do to me!?" Turning to the doorway, she called out, "Dad, you better come in here! Something is very wrong with my headband!"

Ben asked, "Like what?"

Dangling Maxwell from one hand, she held up the other one. "He actually worked fantastically! I mean, I really *was*...right there at Gettysburg! With the soldiers, the guns, the horses, and everything! Then I...?" This time she yelled it. "Dad!"

Ben scowled, "So? That's what these VR's do, you know?"

She shook Maxwell at him. "I know that! This was way, *way* different!"

When both Rob and Connie entered the room, she was first to ask Bessie, "All right, what happened?"

As she fumbled to answer, Ben replied, "It's something about her headset, Mom!"

Connie realized how hemmed-in Bessie looked with all of them around her. "Let's get out of here and give her room to breathe!"

Standing before her parents in the den, Bessie thrust Max-well at Rob. "Dad, you need to look at this! There's some-thing wrong with it!"

Taking it from her, Rob said, "Now Bess, just settle down," He looked at Ben. "What about yours? Any problems?"

"No, mine worked fine." He eyed his sister, "For the few minutes I used it."

Usually shying away from Bessie's teen-girl upsets, Rob figured these were better handled by Connie. After so many months developing this headset, he felt on firm enough ground to handle it himself. "Go ahead, hon, spill it out."

So she did, too fast for Rob to fully follow. Pausing for breath, she began to go on.

He held up a hand. "Whoa, give me a minute here. You saw the soldiers, the horses, and everything else crystal clear through your visor. You also thought *you* were there *with* them, and that's good! It's exactly what Marsh designed these units to do!"

Ben agreed, "I thought that I was there, sort of."

As Bessie started to answer, Rob again raised his hand, "And as for your...bubble thing, I've got no clue what that's about."

Nor did anyone else, though Alex was starting to under-stand. "I think I do, Mr. Howard. A Russian physicist actual-ly referred to what she's calling a quantum bubble." Seeing Rob roll his eyes, he quickly added, "It's still just theory, of course."

As Bessie began to feed into this, Rob held the floor. "Wait! I know you've heard my company spiel, honey, but you need to hear it again!"

This time she squeezed in by yelling it, "Dad, I have, a

thousand times!"

"Well, listen this time and you'll learn something! That's the trouble with you kids, always thinking you know every-thing!" Ignoring the muttered reactions from the ones around him, he went on, "Our older VR models are from the Dark Ages compared to this one. It boosts everything higher, all of your senses, and you name it. Marsh has these making everyone and everything around you looking real as life, and that's why your game's CGI's seemed real. I'm telling you, today our testers swore up and down they'd really been to Paris. Once they're used to this headset and you are too, games like this Gettysburg one won't seem crazy at all!"

Bessie began feeling lectured to. Hands planted on hips she glared back, "Dad, I'm telling you, Ben's game disappeared to be replaced by something else! I wound up inside that...that bubble, which...took me back in time to Gettysburg!" Biting her lip over this part, it sounded as crazy to her as she knew it did to him.

As she expected, he shook his head. "Nah, that's impossible." Also beginning to give up, he gave Connie a beseeching, silently mouthed...H-e-l-p!

Connie could not recall her *usually* even tempered daughter ever looking so over wrought. She said calmly, "You're okay, honey, get back to telling us what happened."

Her mom's reassuring ways usually had a calming effect on Bessie. Now, eyes darting from Rob to Connie, she knew, They still won't get it! Even so, she tried again, "It's hard to describe, Mom. Like Ben's, my headset worked amazingly well, As for this bubble thing, I felt something like it with our old unit, but really faint. This time I felt it very strong all around me!"

"And so?" Connie asked.

Frustrated, Bessie bunched her hands against her head, "I don't know how to put it!" She looked over at Alex.

"Like we just studied in physics, maybe I was inside an energy field."

Alex quickly explained, "We've studied quantum fields, Mr. Howard, and energy bubbles aren't just theory. They're scientifically proven to exist!"

Rob knew Alex well enough to concede the point with a shrug and a nod. Connie merely shook her head.

Though knowing she was getting nowhere with this, Bessie needed to keep talking. Trying again, she asked, "Dad, did your testers mention anything about this bubble? I could feel it all around me!"

"No, Honey, none of them said word one. Since you couldn't see it, how can you be so dead sure it was really there?"

Bessie had to admit the more she recalled her swirling impressions at Gettysburg, the less sure she was they'd happened. Worse, try to describe them was maddening. "Dad, I *told* you I *couldn't see* it! I *felt* it!"

Rob made the mistake of pushing this off. "Come on, everything looks like something! How big was it? What was it shaped like?"

This time she yelled it, "How would I know! It was invisible!"

Throwing up his hands, Rob knew he was batting zero. He gave Connie a helpless look. "I'm done, honey, she's all yours."

As he made to return to his recliner, she narrowed her eyes. "No you don't, *honey*! Before disappearing into your sports channel, you need to run another diagnostic on her headset!"

Rob knew that look. Holding the headset, he sighed, "Say no more," and headed for the computer room.

Looking at Nina, Bessie blew out a breath. "That's it for me too. Let's go for a walk or something."

Taking her cue, Nina took Bessie's arm and guided her

toward the front door. Looking back over her shoulder, she said, "Not to worry, Momma Howard. I'll walk her over to Julio's and we'll grab a cappuccino. We won't be too long."

Also knowing when to bow out, Connie tossed her a wave. "Honey, you girls take as long as you like."

Not that it happened very often, but Ben and his sister did help one another out with problems at times. This shaping up as a big one, he asked, "Mom, can I have your keys? I'll drive us over there."

Connie pointed to the doorway end table. "Sure, dear, they're over there."

Alex said, "I'm clued in about what she mentioned, so I'll tag along."

All smiles about getting away, Bessie jibed him, "You're hungry again, right?"

He grinned, "Enough for a double Italian sub! Let's go!"

Even more in the spirit of this, Bessie told Nina, "I'll tweet Lucy and Ravi to get in on this!"

First out the door, Nina was already taking charge. "Do it! With me there we'll straighten everything out!"

Chapter 13

One of Covington's most popular eateries, Julio's Pizzeria's candlelit tables, wickerwork wine bottles hanging from oaken beams, and a background of old favorite songs provided all the cozy Italian charm anyone could ask for. Weath-er permitting, clients also enjoyed their meals at outside tables beneath bright colored canopies piazza style. And en-joy them they did, the variety of 'specials' not only tasty but served at prices even high school students could afford. More helpfully, these were also hired by owners Julio and Sophia Panetta both parttime and fulltime when needed.

With so many others lured out by the warm evening, Bes-sie's crowd found no empty outside tables. Only sheer luck allowed Ben a parking space at the far side of the parking lot. Peering in through Julio's picture window, Nina stamped her foot. "The worst! Not enough room in there to breath!"

Seeing all the outside tables filled by happy eaters, Alex groaned, "Forget it, guys, we're gonna starve!"

No sooner said when one group began getting up from one of the larger tables. Nina shoved both Alex and Ben, "Grab it you two!"

A flurry of texts on the way here said that Ravi had finished beating up his opponent and that Lucy needed a break from her cyber project. Eager to hear about Bessie's amazing VR episode, they were on their way.

Marching to the head of the table, Nina again commandeered the two guys. "Now find a couple of chairs for Lulu and Ravi! Go on, go!"

Just as all four were seated, Ravi pulled his scooter to

the curb with Lucy hanging on behind. Next, with them joined in, everyone began talking at once.

Nina banged a spoon on the table. "All right, people, settle down!" When they quieted she pointed the spoon at Bessie. "You have the floor, girl."

Looking around at everyone, she began slowly, "I know this will sound crazy, you guys, but just let me..."

Ben cut her off. "Louder, it's too noisy in here!"

She started again. "This will sound totally nuts as I tell it, so I'll only do this once! Just hear me out and then ask whatever you want!"

Pulling potato chips from a basket, Alex said, "They can hear my stomach growling over in Madison, and I can't think without food! First let's order!"

Ben horse laughed, "Earlier you almost ate one of our pizzas by yourself, so I'm for that!"

Ravi chimed in, "Out of mom's leftovers, all I had was a cup of yogurt!"

Nina told them, "Eat, eat, eat, you guys are unreal!" Rising up, she called to the nearest server, "Hey over there! Yoo-hoo!"

Tending to customers two tables away, a tall blond girl in a red checkered smock looked back over her shoulder. Seeing who called, she narrowed her eyes. "You talking to me!?"

Nina had recognized her the minute they'd walked in. In-stantly playing a favorite role, Queen Elizabeth of medieval England, she summoned regally, "Yes, my *deah,* could *yew* come *ovah heah?"*

Wordlessly signaling with a raised finger to wait, the server pointedly turned her back and returned to her customers.

Reseated, Nina winked at Bessie, "She'll take her time since it's me, Talk to us."

Starting again, Bessie described the bubble, or started to.

Ravi interrupted, "Hold it a second, is your PC's bandwidth one of those...?"

Nina shook her spoon at him, "Hush, Wiz, let her talk!"

Bessie said, "Whatever it was, I saw through it perfectly!" She reached out her hands. "I felt it all around but everything outside it was blocked out, any noises, or smells, or even the wind. With a war going on I should have at least heard that! But no, not a sound!"

Alex began, "But what if...?" Nina's sharp glance kept him still.

Bessie went on, "Trying to take it all in, I saw that officer riding toward me. Then when he looked up and *saw me...*?"

Ben laughingly cut in, "He hollered, 'Hi up there, how's it going!'"

She nodded back, "Right, and I yelled, "Fine, thanks! So how's your war going?" Gaining needed relief as this drew laughs from the rest, she wrapped it up, "But no, when I waved...*and he waved back*, nothing was fine! Panicked, I tore off my headset and that's it. So am I totally nuts or what?"

Alex spoke first. "Nah, you're no crazier than I am!"

Ben snorted, "That's not saying much! You're just as nuts with your physics stuff." And then to Bessie, "And you, too, still playing with that old wizard stick."

Nina corrected, "A staff, not a stick, and back in middle school she said she wasn't a wizard but a...?" She looked at Lucy. "...what was it back then?"

Lucy also paused, "I, er...oh, a cyberspace sorceress!"

That quieted everyone, until the cross talk started again, Nina's spoon clacked the tabletop. "One at a time! Alex, you look like you've got something! What?"

He looked up from his phone's display. "I might but it's mostly physics."

Bessie nodded, "I thought so! And?"

Munching another chip, he waggled the phone, "If we go over this..."

Now at their table, their server cut him off, "So all you scientists are here I see!" She added a dry smile to Nina, "My-my, and Miss Hollywood too!" Before Nina could answer, she asked, "So what can I get you?"

As all looked up at her, the guys lingered with that, Sierra Hutchins' attractiveness tending to turn male heads. One of their school's star athletes and a socially hip senior, she viewed this group (except Nina) with benevolent bemuse-ment. On seeing Bessie, her smile suddenly brightened, "Well hi, cuz, and how goes it?"

Technically they were related. Sierra's mother had died four years ago, and father Jack Hutchins, Covington's current chief of police, later met and married Bessie's aunt Melissa, Connie's older sister. Despite a two-year age difference, both girls had instantly liked one another. Back when Bessie entered high school as a lowly picked-on freshman, Sierra instantly became her protector.

Bessie shrugged, "Only so-so, cuz, for the moment anyway!"

Sierra showed instant concern. "Uh-oh, anything I can help with?"

"No, I'm just now running it past these guys. Let's say it involves...physics!"

Sierra shook her head. "That I can't help you with, but we'll get back to each other real soon. That UW tuition keeps me here a lot, but I'm mostly free during the week." Tuition for the University of Wisconsin wasn't cheap, not even for resident students. By working every day she could, she hoped to save enough to cover it.

As the others decided what they wanted, Sierra smiled sweetly at Nina, "So, Miz Hollywood, hanging out with your fans tonight? As *few* as they are?"

Nina's smile was even sweeter, "They never give me a

moment's rest, but..." she faked a wide yawn, "...I get that a lot! Sooo, how are *you* doing...*without* your driver's license, hmmm?" Drawing out that last, she liked reminding Sierra that hers was suspended by her dad after two speeding tickets!

Having hitched rides or walked ever since, Sierra smirked, "Unlike the child you are, I at least *have* one!" Not waiting for a reply, she asked the others, "Want some pizza really cheap? Two extra large thin crusts were called in but they just canceled. Either we eat them or pitch 'em, two perfectly good ones, and still hot!"

Ben had eyed this lovely looking classmate of his since their freshman year, Turning on the charm, he grinned, "Sierra, I could eat one of those by myself! Bring it and I'll throw you some cash anyway!"

Watching, Nina rolled up her eyes. Wearing his usual look of being at starvation's door, Alex said, "Bring 'em both and I'll kick in too!" All the others got in on it.

After Sierra brought the pizzas and what else they wanted, everyone snatched up whatever was in front of them. Immediate hunger pains soon relieved, they all got back to discussing Bessie's experience with Gettysburg.

Always seeking practical answers to puzzling questions, Lucy asked, "Could you have had a hallucination or something? That's what it sounds like."

Bessie replied, "Now I'm hallucinating? Come on, Lu!"

Seated next to Lucy, Ravi stopped eyeing her long enough to say, "We're only talking a video game. Also, Ben said it seemed pretty real to him too."

Finished with his final slice, Ben shook his head at Ravi, "My VR didn't do as much with me as hers did, and I still don't get that." He grinned at Bessie. "I've heard how some users fried their brains with these latest models. Maybe that's what happened to yours!" They all laughed except for Bessie. Swallowing his last mouthful, Alex motioned for her to give him a few seconds yet.

Lucy stayed stoically pragmatic. "That amazing glitch with yours could be due to its highly upgraded sensors. You'll know more after your dad's diagnostics."

Ravi laughed, "If there is a problem, my mandarin muffin here can take it apart and fix it. Then I, your friendly Wizard, will give it the best test run ever!"

Looking at Alex, Nina smiled disgustedly, "*If* you're through filling your face, what about you, genius guy? Any-thing?"

First checking his notes, he nodded. "Yeah, but these can wait." Entirely in earnest for once, he added to Bessie. "Till we run 'em past each other...before getting too nuts with this Gettysburg thing."

Finally feeling partly understood, Bessie returned a smile, "Why not? We'll cover it on the way home."

Lucy asked, "If your headset's diagnostics are OK, will you use it again?"

Mind made up to do just that, Bessie said, "Tomorrow first thing, but just to places in the here and now. There'll be no more war games until I get Maxwell figured out. Whatever happens with that, I'll tell you right away."

Nina looked around at them all. "Anyone else? With anything? No? In that case..." She banged the spoon on the table. "...I declare these proceedings closed! Besides, the night's still young, and I've still got lots to do for tomorrow's show." Getting Sierra's attention, she waved, "Yoo-hoo, Sierra dear! Come over here, please!"

Back at their table, Sierra eyed Nina narrowly for a second, then told the rest, "No charge for the pizzas, but there is for the other stuff." Arching an eyebrow at the crumbs and splattered sauce in front of Alex, Ravi and Ben, she laughed. "I should charge you three extra for cleaning up your war zone!"

Everyone kicked in some cash. Mentally tallying up

their tip, every penny of it bound for her college fund, Sierra grinned, "Thanks, every bit helps!" If grudgingly, she smiled more tightly to Nina. "And you too Miz Hollywood!" For her benefit, Sierra added an insolent flip of her hip before hurrying off.

Right after Ravi and Lucy left on his scooter, the rest climbed into the car with Ben and headed home.

Chapter 14

Seated in front with Ben, only the seat belt kept Nina from scooting closer. Undaunted as ever, she began plying her wiles. Politely putting up with it, he mostly watched out for traffic.

Bessie and Alex were already in a serious discussion in back. She looked at him questioningly. "You just said it again, that time travel isn't possible, so why keep bringing it up?"

Alex was fascinated by Bessie's strange experience. Now completely absorbed with it, he shook his head. "Uh-uh, *you* did, remember? You actually shouted you'd gone back in time to Gettysburg."

"I did, exalted genius, so what are your thoughts?"

He shrugged. "Brilliant as I am, my physics really breaks with time travel. The one exception is something I read."

"What was that?"

Slowing to a stop behind a line of vehicles at a red light, Ben groaned, "This warm weather has the whole town out tonight. We'll be awhile getting home."

To make him pay less attention to traffic and more on her, Nina cooed, "Fine with me, Ben." She gave the other two a backward glance, "You two OK?"

Alex shook his head, "Interruptions, interruptions! What was I saying?"

Waving off Nina, she said, "What you read about time travel, and so?"

"It was a physics experiment that fired a laser beam even faster than light. They claimed this detoured around the laws of relativity to let the beam travel back in time. Later they found something wrong with their experiment, and nothing else was published about it."

"Fine, but what did you learn?"

"Only that most physicists think time travel really is impossible."

"Why is that?"

"For one thing it brings in what they call the grandfather paradox."

Staring back at them, Nina snickered, "Get a life back there! With such a nice evening and all, why go on and on about that boring stuff?"

Bessie gave her a brushing motion, "Keep flirting with my idiot brother, OK? We're solving the world's biggest problems back here!"

Ben snorted, "Well solve 'em quick, we're finally closer to our place!"

Alex shrugged apologetically at Bessie. "Miss Hollywood threw me off again. What was I saying?"

"Something about a paradox. Say more."

"Okay, so you go back in time and shoot...? Well, you're close to your grandmother, so you wouldn't shoot her. But let's say that you did, OK?"

"Granny Michelle would hate that, but then what?"

"Then you'd' never have been born, which means you couldn't have gone back and shot her in the first place." He made a circular motion. "This round and round it goes thing is the paradox. Thinking about it too long makes you crazy."

She frowned. "I can see why, except you do have a but coming, right?"

He laughed. "I always do...with you! Anyway, to get a feel for this, I tracked down some sci-fy stories about time travel."

"How'd you do?"

He stabbed his forefinger emphatically. "I found one

whose main kicker was that by going back in time, a traveler could screw up and change their own future. So this guy gets on a newly invented time path and goes back to the Age of Dinosaurs. He's been warned to never stray off this path to accidentally crush a plant or squish an insect. This, he's told, will cause ripples moving forward in time like a rock tossed in a pool."

"I get it, those ripples eventually affect our own time!"

"Yep, that's exactly what this time traveler does. Getting off the path and stomping around in this pre-historic jungle, he squashes a butterfly. When back he finds everything in America is different from when he left. Believe me, if time travel was possible, it's stuff like this that scares theoretical physicists to death."

Bessie's eyes widened, "It scares me, too, and so?"

"They're afraid if they do figure out how to travel in time, it'd be a total disaster. You're taking modern history, so let's say you go back to...OK, if not to Gettysburg, but to World War II. Then by accidentally changing something, that maniac Hitler winds up winning it! Think about it!"

Bessie realized he was right, that going back could have horrific results. She posed her other uneasy thought, "Except, in my case you're still not convinced I went back to Gettysburg. Go ahead, say it."

Honestly puzzled he slowly shook his head. "I have my doubts, I guess, but I know you'd never make up a story so nuts!"

Stopping in front of their house, Ben said, "You girls get out and I'll drop off Alex at his place. I've got to be up early tomorrow for our game in Middleton."

Bessie replied without looking at him, "Shush a minute," and then to Alex, "I really did wave to that trooper and he waved back. That's the truth."

Though still unsure of all this, Alex wanted to hear her out. "OK and so?"

"All right, let's say he kept a diary and writes about seeing me up there in the sky and waving at him. If anyone read this later it could affect the present!"

He shrugged. "Maybe it would and maybe not! History is full of stories about fiery wheels in the sky, or paintings of ancient gods flying around. When I think about it..." He stopped.

She leaned toward him. "Come on, what!"

He held up his hands, "Look, our own present has pretty weird happenings at times. Compared to these, your Gettysburg diary story isn't strange at all."

Bessie smiled wryly. "Just another nutcase one with aliens in the sky, right?"

Ben complained from up front, "Yo, sis, save it for later!"

Already out of the car, Nina said her good night to him and then to Bessie, as she and Alex climbed out, "I'm starting early myself, girl. Catch you later!"

As she headed home, Alex climbed in front, and Bessie leaned down to the open window. "You've got me thinking about this, you know that?"

He nodded. "So am I with those whatever we call them, those...time ripples."

She nodded back, "And?"

"It's that any from your trip might've been too small to change anything later on."

Too caught up with this to cut it short just yet, she said, "What if you go back to the Age of Dinosaurs and leave behind, say, a pen? Then it's fossilized and today's paleontologists dig it up? The ripple from this would be huge!"

He agreed. "Yeah, it'd turn modern day studies upside down!"

Ben was louder this time. "Bean, knock it off so I can drive him home! I need to get to bed sometime tonight, you know?"

Alex told him, "Give me a second," and then to her," Listen, with you and this Gettysburg bit, don't take any more time trips till we talk this out some more, OK?"

"I shouldn't," she smiled, "but I can't promise I won't."

He frowned, "Going to bed wondering if I'll wake up a chimp is a bummer, so please try not to. Shake on it?" He held out his hand.

Taking it, she felt its warm firmness. Holding on for an extra few seconds, she nodded, "We're on. See you tomorrow."

Going inside, Bessie took no notice of the dark colored car parked across the street and the two men in the front seat.

Chapter 15

Ending a long and trying day, Bessie knew she ought to jump into bed herself. But no, she'd then be all night staring at the ceiling, wondering how to explain this Gettysburg thing. With cold water splashed on her face, and much re-freshed, she met Connie in the hall. "Mom! How come you're still up?"

"Actually, I was waiting for you. Did all of you solve your headset problem?"

"No, the only one who came closest was Alex. We'll talk about it some more tomorrow. What did Dad find out about Maxwell?"

"He's fine, dear. Your dad couldn't find anything wrong."

Bessie returned a smug smile. "I was pretty sure he wouldn't."

"Are you using the headset again tomorrow?"

"When you fall off that horse, get back on it, they say. I'll try Maxwell with that movie I made of our hike into the Grand Canyon last year. If any more strange stuff happens with that, I'll back off."

"Fine, but remember your Dad's warning to not just yank off your headset. Ben said he saw you do that, by the way."

"Really? He's such a squealer!"

Connie gave her mom the look. "Elizabeth Ann, don't say that! When your Dad asked Ben if he saw you just yank it off, all Ben did was tell the truth. That's probably why you were so disoriented afterward."

Hearing her full name said, Bessie knew she'd over stepped. "Sorry, Mom, and you're right. Ben's not the bright-est at times, but he's honest. Besides, I'm the one who blew it by just tearing off Maxwell. I'll watch that from now on." At the same time she doubted this fully accounted for what had happened.

"Fine, but any more of this crazy stuff and I'll set up another appointment with Dr. Myers."

"Oh come on, if nothing's wrong with my headset, there is with my head?"

Connie again gave her the look, "No nonsense, if your oversized whatever it is did cause all this..."

"It's my ITC!"

"Yes, that! If it causes you to see things while wearing a VR unit, then you and I *and* Dr. Myers need to find out what's going on."

Having had it with her ITC, her mind's wellness, and the whole thing, the last thing Bessie wanted was to argue about Dr. Meyers. Forcing a smile, she nodded. "Fine, Mom, and I'm off to bed."

Pajamas on and feeling better about how her day turned out, Bessie literally fell into bed. Turning once to snuggle more comfortably beneath the blankets, she started to check the time on her luminous clock. This as far as she got, she fell sound asleep.

Chapter 16

Bessie awoke with a start. Rolling over, she saw it was only half past six. Usually she stayed cozily snuggled up for a while. Wanting none of that today, she bounced out of bed and jumped into her clothes. Hurrying into the kitchen, she spooned up cold cereal while standing. Next seated at the computer console and about to put on Maxwell she heard the rest of the family also up and bustling around. After her virtual Gettysburg trip, the last thing she wanted were any of them looking on during this one. Stifling her impatience to set off on it, she left the computer room to see what everyone else was doing.

Already heading out the door, her dad called out over his shoulder, "I'll be back early this afternoon! Remember, we're heading to Green Bay!" He left.

Hard on his heels Ben said, "Mom, I won't be home for dinner tonight either. After our game I'm looking at cars again." A teammate honked his car horn out front. Hurrying to the door with "Yeah-yeah, I'm coming!" he saw Bessie. Stopping, he looked her in the eye. "Don't go playing around with Gettysburg again, OK?"

She smiled back. "First, Butt Brain, I don't just *play* with virtual! And count on it, no way will I ever go there again!"

"Good, because you'll get messed up even more if you do! Not that you aren't already!" Once again the horn sounded and he too was gone.

Connie said, "I'm off too!" Looking back, she wagged a finger. "And you be careful using your headset!"

Bessie returned a tight smile. "Don't worry, Mom, I

will!"

Seated at the computer again, she loaded her Grand Canyon DVD.

Donning the headset, she felt her heart racing. Calmer after some deep breathing, she considered what this trip entailed. For one thing, she would not be traveling back in time. Instead, she'd be simply crossing a distance in the pres-ent. Thinking about this for a moment, she posed herself the question; having made this movie *last* year, would this somehow count as time travel? The only way to find out of course was to try it.

She first eyed the staff next to her against the wall. It had never emitted an eerie glow or given off an aura from the amulets, or any of those Hollywood special effects. Feeling silly, yet knowing it wouldn't hurt, she reached out and touched it. Taking a deep breath, she said, "Let's do it!" and pressed PLAY.

The movie showed snatches of her family hiking the Grand Canyon's Bright Angel Trail. Never intending to take it all the way down, her parents had halted at the halfway point. Enthralled by all she'd seen so far, Bessie had vowed, while trudging back up, to return someday and hike the whole distance. Virtually, as it were, Maxwell would now help her to do that. The DVD opened with a satellite view of the whole canyon. Bessie's movie directing guru, Nina, had added this to lend the opening, in her words, *cinematic artistry.*

Eyes fixed on the overview, Bessie summoned up her glow line. Aiming it at the south central edge of the canyon, she mentally pushed forward on the beam and started down. Nothing strange happened at first, and suddenly pitch blackness! The assemblage of frozen images rose up and sailed away. Seconds later there was only her, the chair, and the monitor, and the bubble's strong presence all around.

The monitor still showed Ben and her folks down the

trail just ahead. Oblivious to this, she gasped, "OMG!" The computer room gone, spread to the far horizon beneath deep blue in splendorous colors was the Grand Canyon.

Bessie jumped up from her chair. "You did it, Maxie, we're here!" Somehow tearing her eyes away, she saw directly below that tour buses were unloading passengers at the visitor center. Down to her left three women hikers were walking the South Rim's paved trail. Watching for a moment, it struck her that she was up here in plain sight!

Quickly re-seated, she saw her display read 7:30 AM. This was Wisconsin time, but since Arizona did not use daylight savings their time was the same. There wasn't much of a crowd yet. But even so, the same as that trooper last night, someone down there would look up. Frantically looking for a hiding place, she spotted a stand of small junipers near the Bright Angel trail head. Focusing there, she voice commanded, "Quick, Maxie, take us down there!"

Bessie would later recall having also thought this command. In any case, possibly obeying both types, the bubble promptly descended at the rapid but controllable rate she wanted it to. Hovering over the junipers, she just as effortlessly floated to an open spot and grounded herself. She then realized the three women, now at the guardrail for the trail overlook, were uncomfortably close. Noting their backpacks and belted water bottles, she figured they were readying to start down. Or so she hoped, not hidden as well as she liked by the short junipers.

Thinking, it'll have to do, she keyed her phone's movie and audio apps, Standing, she aimed the screen at the canyon and moved it from left to right. Voice kept low but shaking a bit, Bessie began, "Hi everyone and here I am at the Grand Canyon! As you can see..." She pressed STOP. Not high enough for a good overall shot, she leveraged herself up another foot or so atop the console.

Peering down from the guardrail, the three women were

still focused on the trail. Far to the right others were starting her way from the visitor center. If any of them saw her,
would she be just some girl in a headband with shades
taking cell phone views like everyone else? With her the
monitor, and part of the console also floating in mid air?
Forget it, she had to wrap this up!

That thought no sooner escaped when she saw one of the
women look back toward her. Doing a double take, she got
the attention of her friends. As all three stared at Bessie, she
knew with a heart thud this trip was over. Yet, with nothing
to lose by stalling another few seconds, she faced them.
Sweeping an arm toward the canyon, she grinned, "So gorgeous, I love it here, don't you?"

Picturing them seeing her silently mouthing who knows
what and grinning like an idiot made her nearly burst out
laughing. Getting a grip, she saw the three of them hurrying
toward her. The first to have spotted her stopped several
feet away and took off the shades. Face wreathed with puz-
zlement and concern, she mouthed, "What is this! Are you
all right?"

Still, Bessie wasn't half so panicked as last night. Already seated before the monitor, she saw the woman tenta-
tively reach out to touch the bubble...and instantly yank her
hand back!

That was the last thing she saw. Heart thumping wildly
and eyes squeezed shut, she forced herself to focus on the
computer room. Imaging up the glow line and gripping the
chair, she hung on tight during the parade of images. During this brief stretch, she could hardly guess what those
poor women thought of her vanishing before their very
eyes. Then, too, if reporting this to the visitor center, would
anyone believe them? Having more or less been there and
done that last night, she thought, Good luck with that,
ladies! Whatever the case, she'd be sure to conceal herself a
lot better during any more of these virtual trips.

Chapter 17

Though feeling scattered on her return, Bessie remembered to leave the visor down. Soon oriented she cautiously removed Maxwell. Shaking the hair out of her eyes, she blinked a few times until fully aware of being back home. Getting up from the chair, she saw the monitor still playing her bouncy handheld movie. By now her parents and Ben were walking the trail below her. As they came to an opening cut through the rock, her brother turned with a grin and flipped her the bird. Stepping over to him, Mom slapped his arm down. Giving Bessie a time-out signal for the movie making, she beckoned her to come along.

Incredibly, it was still only 7:45. Feeling as if ages had passed, she was dying to tell someone what she'd done. Her first choice was Alex, but his text on her phone display read busy outside chores/CUlater. Stamping her foot, she said "Well nuts!" then sent back *wild Grand Canyon trip/quick get back*. Nina, Lucy, and Ravi would also be too busy for her to clue them in. Shaking off the frustration, she knew they'd all touch base later.

Bessie felt none of the upsets of the night before, not even after the chaotic ending of this morning's trip. Reaching up to her head, she realized too that today the usually attending aching head was a minor concern. Maybe I'm getting more used to this, she thought. Even so, experiencing only a slight ache while on virtual trips was an annoyance she did not need. Going into the bathroom, she picked out of the medicine cabinet a nearly full bottle of low dose aspirin. Placing one in her mouth, then figuring that two might work better, she washed both of them down. Since the nearly full bottle had been hardly used, she put it into a side pocket to keep with her from now on.

By now what else Bessie felt was a burning desire to go off on more of these trips. Soon seated before the monitor and wearing Maxwell again, she knew that before going anywhere else, she had to figure out a few things. According to dad, Maxwell's effective wireless range was fifty or sixty feet. Assuming her bubble would follow, she had to find out how far she could walk from her chair before he stopped being effective. Staying within working range without the encumbering other stuff would have her able to better blend in with others nearby. The troubling part, beyond a certain distance she and Maxwell could suddenly disconnect from the computer, leaving her high and dry wherever she visited.

Getting stranded in the backyard was no problem but if she walked out of range after hopping over to, say, France? She imagined calling back, "Hi, Mom, I'm marooned here in Paris! Would you mind arranging to fly me home?"

As for trying what dad mentioned about thought commands, hadn't she just done that? Possibly, but to be sure she had to keep them simple. She knew too that, along with snapping photos, she had to bring back samples from these places. These would be hands-on proof she wasn't imagining all this.

She smiled to herself, No worries with travelling, I'm good to go with that! Reaching out of habit to touch her staff, she closed her eyes and made a mental image of the back yard and the large oak in the middle of it. Then, try as she might, she could not form the glow line to take her there. After several more attempts it still refused to work. Having traveled two thousand miles to the Grand Canyon, she could not cross a skimpy fifty feet just to land out back. Was it due to being wireless? With cable to Maxwell's USB, she still didn't budge.

Maybe she needed a movie or at least a photo of her

destination to better focus on it. Hurrying outside, she snapped a few shots of the yard and uploaded them, Wireless again she fully focused on the monitor's distinct images and seconds later...she hung suspended over their oak tree!

Hastily grounding herself, she decided to test Maxwell's effective range. Their backyard extended a hundred feet to the back fence. Standing up with eyes fixed on the monitor and the chair, she took several steps toward the fence. To make sure the bubble had moved with her, she reached out and felt the familiar yielding. Roughly ten feet away, what she'd left behind looked exactly the same.

Trying farther away this time, she counted off ten steps, her long legs covering over another thirty feet. Reaching out again, her fingertips met the bubble's yielding. There was also an odd tingling, as if the bubble was straining to hold itself together. Her chair, monitor, and part of the console were where she left them, but here too their colors were faded to a faint transparency. Apparently Maxwell's working range wasn't much beyond where she stood. To find out where that might be she took two more steps.

With no time to cry out, she was wrenched away to some place completely dark! An instant later the light came back! Head spinning, with no idea where she was, Bessie somehow managed at least one coherent thought – Stand still! I'm OK! Get a grip! She saw through her visor that she was not back in the computer room. No longer feeling the bubble around her nor perceiving a connection to Maxwell meant he was shut down.

Taking him off, Bessie stood just beyond the back of the house. As the aluminum siding's solidly physical existence registered, a hard knot formed in her stomach. If not able to take those final steps and materializing sooner, she might have become part of the siding! Holding Maxwell up, she wagged a finger, "No more strolling with you, my friend!"

After rubbing the sides of her head, she felt better. Enough in fact to perform her next experiment, collecting a sample. Shortly her bubble rested beside a leaf pile she had raked up a couple of days ago. Now for the tough part Bessie knowing she could not push her hand through the bubble to grab these leaves. For all she knew so far, nothing could pass through in or out, no objects, no heat or cold, no sound, nor anything else other than light. Even so, very determined she said it aloud, "Come on Maxie, help me with this!"

She knew she actually could move this bubble. And not only that, it had conformed to her shape before when she'd stood up. The leaves so tantalizingly within reach, she wondered, just slide the bubble forward till it includes them?

Leaning down, she made a pushing motion with both hands. Sure enough, changing shape as if elasticized, the bubble not only flowed in the direction she wanted but also lowered its bottom to just below ground level. "Aha!" she exclaimed. Both hands snatching for the leaves, she had them!

Relishing their crackly roughness, Bessie rolled them around in her hands and buried her nose in them. Inhaling the pungent fragrance, she tipped her face to the sky. "All right, here's my proof!"

Chapter 18

Grabbing a self-seal plastic bag from a kitchen drawer, Bessie stuffed the leaves into it. Bagged sample in hand she decided that before any more teleporting, she wanted to tell someone, anyone, about the amazing results of her experiments. No point in calling Nina, probably in the middle of modeling. Maybe either Lucy or Ravi could be reached by now. But no, instead she tried the one who'd best understand what she'd done.

As Alex's phone rang, she impatiently tapped her foot. *Come on, pick up!* But no answer. Which drove her crazy sometimes, his absentmindedly laying down his phone someplace, but forgetting it when wandering off somewhere else. First to admit that he did this, Alex kept his message alarm at its highest level. Pacing back and forth, Bessie began calling a second time when her own phone chimed.

Sounding out of breath, it was him. "Hey, you've gotta take another course! On patience! You were off before I could find my phone!"

"So tie it to your wrist! What if I was having an emergency?"

"Well don't, because Mom has me up to here with chores. Anyway, I did see your message about the Grand Canyon. How'd it go?"

"In one way, fantastic! I got there, at least. But then the same thing happened like with that trooper last night. Except this time it was hikers, so I had to split. You sound winded by the way. Were you jogging or what?"

"I just finished chain-sawing a downed oak out back. But I meant to call anyway to see how you were doing."

"I've been pretty busy too. Listen, can you come over pretty quick? If I don't show you something this very second I'll go totally bonkers!"

"Well, we don't want you any more nuts than you are! Be there in a few soon as I hose off my sawdust!"

Soon seated side by side at the kitchen table they were, as always, immersed in a science world all their own. First filling him in about her experiments and then showing her samples, she shook her head and laughed, "While you were on your way, I realized how really dumb this is. I mean, they're only... *leaves*."

"Not that I doubt your word, Bean, but they're not exactly proof positive!"

So much was happening this morning that she barely noticed his Bean thing. Her eyes fastened on his. "The best proof would be bringing you along. Trouble is, I can't do that. Not yet, anyway."

Seemingly disappointed, he said, "Not that you could. But if so, why not?"

She frowned. "I've barely started with this, so I need to do more just on my own to get used to it. I've thought up another way. How's your schedule?"

"No lie, I'd like to, but mom has these guys coming over to load up what I sawed and haul it away. "Of course, she wants me there to make sure they take it all."

"All right, but when are they coming?"

"Probably within the hour." He checked his phone. "It's nearly ten, so I should get back there."

"Come on, not even for what, twenty minutes? That's all it would take!"

Seeing her beseeching look, he backed up a little. "Just tell me your plan, all right? I can spare time for that."

Frustrated as she was, this seemed like all she could do. "Alex, I do want you to witness this and with the house to ourselves it's perfect."

Though fidgeting, he nudged her. "So tell me your plan."

Starting to, she looked away and muttered something he couldn't hear.

"What?" he asked.

Still looking away, she slapped the table. "This is so stupid!" It felt so great having someone else, especially Alex, in on this with her. And yet? Turning, Bessie gave him a helpless look, "Suddenly, I'm not sure that I want to."

He groaned, "You practically drag me over here and now you back off? What gives?"

She grimaced. "If I just talk about it you'll think I'm an idiot. If Ravi and Lucy were here so would they. Catching that last night, I really hated it."

"OK and sorry about that. But you never lie, so I believed you. And you believed what you said. This morning I even thought there might be some real physics involved. Speaking of which, you beat the snot out of Lucy and Ravi in that exam, so who cares what they think?"

Like her mother she gave him that look. "You're changing the subject."

He admitted, "You got me there. People also laughed at Einstein, right?"

"Yes but don't do that with me!"

Alex rolled his eyes. "Bean, if it'll make you feel better, I do that with all sophomores,

She narrowed her eyes. "You're changing the subject again."

He threw up his hands. "OK, so let's knock off the whining and get to your plan." Again he glanced at his phone. "But keep it short!"

She tried, but it took longer than she thought, Alex's scribbled diagrams covering two large pages of a legal pad with her own notations added in. She had also mentioned some other much, much farther off places she wanted to visit, like Mars for instance. About to tell him she was considering actually going there, she glanced at her phone. "Oops, sorry, I lost track of the time!"

He got up from the table, "So did I. But you're right, I've got to go." He slid the legal pad toward her, "Keep all of this stuff and maybe it'll help."

She smiled. "Thanks, it might. During the next couple of hours I'll be visiting other places I've always wanted to see. By the end of the day I'll have most of the bugs with these virtual trips worked out. I hope."

"OK, catch you later," he said and left.

Chapter 19

Bessie hoped Alex's sketches and equations would at least partly explain the strange phenomena with her trips. She sorted through her mom's computer files of places she and Dad had visited. The earliest ones showed them here in the Midwest to as far as each of the coasts. Later dated ones included her and Ben but these she ignored. Choosing the places she'd not been to yet, she uploaded the photos.

The first place and the easiest, she hoped, was close to home. Setting off for La Crosse, Wisconsin, on the Mississippi River, she intended to keep this trip short. Once there, she would practice shifting the bubble around and also stay-ing hidden from prying eyes.

Soon suspended above the town, she hastily searched for a place with no one else around. Spotting a vacant overlook on the mighty waterway, she descended until several feet above the ground. Following a brief time of practicing, she learned how to shift across local distances with ease.

Confidence raised a notch, she headed for California's Carmel Highlands. The uploaded photo was a postcard mom had kept when she and dad honeymooned there twenty years ago. A moment after appearing above the municipality she quickly grounded atop a visitor free cliff above a beach.

Relaxed for a change, she simply took in what she'd always wanted to see, the limitless expanse of the Pacific Ocean, its great gray green waves sweeping in past rocky promontories and pounding the shore. Looking farther out, she jerked up , Well look at that! Whales, a whole pod! She guessed they were humpbacks swimming south from feeding grounds near the Arctic Circle.

Bessie's zoom app brought them closer but not as much as she liked. Having seen these huge, intelligent creatures only on PBS or the Discovery Channel, she instantly rose up and glided out till over the pod. Still not near enough, plus, with heart in mouth, she dropped down to just above the waves. Spouting and diving their way south, the whales passed close enough beneath her to practically reach down and touch them.

She yelled, "Go, go, go babies, how I love you!" She would, at first chance, look up more about these lovely crea-tures.

Once back home Bessie noted the time, surprisingly it was still only just past noon. Time enough she supposed to squeeze in another excursion? Or maybe not. Standing, she shook out arms tightened from gripping the chair arms all morning. Realizing all she'd seen and done, along with the nonstop thrills, Bessie felt pretty much wrung out. Besides, her family was due home soon and her friends would be calling or coming over. So enough was enough for now with VR trips.

Chapter 20

Shortly Nina called to say she was back from her fashion show. Meeting her in the front yard, Bessie politely listened while being clued in about the latest styles. As she, in turn, told of her own doings, she made the mistake of trying to explain how they possibly had happened.

Nina interrupted, "Well, girl, you've had some adventures! But I'm no physics person, so you should stick with Alex about this."

They were partway into Nina's other favorite topics, boys, when Connie pulled into the driveway. Getting out of the car, she greeted them, "Hi, girls!"

Just then Sierra Hutchins was walking by on her way to work over Julio's. She called out, "Hi, cuz! And you, too, Aunt Connie!" Ignoring Nina, she began saying more when a white van drove slowly by. The side said Ultra Tech and below that Tel-Com Installation and Service.

First looking after it, Sierra turned to the girls and Connie. "That's the third time they've gone by since I left my place. I wonder why?"

Connie shrugged. "They're probably repairing something around here."

Staring after it again as it rounded a corner, Sierra shook her head. "I don't think so. Did any of you notice that dish on its roof?"

"Not really, but why?" Bessie asked.

As the daughter of the chief of police, Sierra knew all about the equipment atop the department vehicles. "The dish my dad's people use picks up conversations half a block away. But with that van using them around here, I don't get it."

Bessie nodded. "Since nothing much happens here anyway, right?"

Nina laughed. "Except for me of course!"

Again ignoring her, Sierra waved to Bessie and Connie. "Whatever, I've gotta go! See you later!" She paused and then to Nina, "And you, too, much as I'd like to avoid it!"

As Connie headed inside, a car horn blared twice and a third time. The girls turned to see a shiny red car pull into the driveway. Proudly grinning after climbing out, Ben swept out an arm. "Here she is, a nearly new Chevy! Bean, even you could drive it! Jump in you two and we'll go pick up Alex!"

Before long, they were back and Alex was with them. Ben quickly busied himself with a new chamois to remove imaginary specks from his car. Passed over by Ben in favor of his new wheels and seeing Bessie and Alex caught up in another of their science seminars, Nina gave up and went home, Soon after, Alex left Ben to his busy work and went inside with Bessie.

Seated with Alex at the kitchen table, Bessie picked up on where they'd earlier left off. "There's still one big question I can't answer and I need to."

"What's that?"

"How I can do my own kind of virtual trips in the first place? Maxwell is probably helping me." Purposely leaving out any mention of her staff, she tapped the side of her head "But the real answer might be up here, or mostly anyway."

He said, "We've talked about you going over to the Center. Trust me, if anyone has any answers it's them. If my mom sets it up, would you go?"

Connie came over to join them. "So what are you two up to?"

Alex nodded toward Bessie. "I just now asked her if she'd go to the Research Center." He added with a laugh, "To get her head examined."

Bessie rolled her eyes, "Nice way to put it!"as she nodded to Connie. "Actually he's got me thinking about it, and I'm tempted."

"Why is that, sweetie?"

"Alex and I talked about what I experienced last night while wearing Maxwell. When I used him today, the same strange stuff happened. Maybe I could get some answers at the research center."

Alex said, "She could, Mrs. Howard, and they'd even pay her. My mom already knows how good Bean...I mean... Bessie is with these virtual units."

Taking half a second to agree, Connie nodded vigorously to Bessie. "A very good idea! Your dad just sent them his new headsets, which you've already used. Most likely, Dr. Myers would be there too. Oh – except you told him you wanted no part of being whatever, a guinea pig or a lab rat? What changed your mind?"

"Mom, I did fine today with Maxwell. But Alex and I still can't explain these odd things that happen." Leaving out how less strange they were the more they'd occurred, she went on. "I'm guessing it has something to do with my oversized ITC. Plus, if Maxwell is tied in with this, I'd like to know how."

"Believe me, dear, I know you already have some ideas about this."

"That's why I changed my mind about Dr. Myers's bio-med research. So what do you think?"

"I'll call Carmen to see if she'll set you up and I'll talk to Dr. Myers too!" Connie went off to find her phone.

Left to themselves again Bessie began, "We keep getting stuck on impossibly long distances and vast amounts of time with relativity. So what about the incredibly small?"

Alex answered with his own question, "How small, the Planck length? Like 10 to the minus thirty-third centimeters?"

Lighting up, she nodded, "Yes! Since anything that small is where Einstein's relativity no longer applies. And neither does our enormous energy requirement for teleportation. Or even what we normally call space-time."

"OK, I get all that. But even something as small as the Higgs boson still needs too much energy to jump it instantly to someplace else."

"Yes, yes, yes, I know all that! Give me a second here!" Sliding over their ever-present sketch pad between them, she explained and diagrammed at the same time. My mom still draws these Zen tangles...like so." Never minding his impatient squirming and grumbling, in rapid strokes she sketched twisting, entwining ribbons of fine parallel lines, ending with a figure the size of her hand.

As she added shading for depth, he started, "Listen, are you gonna...?"

"Shush!" she told him while finishing up.

Taking in what she'd drawn, he nodded, "OK, it does look pretty neat." He tapped his forefinger where a pair of her ribbon lines disappeared into a shaded junction. "And here it's...a black hole?"

"It could be," she said. "Or else extra dimensions. Either way is where Hollingsworth says..."

Her pause let Alex finish, "That space, time, matter, energy and gravity are nothing like what we think they are. Or so outside them that for us they don't even exist. And so?"

"All right but back to tiny, tiny again. For instance, my brain's neurons?"

He groaned, "Now we're into biology? Come on!"

She returned huffily, "And why not? I can combine biology and quantum physics if I want!" Giving him no time to interrupt, she continued, "Look, I'm not to your level with physics, but I do know this. Or think it, anyway. That with neurons so tiny, tiny, the ones in..." Pausing, she subbed in for ITC. "…my brain might need only the energy from a household 110 V. outlet to transport even me to someplace else. In, say, a Zen tangle!" That last said with a self-satisfied smile.

Caught up in spite of his doubts, he smiled back, "OK, or for a fraction of a second within an entirely different dimen-sion."

Letting out a joined "Whew!" they both laughed. Even with Alex helping with his own comments and sketches, their efforts were making their heads spin. By unspoken agreement they brought all this to a halt. After Bessie walked him outside, he told her, "This thing at the Center won't happen till Monday at the earliest. What are you up to first thing tomorrow? As if I didn't know."

She shrugged. "I'm still not sure. After all that happened today I have some ideas of course. Mom, dad, and Butt Brain will be gone all day for the Packers game, so what about you?"

"Tomorrow is mom's day off at the Center, but she's working anyway. She and Dr. Paul are really excited about your dad's new units. As for me, I'm still stuck with her chore list for outside work, so I'm tied up 'til around noon."

As he said this, Bessie saw the white van again going slowly by. Looking more closely this time, she noticed the two men in front. The driver's eyes were straight ahead but the other one was looking directly at her.

Frowning after the van, she shook her head. "That's funny."

"What is?" Alex asked.

"Probably nothing, but earlier on her way to work Sierra told me she'd seen the van too, kind of circling around our neighborhood." Turning back to Alex, she wagged her finger. "Anyhow, tomorrow keep your phone handy, OK? Just this once? For all your brilliance, you always let it run down or leave it someplace!"

He laughed, "Okay, Professor Bean, I'll obey!" Then he left.

Shortly after, Connie returned still holding her phone. "It's set up with Carmen, but what about you? Can you take Monday off from school?"

"Actually mom, I'm caught up into next week. So sure!"

Raising the phone to her ear, Connie said, "She's on for Monday, Carmen. When? All right, I'll tell her. Bye-bye!" She fed Bessie a wide smile. "More than happy to take you to the Center, she'll be here Monday morning at seven."

Bessie was equally pleased. "I'll be ready and it'll be fun!" Liking and trusting Auntie Carmen, she'd added the Auntie after Carmen Ricci and her mom became friends. So now maybe she and Dr. Myers could help to chase off all the question marks ping-ponging around in her head.

Chapter 21

Gladly using his new car, Ben drove to Julio's and brought back pizzas for their evening meal. Uncharacteristically, Bessie barely touched hers. Too caught up with other things all week, her star-gazing had fallen off. Only wanting the sky to darken, she restlessly shoved around with her fork the slice on her plate. Excusing herself from the table to look outside, she saw the first points of light in the darkening October sky. These earliest ones at this time of year were four of the planets, Jupiter, Saturn, Venus and Mars.

Quickly out back she set up the telescope. Now well over a century old, and passed on to her by Connie, Bessie treasured it. As she first viewed Saturn, the scope's high powered optics and the clear sky afforded perfect viewing. From the back door Connie called, "Hey out there! Care if I join you?"

Bessie yelled back, "Quick, Mom, come see Saturn! It's gorgeous!"

Taking turns at the eyepiece, they shared their ooh's and ah's over the ringed planet. Revved up as always Bessie exclaimed, "You'll love Mars, too, Mom! In opposition to the sun it's only 40 million miles away! Give me a second with this Star Finder to set it up!"

Compared to modern instruments, the viewing qualities of the antique scope more than held its own. The old original mount had not. Teamed up to buy a new one, Bessie and Connie had made sure to include a programmable Star Finder.

Connie said, "Sure, dear. Oh, and tonight where's your other half?"

"She'll be here any minute. Soon as she picks the proper wardrobe for star gazing." Keying the coordinates with one hand, her other with the remote, Bessie's low interference red light was tucked between shoulder and chin. Slipping loose, the light fell to the grass.

Picking it up, Connie steadied the beam. "Try it again."

Making the adjustment, Bessie grinned, "I love this new Finder, but I need three hands to work it."

In answer, Nina's voice rang out from over the hedge, "You two sound ready for me to get you organized!"

Bessie called back, "Just come over and lend a hand!"

"Be right there!" Rounding the far end of the hedge, she pranced jauntily toward them in a bulky knit cashmere sweater and new-faded Monique St. Laurens jeans from today's modelling. In other words, perfectly attired for star gazing. Following short greetings, Bessie's infectious enthusiasm quickly had all of them looking at Mars. Relatively close to Earth this autumn, it was the brightest object in tonight's sky.

"Maybe it's my eyes," Connie said, "but it looks redder than usual."

Bessie motioned her back to the eyepiece. "Mom, take another look. Can you see the polar cap?"

"Barely, just a bit of white."

"It's evaporating. A Martian year equals two of ours, so its warmer summer seasons are twice as long."

Connie laughed, "I taught you that when you were five. It's still only halfway through its own summer, right?"

"Exactly, and all the evaporating at both of its poles creates howling wind storms. This doesn't happen as much during the Martian winter, but there's a lot of dust and sand blowing around up there right now." She gave Connie a knowing smile. "I'm just filling you in on NASA's latest data."

Seeing Bessie's better mood than last night brightened

Connie's. Playing along, she grinned, "Please do, oh wise one. So this is why Mars looks redder?"

"Right, and those red dust storms blow over 200 miles an hour!"

Nina gasped. "OMG, girl, and you've you'd like to go there?"

"I'd love to! Of course, I'd be driving a Rover to be out of the wind and to also be shielded from radiation by the sun. There's hardly any atmosphere to block out its rays, you know. Even so, Neen, roaming around up there would be the greatest adventure of my life!"

More revved up as she spoke, and oblivious to Nina and Connie trading wry smiles, Bessie literally bounced up and down. "And what I'd give to be up on that gigantic volcanic shield, Olympus Mons! Nearly three times higher than Mt. Everest! Or hiking that Martian canyon, Coprates? Do you know it's longer than across the entire United States?"

Connie smiled, "You hiked a pretty huge canyon of our own, remember?"

Smiling back, Bessie nodded. "Almost like it was just this morning."

Able to fit fashion into any topic, Nina cut in, "I've never been there. Pictures of it show colors I'd die for to wear!"

Bessie said, "The photos from our Mars orbiters and surface rovers make me want to go there!"

Connie gave Bessie a thoughtful look. "Mm-hm. Anyway, girls, I'm going in to put things together for tomorrow's game in Green Bay."

After admiring Mars, Bessie decided to view Pluto. Before having the Star Finder, locating the far distant dwarf world was difficult at best. Engaging the Finder's system, she saw within seconds by the remote's display that she was right on target. Even with eyes adjusted to nighttime vision and the old scope's superb optics, neither girl saw Pluto as other than a tiny speck. Enchanted all the same Bessie grinned, "Think of it, Neen! It's currently three and a half-billion miles away! That's where deep space really begins!"

By now not many cars were passing by on the street. As a van drove slowly past, neither girl could see it. Once past the Howard place it slowed and turned around.

From the dark alongside the house a voice called out, "Hey, you astronomers got room for one more?"

As Bessie welcomed Alex to join in, Connie hailed from the back porch, "I'm in for the night! Will you all be out there awhile?"

Bessie answered, "Maybe not these two, but I'll be busy awhile with Pluto!"

"Okay, dear, and good night!"

"Good night!" they all chorused.

Across the street, Trainer and Girardi were parked with engine and lights shut off. Behind the wheel and watching the dashboard monitor, Trainer shook his head. "Charlie, I'm still getting nothing from e-mails or tweets. How are your audios?"

On the passenger side, Girardi adjusted his headphone. "All I get is a bit of the usual kid stuff. 'Course, it'd help if we knew what Manley is looking for."

"I think she wants to know what all this Howard girl can do online with VR stuff. All we have so far is what we heard last night."

"It wasn't much with all the background noise." Then he laughed. "Something about her going back in time? Gimme a break!"

Trainer admitted, "Farfetched as it seemed, Manley got very excited later when we told her about that. So much that starting tonight she's letting us have Lewis and Moritz for our relief back-up."

"Are they standing by right now to come over here?"

Trainer's turn to laugh. "Uh-huh, and they're as unhappy as we are. Losing a night's sleep staking out some teenager just for being a cybernetics hotshot."

"The good news is Manley's talking Moorland into giving us some mighty nice double-time pay!"

Chapter 22

Bessie told Alex, "Earlier I thought I'd seen the last of you."

He nodded. "And so did I, but then I remembered how charged up you've been about you scope's locator. You like how it works?"

Deciphering all this and seeing them watching each other, matchmaker Nina pushed both of them toward the telescope. "Do it, girl, show him!"

Startled, Bessie looked back at her guilelessly. "What do you mean, Neen? Show him what!?"

Nina returned a look of her own. "*You* know what! Do it!"

"Oh! You mean..." Realizing what she meant, Bessie then tried her best. Running a hand lovingly over the telescope, she grinned hugely at Alex. "Anyhow, this tri-axial is as stable as the Rock of Gibraltar! Counting in the Star Finder's positioning ability, this is my proudest possession! Next to Maxwell I mean!" On finishing, she hadn't the faintest idea what she'd just said.

Alex merely raised his eyebrows, "Sounds pretty cool, all right." He laughed to Nina, "So what are you doing out here? You suddenly interested in something besides show biz?"

Tossing a careless wave, Nina grinned, "No-no-no, dear boy, not hardly." Facing Bessie, she pointedly rolled her eyes toward Alex. "Anyhow, I'll leave you two alone. Tomorrow's another early start, you know."

Glancing back and forth at Nina and Alex, Bessie began floundering. "No, no, Neen, just stay a while! Please? We can all.... I mean, I feel..." Thinking, Like an idiot!, she finished, "We can all do more viewing!" Her look back at Nina said, You better stay or else!

For Nina tonight's viewing had spurred a bit of interest, but not enough to stare at something smaller than a sand grain. Satisfied her job as cupid was done, she made her exit. "Ta-ta, you two, see you later!"

Left to themselves, Bessie and Alex reverted from long habit to being more comfy sharing their time as scientists. Instantly more at ease, Bessie decided that even though Pluto was on her mind she'd not say anything to Alex about it. So incredibly far away, the dwarf planet's surface conditions were still very new and strange, notwithstanding NASA's near fly-by in 2016. She would do more research before saying word one to Alex about visiting that place. Nimbly refocusing the scope, she said, "This is as good as I can get it. When you take a turn, you'll see why I'm so nuts about Mars. See for yourself!"

He did and then, "Man, I see what you mean!" Truly impressed, he took his time with viewing. Straightened back up, he admitted, "This is the first time I've taken a good look at your favorite planet!"

"So what do you think?" she asked.

"I get it, you viewing it so much. Through this scope it's still no bigger than a marble. But it's clear, the red color and the white polar cap, kinda fascinating!"

"Which is exactly why I'm dying to go there!"

"You mean with your VR unit, right?"

"Yes, that!" Looking up at the Red Planet, she added, "Which might be one and the same thing now that I think about it." Hearing him laugh at this, she faced him. "What's so funny? I'm serious!"

Still ruled more by skepticism than belief he smirked, "Uh-huh, like Gettysburg, right?"

This was too snide for Bessie's tastes. Fuming and hands to hips, she leaned toward him. "Yes I do, and why not!?"

Abruptly a bit heated himself, he retorted, "It's the distance for one thing. Forty million miles is a lot farther than Gettysburg. If you actually went there in the first place."

She wagged a finger. "We've been all over this distance thing before, remember? With all that you said about quantum...something or other!"

"Entanglement or QE."

"Right, and with QE distance means nothing whether it's out back, or hundreds of miles away, or even light years from here."

"Exactly, but never mind all that. Let's say your headset actually does get you to Mars. Then you'd be dealing with solar radiation."

"And?"

"Well, you're the one who told me there's not enough atmosphere to shield you from that. You say your bubble protects you from everything else, but this better include gamma rays. Because if not, you'll get cooked!"

She put on a sideways smile. "Uh-huh, so now you're worried about me?"

"Wait, I didn't mean..." They both looked away for a moment. Eyes meeting again, both were back to being scientists,

Bessie said, "Tell me, if I do go to Mars, what can I do about the sun's UV radiation? Our own ozone layer protects us but Mars doesn't have one."

"OK, after you tell me what you figure on doing there and especially for how long. Time of exposure is really critical...if you actually go there."

"At night on Mars there's no UV to worry about, but I wouldn't be able to see anything. During the daytime hours what do I wear to shield myself?"

"First, you told me the suns a lot farther from Mars, but the UV rays would be just as strong. The good news, you can shield bare skin pretty well with high blocking sunscreen."

"Which I have," she said.

"OK, and with the right clothing like a long sleeve shirt, full length pants, and a wide brim hat. Oh, plus lightweight gloves and sunshades of course."

"All of which I also have."

"And you'd be protected so long as you stay only a few minutes at most. Any longer is asking for trouble by getting your genes hit with too many UV rays." He laughed. "You don't want funny looking babies later on, right?"

She laughed back. "Of course not! If I ever have any, that is."

He became completely serious. "So you're actually going there?"

"Tomorrow first thing, soon as my parents and Butt Brain leave for Green Bay. And stop worrying, I'll check out NASA's latest data about Mars. As for the right clothes and what else I need, I'll save that till they're gone, especially mom. If she saw me at the computer in a wide brim hat, wearing winter clothing, and carrying my knapsack, forget it."

"Probably. Anyway, once you're back," came the chuckle, "from outer space give this earthling a call, OK? I want to hear all about this trip!"

Stalling with calling it a night, they stayed side by side staring at the Milky Way, a vast glittering highway across the night sky. Bessie inhaled the cool, fall-fragrant night air. Letting it out, she said, "I will," and gave him a shove, "Now go home so I can get organized!"

Seated at the computer, Bessie opened her Mars file. Constantly adding NASA's data plus everyone else's was obsessive, she knew. One could do worse than obsessing over outer space adventuring. It was comforting too that her first off-worldly destination was not terribly different from

Earth's. The dry and rugged Martian high plateau regions resembled the Grand Canyon's she'd visited this morning. Her canyon trip had also obviated something extremely important, that whatever distance she crossed, whether very long or very short, meant nothing at all. She smiled at Maxwell beside the monitor, Not with you they don't.

Connie stuck her head through the door. "Honey I saw the lights on. Aren't you ready to turn in? It's late."

Mind churning over the hundred and one questions about tomorrow's trip, Bessie forced a casual reply, "I should, I guess."

Seeing Mars on the monitor with Maxwell beside it, Connie could pretty well guess what her daughter planned. Then again, if left alone tomorrow for just another VR trip, what harm would that be? With none she could think of, Connie nodded, "Fine, dear, but that's it, OK? Instead of sleeping in tomorrow, I want you up and going before we leave for Green Bay."

The whole family, including Bessie, wanted the Pack to cream the hated Minnesota Vikings. Having furiously fought it out last year to clinch the division, their Sunday rematch would be a thriller. Connie tried one last time, "Are you sure you don't want to go? It'd do you good to skip this VR stuff and get to a game."

A solid Packers fan, Bessie enjoyed their games as much as anyone. A perfectly good reason to do just that were these latest Mars Rover transmissions by NASA. Amidst one of its horrendous summertime dust storms, and covered from pole to pole, chances of seeing anything were practically nil. She was tempted to skip this and go to Green Bay instead. But for what, watching a bunch of big guys like her Butt Brain brother beat each other up? This placed a distant second. Even if she did go root for the Pack, she'd spend the whole game wishing she'd done this, dust storm or not. No, Mars was a GO!

"Maybe next time, Mom," she replied, and then grinned, "Besides, I'll be traveling a lot father than Lambeau Field. Anyhow, I'll be fine, OK?" Bidding a final good night, Connie left.

Alone again, Bessie considered what she knew by now about places other than Mars. What lay further beyond held their own uniquely exciting attractions. Forty million miles farther out and roughly 200 million miles wide was the Asteroid Belt. Spread thinly throughout, the vast majority of countless objects were only sand-sized. Between 0.7 to 1.7 million others ranged up to 1 km. in diameter. Space probe surface scans showed these larger ones composed mostly of water ice and carbon compounds. Essential for life support they could be used, she hoped, to provide habitats for research and colonization projects and even mining operations.

Yet farther out the giant gas planets and their larger moons held her equally in thrall. None of these, however, excited her imagination like one of the outermost objects of all. Unimaginably distant and still utterly mysterious. even after NASA's 2015 fly-by, Pluto called to her more strongly than all these others, including Mars. Because the dwarf planet was that much closer to where she had always dreamed of going – to the stars!

Bringing up Pluto's image, she stared at it for a moment. Then she thought, No, I'm not ready for you just yet. But pretty soon you and I have a date to keep!

Chapter 23

Doing her best to get everyone out of the house and off to Green Bay, Bessie practically shoved Connie toward the door. "Mom, you guys need to go! There'll be tons of traffic as it is!"

Connie fed her a level look. "You're arousing my suspicions. Why the heated rush to get us out of here?"

Bessie's eyes went innocently wide. "I'm just being help-ful!"

Catching their exchange, Ben grinned, "You and your pals can't start partying till we're gone, right?" Also hurrying, he'd gained the OK from Rob and Connie to drive the three of them to Lambeau Field in his new Chevy.

Bessie retorted, "*You* would, but that kid stuff bores us!"

"That's enough you two," Connie said and then to Bessie, "I'm sorry you're not coming along. For today, anyway, I'd like to see you skip using your headset. You're overdoing it and that worries me."

Torn between telling all she'd accomplished with it, or else picturing her mom worrying the whole time at Green Bay over this Mars trip, Bessie chose walking the tight rope. "It's that Dad's new headset works so great and I'm no longer messed-up with it. After practicing yesterday I can visit any place or any time that I want, no problem!" True enough, she thought, sort of.

They heard Ben honking his horn. On his way out the door, Rob laughed, "He's fired up to get us to Green Bay. Honey, you ready to go? And what about you, Bess? Sure you don't want to?"

Connie said, "Give me a minute, dear."

Impatiently bouncing a leg, Bessie shook her head, "Dad,

I can't! I'm totally caught up with my astronomy project."

"Okay, but you're missing a great game against the Vikings!"

"I know, so maybe next time." She blew him a kiss. "Go Pack!"

Returning a thumbs up, Rob went outside.

Not quite ready to do the same, Connie felt something bothering her about this astronomy project. She frowned. "Last night you were online with your favorite planet. So how does Maxwell fit in?"

Bessie stayed with the truth. "I'll play NASA's latest transmissions from their Rover III. With Maxwell's close-ups added in, my recorded data won't be that same old stuff. Mr. Nesbitt will appreciate that enough to give me extra credit."

Connie was pleased to see her own students work toward extra credit. With Bessie earning straight A's, she persisted, "Actually, I don't see why you need that." After another honk she muttered, "These guys of mine, I swear," and then, "I know your general science teacher and that's what puzzles me. You say he'd be impressed with your essay?" Bessie knew her mom wouldn't leave without an answer she could live with. "Why wouldn't he? He is a science teacher."

Connie nodded. "Uh-huh, but trust me when it comes to astronomy," she added a wry smile, "Walt Nesbitt doesn't know Mars from Milwaukee."

Ben stuck his head through the front door. "Mom, are you coming or what! We've gotta shove off!"

"I'll be out in a second, dear! I'll make up for it by treating you guys to lunch!"

"Okay, Mom! See you, Bean old girl!" He left.

Bessie also wanted to wrap this up. "Actually Mom, he didn't assign it. To be perfectly honest, I volunteered...because I knew it'd be fun!"

Connie was through with pressing her. "Sure. Compared with this one your other trips are like only out to our back yard." Missing her daughter's little smile, she too wrapped it up, "I'll call later to see how you're doing, so leave your phone on. Will you do that?"

Bessie frowned. "I planned on leaving it off while on...while thinking "I'm on Mars". The last thing I need are interrupting calls." Seeing that look of her mom's again, she hastily amended, "All right, I promise to bring it along!" While thinking, But it stays off! She doubted incoming calls would create electrical disturbances disrupting her pro-tective bubble. On the other hand, gasping her last breaths on Mars was one risk she wanted no part of.

Bessie waved her goodbyes as Ben started down the street. Then dashing inside, she changed into long-legged cargo pants, hiking boots, and a Packers sweatshirt. When a hat and insulated ski gloves were added, all of these would protect at least for a short time from the sun's UV rays.

Equatorial surface temperatures during Martian summers actually reached as high as an average spring day in Wisconsin. Martian winters, however, plunged nighttime temperatures to minus 225 degrees F at the polar caps. As for a breathable atmosphere, there wasn't any. Inside the bubble, the air she breathed and the temperature she felt would be those of the computer room. Neither Martian surface conditions, including dust storms or anything else, not even a stray meteorite, could penetrate her quantum energy shell. With no mass UV rays would zip through her bubble's wall like it didn't exist. Which, with the quirky workings of quantum physics, it did not. It would be simpler to visit the planet during its nighttime hours, of course. Except, enshrouded in total darkness, what could she photograph or even see?

Looking around, Bessie wondered if she'd forgotten

anything. Her Packers cap lay atop the dresser. Just shy of enough protection, what else could she use? Hurrying up the hall, she saw her mom's wide brimmed garden hat on a peg beside the patio door. Trying it on, she found the elastic headband stretched enough to fit down over Maxwell. Liking the floral design, while doing a Nina modeling turn before the hallway mirror, she grinned, Looks good on you, girl!

Others wouldn't think so of course. If NASA operatives in the United States, via observational satellites orbiting the planet, zoomed in on her down there, they'd see? Sputtering a laugh, she thought, Me hosting a garden party?

Rummaging through a kitchen drawer, she pulled out several Ziplock sandwich bags and stuffed them into a pants pocket. In after these went a measuring scoop. Then she liberally smeared sunscreen over every square of skin still showing. This kind had the highest rated Sun Protection Factor on the market. Half emptying the squeeze bottle doing hands, face, and neck, she began dripping the stuff an the floor. Hastily swabbing it up with paper towels, she imagined her friends watching all of this. And her looking back to ask, "What, me nervous?"

Her racing heart answered that. Before doing another thing she had to calm down and get a grip. Breathing deeply in time with side to side twists, she finished with no knee bending by slapping palms to the floor. Somewhat settled back down, she made herself walk not run to the computer room.

Seated at the console she fastened her hair in back with a rubber band. After donning Maxwell with visor flipped up she fitted on the garden hat. Poised to press PLAY for the DVD, she drew back. To be professional with this, if also stalling a bit, she entered the date and time on her phone, then titled it *Mars Expedition #1* and combined virtual reality viewing with NASA's Surface Rover III imaging.

Her self congratulatory mood for being scientifically disciplined lasted for maybe three seconds. Her next realization didn't help, that nobody but nobody had set off to cross 40 million miles of outer space. Setting the phone on the console, she took a deep breath and let it out. Lowering her visor, she said, "Maxie, let's do this!" and pressed PLAY.

Chapter 24

As the DVD's documentary unfolded, Bessie punched Fast Play to skip the introductory blah-blah-blah. She stopped forwarding where the orbiting module panned an upper portion of the Martian hemisphere. After creating the glow-line, what mostly caught her eye was the polar cap. From this distance the covering of brilliant white beneath star filled black was an inspiring sight. Yet, landing down there only to look around at a Texas-sized landscape of snow drifts was the last thing she wanted. Sliding the glow-line over the plains, canyons, and craters, she found the vast Victoria crater.

She ordered, "Right there, Maxie, take us down!"

As she rode the glow-line the freeze frames briefly came and went. Abruptly vanishing, this left the vast red-orange mix of Martian craters, canyons, and plains rushing up at her! She cried, "No, no, no, Maxie, slow down!"

He did the rest, adjusting to more sensibly floating down as if in a parachute. Down past her boots was a boiling mass of brown yellowish clouds. She knew just to land, let alone see anything, she needed something more distinct to focus upon. With no other choice, she went to Plan B. "Stop, Maxwell!"

Knowing about the huge dust storm ahead of time, she had a way (she hoped) to cope with this very situation. Gloves off and fingers playing over the keyboard, she opened her NASA data file. Bringing up their extra-planetary GPS grids, she quickly sorted out those pertaining to Mars. Maximizing the specific equatorial region she wanted, Bessie said to the screen, "Voice command!"

A pleasant sounding woman's voice replied, "Say a command." The monitor displayed a choice list from *View Map, Find Place, Find Category* and so forth. Too excited to choose for a moment, she drew in a deep breath. And then, loudly and clearly, but voice shaking, "Find place!"

The mellower, calmer voice came back, "Speak the *name* of a place."

So far, so good, she knew, through Alex, that even removed from the computer room by millions of miles the quirky workings of quantum entanglement had her also back there. So the big question, could her cyber system connect with NASA's satellite systems orbiting both Earth and here? Heart in mouth, she tried, "The planet Mars!"

To Bessie, the robot's reply sounded surprised, "Did *you* say *Planet Mars*!?"

Choking off a laugh, Bessie cleared her throat and said loudly, "YES!"

The monitor first displayed a tumbling array of colorful patterns as the system dutifully began its search. Her turn to be surprised, Bessie saw it clear in seconds. On it appeared a topographical map of Mars overlain with a checkerboard pattern of co-ordinates delineating longitude and latitude. Again, almost laughably, the GPS woman instructed quite pleasantly, "Please *say* the *address*!"

Bessie had pin-pointed Victoria Crater near the equator the night before. But would her system know the Martian equator was also called, in astronomical terms, the Prime Meridian? Thinking, Only one way to find out, she answered as clearly as she could, "Prime Meridian," After only a slight pause the voice told her, "Co-ordinates two-point oh-five degrees south and five-point five-oh degrees west!" Instantly high-lighted in blue, a path led to where she'd directed, ending with a checkered flag. The voice asked cheerily, "Would you like to begin navigation?"

Beside herself with excitement, Bessie's voice somehow

stayed steady. "Yes, begin!" And then, "Let's go, Max, but take it slow!" Once more looking down to see nothing but storming clouds, she wondered aloud, "How can I land in a mess like that?" No sooner said when an opening appeared directly below. Enough to reveal in its center Victoria crater and, parked at its nearer edge, Rover III!

A moment later Bessie grounded the bubble. Gripping the chair arms like a vise she stared wide-eyed at what lay all around her. Releasing the arms, she leaped up and cried to the butterscotch sky, "Woohoo! Hello Mars!"

Barely aware of the dust clouds swirling overhead, nor those at ground level farther out, Bessie had all she could do to simply take in her near surroundings. She had seen this barren rust-toned landscape many times before, of course, on NASA's website, PBS, and the news channels. But this couldn't begin to compare to actually standing in the middle of it. A chill ran up Bessie's spine, it sinking in that what was only inches beneath her boots no longer had anything to do with Mother Earth – that every bit of it belonged to the Red Planet!

This thrilling thought was interrupted as the bubble was again struck by wildly blowing dust and sand. Seeing the larger grains carom off its sides, she knew these summer winds could not only reach up to well over 250 miles per hour, but could rage for weeks or even months on end. While grateful for her bubble's protection from being sand-blasted, she felt it totally unfair, coming so far to see what she'd yearned to see for so long – only for it to wind up so hidden!

Stomping a boot and shouting "OMG!" she threw an air punch at what was going on out there. "Give me a break! Go away!"

The whirling maelstrom suddenly stopped. As it moved off to her left, she'd been caught inside a gigantic Martian sand devil. A major portion of the dust also shifted away.

No longer obscured, the enormous Victoria crater lay directly in front of her. Scattered past the far edge were large boulders and rippled red-colored sand dunes, these looking like those she'd hiked on Lake Michigan's shore. Beyond and ap-proaching rapidly however were yet more billowing dark brown clouds. Jaws clenched, she growled in frustration, "Nuts, that'll be here pretty quick!"

All was not lost for just to the right sat Rover III, along with a few minutes to look it over. Exploring here for over a year by now with no air or moisture to cause any rust, its metal surfaces gleamed like new. The Rover's single telescoped front tire rested a few feet back from the crater's edge. Reached out over the tire, the sampler arm was bent down just inches from the sand. Now motionless, it was probably, she assumed, recharging its solar power source. The array providing this was an eight foot rectangle over the motor assembly. Estimating the camera atop the mast to be several feet higher over the panels, Bessie judged she and the camera were roughly the same height.

High in the hazy yellow sky the sun was half its size as seen from Earth. In spite of the wind whipping up so much dust, With the temperature like a cool June day in Wisconsin, the scene minus the dust storm would be inviting.

If more protectively dressed, while wearing a self-contained air tank, Bessie pictured herself sun bathing atop the Rover's solar platform. But no, there'd be no catching rays here for her nor anyone else for a very long time. If ever, before this starved for air and water planet was somehow terraformed.

As the dust storm drew closer she began shooting photos of everything in sight. As with her Grand Canyon photos, these, she knew, would not help to prove she'd been here. Anyone could view the same thing online or on a news channel. Storing the shots, she saw blowing dust already hiding half of Victoria Crater.

Taking a moment to consider future trips to this place, she reached up to the brim of mom's hat. For the next trip she could duct tape a beach umbrella to the back of her chair. Lining the umbrella with aluminum foil would protect even more from UV rays. She smiled at the thought, somebody else looking into the computer room...and seeing her beneath a beach umbrella wrapped with several packages of mom's aluminum foil. Her fellow science geeks might understand. Or else, their suspicions about her lately would be confirmed, that she actually was loony tunes.

Encroaching darkness meant the monster storm would be on top of her any second. Her next thought, Before it is, I need some samples!

Back on Earth the only samples were meteorites shown to have once been a part of Mars. Impacted billions of years ago by another large body, some of the torn off pieces of Mars had landed on Earth. Where she lived, none of these were on display. For her own very special one she would first have Alex check out the samples on her return.

Leaning sideways, Bessie pushed to her right, And yes, her bubble obligingly lengthened its shape, while also lowering closer to her head and back. She gave a start, "Hey!" to see her circle of carpeting vanish to be instantly replaced by red rust-colored sand and pebbles!

To truly *touch* the surface of Mars, she reached down her right forefinger and stirred the sand. Cupping more with both hand and letting it slide through her fingers, she felt its coolness. Purely enjoying a moment of this, Bessie then quickly used the measuring cup to scoop sand and pebbles into a pair of resealable bags. Stuffing these into her pants pockets, she hoped Alex could analyze these samples.

Just then the storm struck her bubble! Even so, she couldn't resist touching Mars one last time. Scooping up more sand bare-handed, she made a fist. Closing her eyes, she pushed off any other thoughts but returning to the computer room. Moments later she was home!

After the biggest thrill of her life, Bessie found it nearly impossible to wait till fully oriented to her surroundings. The instant she was, up went the visor and off came Maxwell. Stumbling backwards over the chair while getting up, Bessie regained her balance. Then she shot out both fists. "OMG, I did it! Woo-hoo!"

Chapter 25

After downloading her photos, Bessie checked the time. To her surprise the whole trip from start to finish had taken just under fifteen minutes. Quickly sending Alex a text, she edgily awaited his response. There was none, the display showing his phone was turned off. Then she remembered him saying he'd be tied up with chores.

The day was still young. Chomping at the bit to keep on with VR trips, she sorted through more of her family's travel DVDs. As none of them grabbed her, she rethought how she'd mishandled tripping back through time to Gettysburg. Immediately following that disaster, she'd been frankly afraid to try any more time travels. But that was yesterday. Having since perfected her techniques with Maxwell, she felt more comfortable with them. And so, time traveling should go as well as crossing spatial distances. She hoped. Besides, having already gone all the way back to 1863, couldn't she now travel much farther back with no problem? In any case her original hesitation over this had vanished. She had to remember to bring the bottle of aspirin along. The only thing left to decide was to where and how far back she should go. Her eyes happened to fall on the PBS DVD about prehistoric Earth's Triassic Age.

Driving a dark gray sedan last night, Trainer and Girardi had followed Ben Howard's car until he dropped off his sister and her blonde girlfriend. Deciding Ms. Howard to be more important than her brother, they'd let him drive off. The trackers had parked across the street from the Howard place. From then on, until later when inside lights turned off, they'd recorded only scraps of conversation from out back, and nil later on from e-mails or tweets.

Back first thing this morning in the Ultra Com van, Train-er and Girardi were outfitted in white coveralls and peaked white caps. On the passenger side Girardi wore earphones over his cap, while staring down at his laptop monitor. Wearing a wire earphone, Trainer was focused on the dashboard monitor. "I've got nothing here, Charley. What about your dish sensors? Anything?"

"A while back for a couple a' times ten minutes apart. Then it went nuts, some kinda electrical disturbance. For now I'm back to being flat-lined here."

Trainer shook his head. "What little we've reported to Manley has not made her happy. All we have with this Howard girl are bits and pieces we picked up last night. This morning before your monitor went haywire I caught scraps about her doing, I dunno, a VR take on Mars. In other words nothing much."

"Maybe not," Girardi replied, "But Manley sure thinks so." Suddenly he stared at the monitor. "Aw for...! There it goes again! What's with this thing!"

The very thought of visiting the tropically clement Triassic era made Bessie feel pleasantly warm. Taking off the sweat shirt and garden hat, she kept a couple of the extra Zip-Lock bags. What else would she need? Patting a pants pocket to make sure of the aspirin bottle. she snugged Maxwell down around her head.

Enjoying historical DVD's recreations of Earth's long-ago eras, she was especially interested in the CGI characterizations of various prehistoric creatures and early varieties of vegetation. As the narrative for this Triassic era began, the waves of an ancient sea were seen rolling in onto a beach fronted by tall trees and giant ferns. From high above, winged reptiles dove down to the water after fish.

Dating back some 150 million years before the true Age of Dinosaurs, this early Triassic recreation was Bessie's preferred era. Versus Ben's, his Jurassic DVD choice quenching his thirst for bloodshed by showing, for instance, the ravenous T-Rex hunting and slaughtering its prey. Put off by this, Bessie liked seeing creatures of any size contently browsing on land or swimming leisurely in the seas.

As the narrator explained various details about the early Triassic, Bessie's background soft rock joined in. Foot tapping in time, she focused on the monitor's overview of Earth more than 250 million years ago. Mainly one great land mass, Pangea, all else on the planet was ocean-covered.

Creating the glow line, she centered it on an equatorial region where the land met the sea. Automatically leaned forward she pushed off.

Seated behind the wheel in the van Trainer asked, "Getting anything else? It's been awhile since the last time."

Watching his scanner, Girardi said, "Among her smaller signals, I got a couple of strong ones. Since then not much." Suddenly a hand flew up to his earphone. "Whoa! There it is again!"

Slowing her downward glide, Bessie grounded the bubble on a long stretch of beach and low dunes. To her right the sea rolled in on gentle swells. Directly above, through a patch of blue, the sun's rays brightened her portion of the beach. Making landfall not far off, an enormous mass of storm clouds rapidly approached.

Doing a double take at the darkening oncoming cloud mass, Bessie thought, *Nuts!* Twice *in* two *trips?* She twisted in her chair for a quick look around. Off to the left rose bare tree trunks, their palm-like tops leafed out in a mélange of pale greens and decaying tans and yellows. Several in the foreground were toppled over into deep green stands of gigantic ferns.

She spotted a creature the size of a possum scuttling over the sand. It left behind a symmetrical pattern of small tracks leading back to the water's edge. According to what she'd read, it was an early-evolved amphibian. Turning her head slowly to find other creatures, she saw none. Gazing up, she spotted a winged creature high aloft and gliding the air currents.

Lowering her gaze to the sea, she saw a pod of creatures rising above and plunging below the waves. Resembling the humpbacks off the Carmel Highlands, they were nearly the same size. Surging in the same direction farther out, the monstrous long jawed heads of much larger creatures rose and dove under.

Identifying these, Bessie gasped, "OMG! Mosasaurs!?" Indeed they were, the largest, most voracious denizens of the early Triassic seas. Unlike her whales, the thought of being out there even in a very big boat chilled Bessie's spine!

Right here safely ashore she'd have liked nothing better than staying put and taking it all in. Had she a better supply of munchies and a water bottle she would have spent the whole day. All she'd thought to bring was aspirin and the extra Zip-Lock bags. In fact, the beginning of a headache pressed the back of her head. No sense in letting it grow until it worse, she promptly shook out an aspirin and swallowed it.

Suddenly Bessie was alarmed by how quickly the towering, ominously black clouds were moving in. Absently putting the bottle back into her pants pocket, she thought, I better go! Nuts, I've barely arrived!

From the looks of these clouds, she suspected that once the downpour began, it could go on for quite some time.

She'd been lucky to arrive here during a short period of clear weather. Then she remembered, My sample!

Leaning down to her right, she felt the bubble conform to her movement. Moving forward over the reddish sand, she grabbed a handful of it. Just then huge raindrops began pelting her bubble. Bolting upright, she dumped the sand into her bag. The rain suddenly torrential, yet inside all was silent but for her breathing. Leaning back in her chair, she summoned up her glow-line and imaged herself sliding backward on it toward home.

After removing Maxwell, she pressed a hand to the back of her head. While not splitting, it hurt enough to reach into her pocket for more aspirin. The bottle wasn't there. Checking her other pocket, it wasn't there, either, only her sample bag. She looked around beneath her chair, but no. So where was it? Letting out a groan, she realized...she'd left it behind. Cursing her carelessness, Bessie recalled all too well what she and Alex discussed the other night. They would probably agree the odds were astronomical against this – that the left behind bottle would cause problems or even incredibly slight changes in the present. But one never knew.

In a bit of a panic, she donned Maxwell. Within what seemed the longest thirty seconds she'd ever spent, she was back at the ancient beach. Head pounding, Bessie realized she had rematerialized precisely where she'd been before. As Dr. Myers had said her expanded ITC could return her to wherever she'd been before. She was lucky, too, that the torrential monsoon driving her off only moments ago had let up. Not for long, though, with more black clouds coming directly at her. She had to hurry and find that bottle!

Turning right, she saw it directly below in the sand. Seeing what was maybe twenty feet beyond it, she gave a start, "OMG!" Upright on large hind legs, its upper forearms fitted with folded wings, a birdlike creature stared back at her! She was, she knew, too far back in the Triassic for pterodactyls to yet exist. A similar but smaller version, it was not as tall as Bessie in her chair, Noting its long hooked beak lined with sharp teeth, she wondered, a pterosaur? Regretting having no time to study it, she grounded the bubble.

Trailing its wings, the pterosaur scurried a short distance away. Recovering, it stared back at her almost thoughtfully. She wondered, who said all these prehistoric animals were pea-brained and dumb? This one seems curious about me.

Even so, she had to grab the bottle and go. Making a pushing motion, she leaned forward and reached down. Snatching up the bottle, she rose up to see? Now glaring at her, the pterosaur had its wings spread wide and open beak displaying menacingly sharp teeth. And probably screeching at her, too, but all was silent in the bubble.

Bessie held up the bottle. "Sorry if I've upset you..." She wagged a finger. "...but no-no, these aren't for you!" Faced forward again, she leaned back and headed back home.

Out in the car, Girardi blurted, "Nuts! It did it again!" Turning to Trainer, he shrugged, "Whatever this interference is, have you tracked it"

Looking down at his dish monitor, Trainer nodded, "It's coming from inside the Howard place. It can't be from her on the computer. Any hard drive energy signals would barely even show."

"OK, but whatever it is, Manley will want us to report every bit of it."

Going into the kitchen, Bessie washed down two more aspirins with a glass of water. As if dying of thirst, she gulped down another glassful. Next she bent to the counter with hands to the sides of her head. Within minutes, her headache dissipated.

Ready to reach Alex to show him both samples, she held up the bag of reddish sand. But then she saw that it looked like only what it was, a handful of red sand. Worse, what she'd also brought back over 40 million miles from Mars was merely a few orangish tan-colored rocks.

She would show these to Alex anyway. Partway convinced she was going to these far off places, he'd at least examine these samples at his home lab. By cutting and polishing one of the pebbles, he could determine its composition with his microscope. Acquainted herself with NASA's drilled-up and analyzed Rover samples, she thought these were similar to rusty mudstone here on Earth. As for the red sand, finding the age for that required what neither Alex or even their school lab had, the highly sophisticated potassium-argon dating equipment. If nothing else, as fellow scientists, she and Alex had samples to truly touch for added encouragement to keep going with this.

Chapter 26

Back home by 5:30, the three Howard's figured their beloved Packers, at 24 to 3 over the Vikings, were headed for a winning season. On the way home Connie had called Bes-sie to have her whip up something simple for dinner. Soon after they pulled in, she set out a platter heaped with hot spa-ghetti and the sauce to go with it.

As they ate, Bessie asked Ben, "So, brother dear, how'd your car work?"

Between mouthfuls he said, "Great set of wheels with easy handling! Even a kid like you could drive it! These meatballs are pretty good, by the way!"

"Glad you like them, Butt Brain. So, when can I drive it? You promised you'd teach me, remember?" Now that he had his car, she was eager to learn how.

"We'll do that right after dinner if you want. I need to gas it up again anyway. Then we'll go to the school and you can drive it in the parking lot."

She frowned, "I'm not a little kid, you know. With my Learner's Permit I could practice right here on our street."

Ben shook his head. "Not! You'll run over somebody! Worse, you'd probably scrape it against a parked car or something!"

As the usual squabble got underway, Connie and Rob, rolling their eyes at one another, got up from the table. He asked, "Need help cleaning up? If not, I'll catch what's left of another late game on the tube."

"No, Bessie and I can load the dish washer. Then I'll correct essays from my seventh graders." She turned to Bessie and Ben. "If you two are off to do some driving, be careful!"

As they were already partway out the door, Ben said, "Alex is coming over to try the new games we bought, so we won't be long. Unless she piles us into a tree or something!"

Following him out, Bessie let out a "Grrr!"

Back forty-five minutes later, Bessie was flushed with excitement. After Ben coached her at the school's parking lot, he'd relented to let her drive home.

Greeting their parents in the den, Ben laughed, "Well, we're still alive!"

Bessie laughed, "Driving home, I hardly ran over anyone!"

Soon Nina and Alex were on hand too. He was ready to play one of Ben's new UK games. At the top of her form this evening, Nina motioned toward Alex, then flashed Ben a teasing smile. "You always play Genius Boy, here, so give Bessie another chance. I still think she can beat you!"

Looking at Alex, Ben shrugged, "Miss Hollywood is right for once. You mind?" He smirked at Bessie. "It won't take long."

More interested to see how Bessie would do against Ben, he nodded. "Go ahead, I'm okay with watching you guys."

More ready than before to play Ben, Bessie smiled back, "You think it won't take long? Then bring it!" This another historical game, she had moments ago taken a couple of aspirin. And as much for a good luck token as anything else, she made sure her staff rested against the wall.

Seated before the monitor both wore their headbands. Becoming all business, Ben loaded his series of British World War I games. "Bean, I'm feeing generous tonight. Which of these battles do *you* wanna fight?" He couldn't help adding, "Not that it matters, you're still gonna lose it!"

Enjoying her modern world history class, Bessie especially appreciated the way Mrs. Ames, took the time to discuss historically pivotal events. This spurred Bessie to immediately search out any additional material she could find about them. She'd thus developed a sense as to how widespread conflagrations in both world wars had shaped history right up through the present.

Standing behind Ben, Alex stayed silent. But not Nina. Grasping the back of Bessie's chair, she urged, "Do Gallipoli! You and Ms. Ames really kicked it around in class! Or you sure did…With your beloved Winnie and all!"

For a change, the Gettysburg fiasco over done with and virtual techniques firmly in hand, Bessie felt she was meeting Ben on an even playing field. Despite what were seen as Churchill's failings in this battle, she would play as him. "You're right, Neen! So, Butt Brain, with this Gallipoli battle, can I be the British?"

"No, I want(to) be them! They lost for real and I can turn it around! We'll flip for it!" He looked up at Alex. "You got a coin?"

"Yeah, some place!" He fished a quarter from his pocket. "Okay, it's between the Turks and the British. Who gets to call it in the air?"

Ben grinned. "Bean, you call it since you're the underdog!"

Psyched up even more for battle after that, she said, "Flip it!" When Alex did, she called, "Heads!"

"It's…tails!"

Nina patted Bessie's shoulder. "Too bad, there goes your Winnie. But he's too old for you anyway."

Disappointed at leading the Turkish forces, Bessie protested, "He wasn't that old! Only 41 as First Lord of the Admiralty."

"That's still pretty old."

Totally unconcerned Ben said, "Let's play!"

Showing inside their visors and on the monitor, the sweep of the Dardanelles Narrows at Gallipoli took form.

CGI British battleships were shown entering the Narrows. Meantime, icons of Turkish defenders were atop the peninsula's high ridge above water's edge.

As Ben and Bessie moved their cursors, she fumed about the position given to her by the coin flip. As defender, her Turkish forces would oppose her Winnie and she didn't like it. Right away she also had to set up additional gun emplacements atop the ridges guarding the Narrows. With Ben so mindlessly aggressive, he'd give her little or no time to do this. For her this game was not starting out too well.

Beside her she partly heard Ben chortle, "Okay...(something)...my battleships...(something)...to get you!" Sliding his fleet into the Narrows, he deftly double keyed to increase his ships' armor and the firepower of his big guns.

She *could* hear his arrogance. Combative resolve heightened even more, she retorted, "Soon as I'm ready, brother dear, just come and get it!" Putting all else out of mind, Bessie began riding her glow-line down.

Standing behind them, Alex and Nina saw Bessie jerk up to exclaim, "OMG, you've got to be kidding!" To which Alex merely offered a nod, "Mm-hm!" compared to Nina's vigorous one, "Here she goes again!"

Bessie hung suspended over a rocky and dusty brush-covered ridge atop the Gallipoli peninsula. Fronting it below was the green-blue Dardanelle Narrows, through the middle of which steamed a file of British battleships. Spread out here on the ridge, Turkish troops were shoveling and pick-axing trenches, Further to their right, others were manhandling field guns into position.

Exposed to anyone chancing to glance up, Bessie grounded her bubble beside brushy cover between her and the Turkish soldiers beyond. Only waist high the scrubby brush hardly covered her upper self and the monitor. The soldiers looked to be far too busy to notice her. Eyes back on the monitor she saw Ben's ships beginning to fire bright green lines. To accompanying amplified bursts of gunfire, he added his own, "Ka-chow! Ka-chow! Hah! I'm nailing your Turks!"

Dimly hearing him, while looking past the monitor and down at his ships, she retorted, "We'll see about that!" With good reason, too, in knowing not only her poor Winnie's tragic results here, but the Turks' more fortunate ones. And then she realized, Butt Brain's forgotten about my mines! Instantly, she moused clustered little orange circles, her mines, toward his lead battleships. There was a delay by the game fitting in Real Time for the mines to make contact. This gave her a moment to take in what was around her.

With the sun directly above, she imagined feeling warmed by it. But no, only the sun's light, not its heat, could reach inside the bubble. Yet *really* here at the Dardanelles, she clearly saw the nearby scrubby brush and pebbly parched-looking soil. Another fifty feet to her right soldiers in khaki shirts and leggings were pick-axing and shoveling out entrenchments.

Pick over his shoulder and ready to punch into the stony ground, the nearest soldier glanced her way. Frozen open mouthed in mid swing, and dark eyes widening, he stared at her. Seeing his small mustache, Bessie thought he looked little more than high school age. As if déjà vu, Ben sounded off loud and clear, "Now all my ships are in the Narrows! This is it, Bean, your guys are history!"

Pick lowered, private Ruzgar stared disbelievingly some fifty feet to his left. Next to him his best friend, private Berkay, was shoveling out their trench. Their leader, Sergeant Baran, stood further off to their right.

Baran's own shoveling stopped, he grimaced at the British ships far below. In Turkish his name meant brave fighter and warrior. And fittingly, the crusty combat veteran was driving his platoon of recruits without let-up in hopes of winning here.

Not daring to draw Baran's attention, Ruzgar held his voice to a hoarse, dry throat whisper. "Berkay, look quick! There's a girl over there!"

Shirt sweat-soaked like everyone else's, and too busy to rise up and look, Berkay's own throat was raw from thirst. He rasped, "A girl up here? You've got heat stroke! Shut up and keep chopping! This ground is like iron!"

With Baran still paying them no attention, Ruzgar ventured more loudly, "No fooling, that girl is watching us!" This time his boyishly pitched voice carried.

Focused on what was happening in the channel, Berkay boomed out a deeper exhortation, "You young idiots quit gabbing about girls! You get those trenches dug for our guns!" Heavy set and also sweat-stained, Baran remained leaning on his shovel. Staring at the Narrows, without deigning to look at his upstart recruit, he growled from the side of his mouth, "More of our Skoda guns will be up here tomorrow!" He then jabbed a finger toward the British ships. "And when those Tommies do come ashore, by Allah, we'll give 'em a nice surprise!"

For all his bluster, Baran knew that to do so would require whatever additional help that Allah might render. Was digging these lousy trenches a worthless effort? Though increasingly fortifying these heights, there were too few troops to oppose a landing force. Once ashore, a couple British battalions could easily take this position. Most of these conscripted kids had yet to be issued rifles, let alone be taught to use them. Then again, he mused, they might not have to. If those big battleships steamed through the Narrows and all the way to Istanbul's harbor, this battle was over. And, perhaps, the whole blasted war?

Pushing off her panic at being seen, Bessie realized, Wait! What can they do to me...inside this bubble! Having a game to win, and refocused on the flotilla of ships on the monitor, she sent a strong simple thought, I'll sink you unless you turn back! Inhaling deeply, she voice commanded as strongly, "No-no-no, Winnie dear, you stay out of these Narrows!"

Caught up in the heat of battle, she moused her mines closer to Ben's ships. Feeling as if commanding in Real Time from here on the ridge, she said the same to her Monitor's CGI soldiers, "Hold your ground! They can't beat you up here!"

As Ben frantically maneuvered to avoid Bessie's mines, the first of his ships flashed and vanished. Alex told him, "Uh-oh, that's not good!"

From behind Bessie, Nina urged, "Yes! Go get him, girl!"

While no defeatist, Baran had certainly felt that way when up here at first. In spite of that, as a hardened veteran who prided his soldiering. he'd driven these youngsters to get these emplacements done. Though just now he'd dropped back to thinking, But what a hopeless mess! For two drachmas, I'd chuck this whole...?

Abruptly straightening, he suddenly felt infused with an all-abiding sense of knowing...those British ships down there will not pass through! Materializing by some form of wizardry, it struck him that his own troops and those of everyone else...had nothing to fear! They would win! The sounds of picks striking the earth and exuberant young voices suddenly bantering heartily made him nod, my young idiots feel it too!

Seeing the arrogant British steaming their fleet through the Narrows like on parade, he growled, "Accursed limeys, we'll stop you anyway!"

As he said it, the bow of the battleship leading the long flotilla burst into a red-orange ball of fire! As huge black clouds of smoke billowed up from its bow, the next battleship exploded amidships! As one thunderous BOOM!

after another rolled up at him, the sergeant bellowed, "Praise be! They're hitting our mines!"

The explosions and the roaring of his own voice had him unable to hear young Ruzgar cry out, "Yes, praise be! But sergeant please! Look over here! I swear, there is a girl up here with us!"

The sergeant finally looked at his trooper, then past him. Seeing nothing, he bellowed, "Miserable pup, what are you babbling about! Back to work!"

Throwing up his hands, young Ruzgar yelled back, "I beg forgiveness, sergeant! Besides, now she's gone!"

As the game's audio issued battle explosions, Nina was all sweetness from behind Bessie. "Ben, dear, you're slipping! She's blowing up all your ships!"

Without turning from the screen Ben growled, "Why don't you go play jump rope or something?"

Staring at her own scene within the visor, Bessie exclaimed, "I just sunk another of your ships! That's three so far!"

Sliding his surviving ships out of the Narrows, Ben slumped in his chair. "OK, OK, I quit!"

After he and Bessie removed their headbands, she winced, "Ouch! Here it comes again!" Making sure anymore to keep her aspirin and water bottle handy, she washed down a couple of capsules.

Chapter 27

Alone at last in the naval war room, Winston Churchill leaned back in his chair at the head of the table. Puffing a plume of smoke from his cigar, the irony of its label, Turkish Domestic, struck him. Flicking off an inch of ash, he growled to himself, "Harumph! How long can I keep purchasing these?"

Negativity not part of his make-up, he struggled mightily today for it not to be. Indeed, was it only last month when, as First Lord of the Admiralty, he'd been brim full of optimism? Despite interminable delays with moving the confounded fleet to the Dardanelles Strait, his proposed attack upon Istanbul had overflowed with his certainty it would succeed. And with good reason, the heights above the Strait not yet fortified.

The assault finally underway that fine day, he had entered this war room. Cigar clenched in his teeth and briskly rubbing his hands together, he'd told his cabinet members, "Let's have at it, shall we!?"

As First Lord, he had covered the great sized map table with ship models. Sliding those flying the British ensign to the opening of the Dardanelles Narrows, he had let it be known, his basic creed militarily, "Attack! Forge ahead and hurl them ever back!"

Quite inexplicably he'd been incapable of imparting even a sense of this to his naval officers, let alone infusing them with it. Tapping another ash from his cigar, he groaned inside, What happened next was abominable! Setting the cigar aside, he bent forward to read for the hundredth time his journal entry.

This said, in effect, that on March 18, 1915, at 4 PM,

fourteen British battleships and four French bat\
under Admiral De Roebeck confidently advance in\
Narrows. But then some of them struck mines which\
been undiscovered. Three battleships (very old ones due\
be scrapped) were sunk, plus, one French battleship and a\
English one were damaged, with total casualties amounting\
to only 61 killed and wounded. Promised for the next\
assault in the Dardanelles Narrows were destroyers\
equipped with mine-sweeping gear and four more British\
battleships! However, Admiral de Roebeck, mystified,\
disturbed, and disconcerted by these losses of which he did\
not know the cause broke off any further action.\
Commander Roger Keyes asked de R. for permission to go\
back in a destroyer to salvage the two damaged battleships.\
At the moment he thought de R. was absolutely beaten.

Sliding aside his journal for the moment, Churchill\
wearily switched to musing once again about his fleet\
Admirals encountering some sort of indefinable, but\
"insuperable resistance." Years later, he gave one of his\
dearest and most trusted friends, Lady Violet Bonham-\
Carter, full access to his personal notes about the by-gone\
Gallipoli campaign. In her own memoirs she faithfully\
disclosed Churchill's remarks, along with those of others\
who had been involved.

One of the more pertinent items she wrote was this: "In\
later years the Turks stated, 'By not rushing more ships\
through the Dardanelles the English gave us time to fortify\
the Peninsula with over 200 Skoda guns in place." What\
had happened to produce the sudden change which took\
place in de R's mind?

"Henceforward," Churchill wrote, "the defenses of the\
Dardanelles were reinforced by an insurmountable mental\
barrier, immovable, towered up in the Narrows...and\
against this wall of inhibition no weapon could be\
employed. The Admiralty laid bound by a spell which fire

and faith were powerless to exorcise."

Churchill never did discover the reason even he had been, for one unforgettable moment, beset by an impending sense of disaster and utter defeat.

FOOTNOTES
[1]Carter, Violet Bonham. "Winston Churchill; An Intimage Portrait. pp.158-9
[2]Ibid.

Chapter 28

Early last night Bessie had told Alex, "If you're free and willing, I want to try taking you back to Mars with me." And then to Nina, "You say you're not ready for that, but I need you here to watch. Then you'll both know, I hope, that I'm really doing this. All right?" Happily for her, they'd agreed.

At quarter to eight Monday morning Carmen Ricci arrived to take Bessie to the Center. Four years ago when Carmen and Alex moved in less than a block away, the Riccis and Howards became neighborhood friends.

Carmen worriedly eyed Connie. "I know it's been a while since Bessie fell off that ladder. In fact Alex has mentioned she's still having headaches. I wondered about that when we talked about her coming in for us today."

Connie reassured, "Not to worry, One of your researchers, Dr. Myers, told me she'd suffered no ill effects from her fall. Other than mild headaches she's been fine ever since. They only happen during what she calls..." pausing, she shook her head, "all right, her VR time travels."

Carmen nodded, "Alex has mentioned all that, but Myers will also be there today and he'll keep an eye on her. As always we'll have our Ultra-Tech observers hovering over us too. Additionally we'll have an observer from the Defense Department. Did you tell Bessie about all these others? Surrounded by quite a crowd Bessie might find this pretty distracting."

"I doubt it, not once she's locked into her virtual unit."

"One who might bother Bessie," Carmen said, "is Ultra Tech's Dr. Manley. Bessie might know who she is from visiting the Center with her class."

Connie asked, "What is it with this Dr. Manley? You've said she's so intense with this testing that she's scary with it."

"Veronica is pretty high-strung. She was when with us at the Center."

"What about her immediate superior? Moorlock? Or Morely?"

Carmen laughed. "Moorland? Roger's all right in some ways. When at the Center along with Manley, he just walks around snooping at this or that. Very congenial, he turns on the charm. The good news, his position at Ultra gives him final say-so over Manley."

"Good enough. Will Alex be there too?"

"No, he said he's busy with one of his home lab projects. I just hope he doesn't blow up my basement."

Connie glanced at the wall clock. "Good grief, we've been gabbing forever!" Turning, she called, "Bessie! Come out, come out wherever you are!"

Just then Bessie entered the den. "I'm ready!"

Connie had gotten her to forego the worn T-shirt and cargo pants. Except, now wearing new shorts and a blouse, she had on her Packers cap. Connie groaned, "Sweetie, you're not wearing that hat!"

"Oops! And besides, Auntie Carmen, it would be in the way of the VR unit." Liking Bessie as one of her own, Ricci enjoyed being called "Auntie". She grinned and nodded, "It probably would, dear."

Connie interjected, "Honey, your hair is really long. How about tying it up?"

"Done Mom! Give me a minute!"

As she headed back to the bedroom, Carmen shrugged, "I wouldn't care if she wore a zebra costume. Bessie's wizardry online overrides whatever she wears."

"I wonder what your Ultra observers would think if she

did come like that?"

Carmen raised an eyebrow. "They'd not be amused. Not Manley, anyway."

"These large corporations seldom are with that."

"Amen, especially with Ultra Tech reached out into technical products the world over. They provided for the Center's original expansion, so we can't deny them. Speaking of funding, the U.S. government is also in our picture these days."

"How is that?"

"By sponsoring grants, including to develop cyber-integrated prostheses for disabled veterans. There's also the Defense Department's need to upgrade its weapons capabilities. But then they need systems to defend against them. One of their people will be there today too."

"Whew! You're right, that will be quite a crowd."

"Yes, sorry to say. We'll be up to here in..."

"All right, Aunt Carmen, let's go!" Hair brushed and tied back she looked much improved. She also carried her gym bag.

Carmen pointed at it. "What else are you bringing, Bessie?"

"My own VR, of course."

"But just as a back up, all right? We'll have you using the very same model but one your dad sent to us."

Connie pointed to part of a string of beads sticking out of her pants pocket. "And those, dear?"

Bessie nodded, "Ah. From my staff, Mom, just...for luck or whatever."

As they drove to the Center, Carmen said, "Bessie, you already know a little about our Ultra observers, don't you?

"They're in my photos from my visits. Mr. Moorland looks dressed for a night on the town. Dr. Manley resembles Morticia in the Adams Family. What a pair!"

Carmen smiled at that. "Between you and me, we call

them the M-and-M's."

"For Moorland and Manley, you mean?"

"That too, but also for what both you and Alex call them, Mr. Moron and Morticia. They'll definitely be there, so please no slip-ups with calling them that. We don't want Morticia any more tensed up than usual."

Bessie promised with a grin, "I'll behave, Aunt Carmen."

She and her class had visited the Center several times to familiarize with the latest cyber systems. While there, Bessie had additionally sought out research technicians to be even more informed. Remembering her, one called out as she and Rossi walked in. "Hi, Bessie, we heard you were coming!" From another, "Hey, good to see you back!"

After she greeted them, Dr. Paul came over. Reaching out a long arm for a handshake, he smiled, "Hello, and it's Elizabeth, right?"

She gripped his hand firmly, "That's right, Doctor, except..."

He corrected himself. "Or no, it's Bessie. I've seen you here before."

Thrilled as she was with meeting him, she had no idea that someone so famous would bother to be here for her session.

Chuckling, he waved her off. "Besides, Carmen has sparked my curiosity about you, so I'm happy to take the time." Smiling, he excused himself to see someone else.

Bessie said to Carmen, "I've heard from Alex how busy all of you are with AI. I'm surprised Dr. Paul would even bother with my so-called VR skills."

"Bessie, honey, both his AI and cybernetics research are inseparable. And that reminds me, your family doctor, Tom Myers, said he'll try to show up. "

Reacting, Bessie thought, Uh-oh, to wire me up? No way! She merely nodded, "Mm-hm."

Seeing Roger Moorland and Veronica Manley come in, followed by a man in military uniform, Carmen turned to announce,, "Heads up, people! Our observers are here!"

Bessie recognized the Ultra pair. On seeing her, Moorland smiled widely, effusively, "Why hello there! You, I assume, are Ms. Howard?"

His slickened white hair was as bright as his teeth, she thought. She smiled back, "Yes, I am. And you're Mr. Mor–" Choking that off, she finished, "Mr. Moorland, I assume." Behind him she saw Carmen, suddenly stern-faced, tilt her head toward her.

He went on, "That's right! We've heard good things about you from Ms. Ricci about being quite the prodigy with VR units and all." He favored Carmen with another of his huge grins.

Return smile not half so wide. "Yes you have, Roger," she greeted Veronica Manley with a barely polite one, "Good morning, Veronica."

Next to Moorland and totally unsmiling, Manley merely nodded. Wearing a black blazer over a white blouse buttoned to the neck and a black skirt, her straight black hair was tied back by a black band. Accentuating the severity of all this, her dark eyes regarded Bessie like a bug beneath a microscope. Manley fed her a fixed smile, "Hello, Ms. Howard. I hope you won't find us getting in your way."

Moorland added agreeably, "No, we certainly don't want you feeling bothered or distracted by our being here!"

Already deciding today's session would be her only one, Bessie smiled back at both, "Not to worry! I won't be bothered a bit!"

Carmen called her over to where she stood with the man in uniform. "Bessie, I want you meet Major Thomas Meachem. With the U.S. Department of Defense, he'll also be with us today."

Tall and athletic looking at thirty-something, Meacham wore his uniform comfortably, with no martial stiffness. Extending a hand, he smiled, "Pleased to meet you. Ms. Howard." Hand warm and firm, his greeting not the least overdone, he seemed forthright and easy mannered.

She immediately liked him. "Glad to meet you too. And please, let's skip the Miz and make it Bessie, all right?"

He nodded, "Fair enough. Carmen Ricci said she's seen you using a VR unit at your house. It seems...Bessie, that you've got a special ability with it. To me it sounds similar to what my nephew and I saw in a sci-fi movie."

"Ah! You actually watched a sci-fi movie with him!?"

He nodded. "I've always been a nut for that stuff. The one I'm talking about has a young guy connecting his mind to a super computer. It's what they're trying to do here at the Center, by the way. The movie shows this guy able to go anywhere, to any time, and so on. The name of it was...uh..."

She laughed delightedly. "*Perils in Space-Time*, one of my favorites! You really liked it?"

"That's right, and also somewhat believable."

"Good, because I've had some...space-time problems of my own lately."

Smile entirely genuine he asked, "Oh? How so?"

Hoping he would listen and not just laugh, she began, "Lately, Major, my virtual trips really have been the most fun and exciting things in my life! At the same time they're not exactly what you'd call...believable. Sometimes not even to me. So now," she motioned toward the people and testing stations around them, "I'd like for someone at the Center to explain to me how I'm doing them."

At this early stage he could only shrug, "Maybe they can. To me, though, you're entirely believable. Let's see how it plays out, OK?" He glanced at his watch. "As far as I know, you're now on their pay clock, so I better let you go."

Carmen cut in, "That she is, major." She then pointed to where technicians were gathered at a computer console, "Bessie, I need you over there with them."

Meacham asked Carmen, "Is Dr. Paul showing up here too? For all the times I've been here I've hardly spoken to him."

Pointing across the room, she smiled. "He's pretty hard to miss, Major." A head and a half taller than either Moorland or Manley, who'd now joined him, he was obviously trying to listen to both. Ricci went on, "As usual he's side-tracked by our Ultra Tech guests. I'll separate him from them and steer him to you."

Along with Bessie at computer #3, George Tanaka, the Center's most highly skilled senior technician was also setting himself up. In his early thirties and married, with two kids just reaching their teens, he was, Ricci felt, her best choice to pair off in this test session with Bessie. Though famously a winner with augmented reality games, George, along with competitor Bessie, would forego using an AR system in favor of Rob Howard's total immersion VR headsets.

As she and Tanaka settled in, everyone else gathered around. Next, none other than Dr. Myers hurriedly joined the group. Holding up a manila file, he said, "Sorry I'm late, Carmen. I had to double back to Med Research for Bessie's brain scans."

As Ricci filled him in, Bessie was somewhat buoyed up by his infectious enthusiasm. Even so, she said to him unsmilingly, "I'm glad to see you, Doctor. A reminder, though, that I originally meant what I said about being a lab rat."

He waved his hands. "No, no, there'll be none of that! Aside from our own visuals, the sensors in your dad's headpiece will provide any data we need, OK?"

Nodding slowly, a trace of her smile came back. "That'll

be fine...I think."

Seated beside her, Tanaka grinned while handing over one of her dad's new units, "Here you are, Bessie. Now let's see what you've got!"

She grinned back, "Maybe more than you think, Mr. Tanaka."

His grin shortened. "Is that so? Because when playing these games, they don't call me Tiger Tanaka for nothing!" He then saw her take a string of beads and also a gold-colored something from her pocket. After she held them a moment, he asked, "So what are those for?"

Even more in the mood, to take him on, she replied, "Just for luck...*Tiger!*"

Chapter 29

As others aligned scanners and recorders, George said, "Carmen, I've set up today's testing session as a soccer match. I'll be leading the home team and Bessie here will head the visiting one." Turning sideways to Bessie, he grinned. "Just to let you know, I play soccer in my neighborhood league."

She simply nodded back. "I've actually played a bit myself." She had, if only one on one against terrifically athletic Ben.

Both lowered their visors and gripped hand controls. As observers crowded closer to watch, Bessie wasn't sure she would undergo the usual reality shift to wind up inside her bubble. She concentrated to be the game's CGI representing her.

Not entirely surprised she saw that all around her went black, followed by the succession of images. Next she found she'd materialized as...really the player! On a soccer field with seemingly real players! Glancing from within the visor, she momentarily wondered, OMG, has Maxwell actually changed me? Or has my ITC changed? The only change she felt with this unit was a lesser sensation of her surrounding quantum shell. Maybe she didn't need it as much as a game's CGI. As for the staff, she'd left it home, but she had brought her trinkets. She would look into all this later, but right now she had a game to play.

As if in answer she heard faintly from George to her left, "OK, Bessie, I'm in! How about you?"

Looking down at her uniform and running shoes, while *feeling* her padded headgear and shin guards, she answered haltingly, "I...um...yes, I am!"

Standing in the short grass in the center of a soccer field, she saw her CGI teammates to either side, all looking as nearly alive as her. Opposite her in front of their goal, the George CGI and his team were crouched ready to play. Nearby, the ref CGI held his whistle in one hand while cradling the ball in the other. From both the George figure and from to her left came, "OK, ref, we're ready!"

Meantime, the DVD played this same scene on their monitor. Feeling oddly set apart both from those observing and from these CG players around her, she heard only faintly the Center's technicians and observers.

Like George, Bessie dropped into a crouch and tensely awaited the signal. Ben had taught her to play this game. Good at it, too, her long lean-muscled legs could outrun most boys her age. Ben had also taught her to dribble, side kick, and even head butt the ball. None of which, while nervously setting up, she'd thought to mention to George.

The ref tossed the ball to the goalkeeper for George's team. At the shrill of the whistle the goalie gave the ball a powerful kick. It flew straight toward Bessie, as George followed at a dead run. Shooting out of her crouch, she reached the ball by its third bounce. During the next few seconds the flurry of feet kicking the ball and the jostling of others had her aware of nothing else...but wanting that ball!

Amid colliding hips, shoulders and elbows, Bessie thought, "Make me faster!" The wild action around her instantly switched to much slower motion!

Seated at a console apart from the observers, one of the technicians, Ryan Hill, had been putting in long hours. Pulling off his glasses, he took a break from peering intently at the soccer game's graphics darting across his monitor. Head back and rubbing his sore neck, he saw the overhead tract lights flicker. Stopping for a few seconds, it began again. Sitting back up, Ryan grunted, "Huh?" Glasses back on, he saw yet other tract lights flickering.

Quickly away from the tangle of *slowly* kicking feet, Bessie toed the ball to her right. Giving it a solid kick, she took off after it. Booted clear of anyone close by, it crossed an open space as others charged in from either side to chase it down. Faster than them, she easily dodged one player. Darting around the next, she saw he was the George figure. From him or someplace else came a loud and astonished "Hey!" but sounding strangely garbled and deepened.

As Bessie sped on behind the ball, beyond waited her opponent's net. As their goalie and two others came in *slowly* from each side to defend, she reached the ball and kicked it sideways. Shifting too fast in that direction for covering players to adjust, she saw their heads turn slowly to follow her. Again spinning the ball the ball toward the net, Bessie gave it a powerful kick shooting it straight into the unguarded side of the net!

"Goal!" Bessie shouted, and leaped her CG figure into the air!

Staring again at the flickering lights, Ryan saw them stop. Looking to see if anyone else had noticed, he saw everyone else watching Bessie and George or otherwise focused on their monitors.

Easily peering over those in front of him, Dr. Paul was focused on the game. From behind Bessie, Ricci gasped, "Look at her go! They can't touch her!"

Not taking his eyes off the screen, a design engineer asked a technician at his side, "Sharon, did you by any chance speed up the motion setting for her CGI?"

Eyes also on the screen she replied slowly, "No, she's...somehow...speeding it up...on her own!"

In front of Paul, Manley watched utterly fascinated. Mildly interested beside her, Moorland directed his glances at the pretty technician working a video cam nearby. Expression rigidly set, eyes riveted on the monitor, Manley blurted out, "This can't be! She's changing the program!"

Paul patted her shoulder. "Veronica, are you all right?"

Giving a start, "Oh!" she looked up at him, "Do you realize she's exerting complete control over her CGI?" Her voice rose, "It's as if...this girl has actually placed herself inside it!"

He nodded. "I noticed that too. Her talents are much greater than what any of our testers have shown."

As the program instantly set up the next round of play, Bessie, thrilled as she'd been by scoring, had no time to enjoy it. Her CGI changed to defending her goal, she found herself rearward and to the left of her team's formation. Heart racing, she waited for the ball to be put into play.

Leaned toward the monitor with hands stuck down into his lab coat pockets, Paul frowned, "Whatever she's doing and how she's doing it has me stumped!"

To his right Meacham asked, "Is this unusual, Doctor, all that she is doing?"

He nodded slowly. "It is. I've seen testers sometimes *seem* to move their CGIs a little more in tune with their thought impulses. But she's manipulating this one faster and more completely than I've ever seen. Speeding herself up like this is...? Major, it's beyond the capabilities of the system, and I'm at a total loss to explain it."

Fascinated by the cybernetic sciences, Meacham had been jolted wide awake while watching this. Later his debriefing with General Hensley would have him answering tough questions from his equally tough boss. "Doctor, what could be the reasons for her amazing abilities?"

"There are any number of them, Major, but I'm only guessing at this point."

As they and others watched, Bessie easily, too easily blocked several of George's goal shots. Then driving the ball from her own goal marker, she zig-zagged all the way downfield and scored another goal!

This ended the game. Taking the time to reorient themselves, Bessie and George removed their headbands. Next, she, George, and the others spent another little while animatedly discussing all that she had accomplished.

His busy schedule requiring him to go someplace else, Myers was first to say, "All right, everyone hold it a second. Now Bessie, I've not forgotten what you said last spring about coming here. After today's session you've learned, I hope, how important we think our work is. My readout data just from today would keep me busy the rest of the week." Seeing her suddenly draw back, he finished, "First, how's your head these days? Having any aches or vision problems or any of that? Especially when using virtual?"

She kept it honest but short, "I've had a few headaches." Now wanting to drop all of this, she quickly added, "Though barely any today, it's nothing, really."

"In that case, would you come in again tomorrow?"

Before she answered her refusal, Moorland cut in, "I had all I could do to break away from my own work today. Much as I'd like to, for me tomorrow is a no go." He turned to Manley. "What about you?"

Staring intently at Bessie, she said, "My assistant could cover me."

Bessie knew what would happen if she did come in. For one more day? She'd wind up here the rest of her school year, or much longer. Looking at all of them, she said, "For me that won't work." After someone else asked the same question she shook her head and stayed silent.

Frequently engaged with the Center's VR exercises, George Tanaka well understood why she did that. "Bosses, I think our intern here has had enough for today. Let's let her be."

As Bessie gave him a grateful smile, Manley quickly put in, "Ms. Howard, you really don't seem to be in the spirit of this. If you have some sort of strong reservations against our research here, I'd like to hear them! **Sox** do you?"

Not much liking her tone, Bessie narrowed her eyes. "Don't get me wrong, doctor, this research work I've been shown today has been very interesting. Thrilling in fact."

As she started to go on, Dr. Paul ventured, "It has been for us, too, Bessie, except I'm sensing a *but* coming on. Am I right?"

For him, she smiled back. "Dr. Paul, I've told Aunt Carmen that spending the rest of my school year here constantly observed is definitely not happening."

Eyeing her with renewed respect, Myers, if disappointed, was equally supportive. "Bessie, let me know if you change your mind. For now get on out of here and have a good day!" She rewarded him, too, with a smile and a nod.

Shallow as Moorland seemed, none of Bessie's amazing skills had been lost on him. Finding out how she accomplished them and then duplicating them at Ultra could raise him higher on the corporate ladder. He grinned widely, "You know, by continuing these sessions...Whenever you can of course, either after school or on weekends, I could authorize some pretty good pay. A girl your age could certainly use it, right?"

As he started to say more, Ricci cut him off. "Roger, as busy as Bessie is, the last thing she needs is being stuck here."

For Bessie putting up with Moorland was one thing but Manley, she knew, was impossible. If only the people at the Center plus major Meacham and Dr. Myers were here, another day might have worked. Whereas, instinctively wanting to steer clear of these Ultra people, she gave Moorland an unsmiling head shake.

Ricci wrapped it up. "Anyhow, Bessie, for all you've done today I'm putting you in for a full day's pay."

Meacham also told her, "And you've earned it."

As Ricci pulled out the parking lot, Bessie saw Manley

talking to two men in a white van. Seeing the dish on top and Ultra Com on the side, she wondered about Manley's connection here. Before she mulled this any further, Ricci asked, "Want to be dropped off at home or at school? It's only noon."

"Not school, Auntie, I arranged to skip my Monday class-es."

As they rode the beltway to Covington, Bessie texted to her crowd she'd finished and was headed home. Lucy and Ravi replied they were stuck at school, but Nina and Alex said they could free up and meet her at home.

Chapter 30

The U.S. Defense Department's Intelligence section had beefed up its Madison office for the express purpose of tracking latest developments at UW-Madison's Cybernetic Research Center. Washington especially prioritized not only Dr. Paul's AI work but especially his experimental testing of both virtual and augmented reality systems. Because Paul's research ranked among the nation's best, the Defense Department director had his most qualified people running the Madison branch.

Brigadier General Brice Hensley had headed it for nearly a year. A couple of months back his reports had shown UW's research work stepping up even more. Accordingly, he'd since ordered his top subordinate, Major Thomas Meacham, to increase his own efforts with observing at the Center. Born and raised in Madison, and having studied cybernetic tech-nology at UW, he'd later served under Hensley as a junior staff intelligence officer in Iraq. On finding Meacham so capable back then, Hensley had kept him in the department's intelligence section ever since.

In the middle of a late stand-up lunch in the break room, Hensley's phone chimed. Seeing Meacham's name display-ed, he barked into the phone, "Caught me grabbing a bite, Tom! What's up?"

Having worked in the same section since Iraq, both had since dropped using strictly militaristic titles in private. Meacham replied, "Glad I caught you, Chief, and that's *why* I called."

Hensley's laugh was more of a growl. "To pin me down before I got away, I suppose. And so?"

"It's news from the Center. With you at our office it'll keep until I'm there in ten minutes or so."

Pocketing the phone, Hensley lumbered down the hall to his office like a bear heading for a stream jumping with salmon. Tall and heavyset, and always in a rush, his special intelligence section did keep him on the run. Nonetheless enjoying his work, he passed his liking on to his staff and they in turn liked him. His gruffness reserved for those newly hired, he'd wink to veteran staffers, "My scaring 'em is just an act, but if they stand up to it they're in!" This rough exterior, however, belied what he was, a sharply intelligent driver who got things done.

Entering his office, he breezed right past Lieutenant Cary, his managing staff officer at her desk. At the door of his inner office, he caught himself with a "Whoa!" and turned back to her. "Emily, Tom Meacham will be right behind me! So hustle him on in and then no interruptions, OK?"

Having been with him all year, she knew the drill. "Sure, General!"

He was no sooner seated behind his broad desk, when he heard from outside, "Hi, Major, and he said go right in!"

When Meacham entered, Hensley motioned, "Drag up a chair, Tom!" He then jerked a thumb toward the ceiling. "Our higher ups just now jacked up the security level, by the way. So no more phone calls, faxes, or snail mail, and texts to be coded. They even want memos moved strictly by hand. Who knows why they've gotten so jumpy over in D.C. but orders are orders. Anyway, what've you got?"

Meacham nodded. "Brice, from what I saw today, things could suddenly be starting to move at the Center."

The general, as usual, had done his homework. Already knowing some of Meacham's material, he skipped the small talk. "Show me what you got."

In turn, Meacham knew the General demanded that data

be straightforward and simple. Removing four sheets of paper from his briefcase, he slid them across. "That first sheet is an update of people at the Center and what they do. The important ones are highlighted. The next shows corporations producing the latest computer accessories, including those VR units I've told you about. List number three gives family members and friends of those on the first two lists. Data from today's testing session is on page four, plus, a footnote about Ultra's people."

Partway through the third one Hensley frowned. "About this young girl, Tom, do we have time to chase down any more info about her?"

"From what I saw today of her skills with VR link-ups, we'd better make the time. Brice, this Howard girl is one very special item."

Hensley raised a bushy eyebrow, "Coming from you, she must be. So what's she like? Really bright, totally cooperative with all the rest of you, or what?"

"Yes to the first and no to that last, at least with Ultra Tech's observers. In any case, to me she seemed a pretty good kid. Hitting it off from the start, we were practically pals by the end of the session."

"Will she be back over there tomorrow?"

"No she won't, sorry to say, and I don't blame her. Bright and energetic with her whole life ahead of her, she told me and the others that being bogged down at the Center with us hanging all over her is out."

"Hmm. But you'll be back over there of course."

Again Meacham nodded. "Without Bessie Howard there I'll be paying more attention to the Ultra observers. I saw both Moorland and Manley definitely taking notice of her, and also overheard them considering raising their own level with watching her. They were so intense over this, they have me thinking we should keep an eye on those two also."

"All right, let's do," Hensley replied, "But back to this Howard girl. If she's not sold on continuing, that's her call. But it's not in the cards to let her out of our sight. These amazing abilities of hers could wind up attracting those who are not friends of ours."

Having sped read Meacham's test data page, Hensley went on, "Along with our regular intelligence info, I've kept up with current STEM findings." He said this offhandedly as if poring through Science, Technology, Engineering, and Mathematics material was second nature to him. "So whatever surfaces about this Howard girl, we'll get on it. I'll be awhile getting any more of our people here to help out." He grinned, "Which means I'll be spreading you pretty thin for now."

Meacham grinned back, "Don't you always?"

"You're right but let's just stay close to her and see what happens, okay?"

"OK and anything else?"

Hensley nodded. "What I said about keeping an eye on the Howard girl also goes especially for these Ultra people."

His full-on pursuit for intelligence about Ultra's leading edge technology, particularly with virtual systems, was understandable. The potential for these when combined with today's modernized military was enormous. Recently, however, he'd sought additional information about those much higher up at Ultra. Puzzled by this, Meacham asked, "During these last few weeks, why all the questions about Ultra people at the very top? Do you know them personally?"

After staring back for a long moment, Hensley replied, "Just between you and me, I definitely know Ultra's owners, Ed and Martha Wells. He was my commanding officer in the intelligence section in the seventies. In fact he's the one who talked me into sticking with intelligence for a career.

After the service he and Martha moved to the east coast and I've stayed good friends with them ever since."

For Meacham this explained enough for now. Mainly, he would definitely keep closer track of Bessie Howard.

Chapter 31

When dropped off Bessie found Nina and Alex waiting out front. Coming up with an idea with them here, and having the house to themselves, she told them what she'd thought up. She could have predicted their reactions.

Staring back, Nina exclaimed, "Me? A virtual trip to Mars? No way!"

Though doubting it, Bessie had hoped she would. Again she tried, "Neen, I've told you how harmless this is. You've even seen that with my Gettysburg trip. OK, except for me so bonkers at first from just yanking off Maxwell."

"All right, and even with going back to Gettysburg, that was fine. But excuse me, all the way out to another planet? I don't think so!"

"Why not? In some ways crossing through space is easier."

Part of Nina wanted to. She also pretty much believed by now that her best girl friend could truly do these things. Lightening up, she grinned, "Of course I'd go to Mars...if they had a Janine's up there. Or what if we went to her boutique at the mall?"

Contrastingly serious, Bessie shook her head, "No, we might be recognized."

Nina laughed, "Then the one in Milwaukee?"

Meantime pacing circles around them, Alex cut in, "If you don't mind, Bean, what about me! I'll go in a heartbeat!"

Bessie grinned. "I know that. So don't feel left out, because you are!"

"Really? You mean that?" Alex exclaimed.

She patted his shoulder. "Yes I do. Let's go inside, you

guys."

Following her and Alex, Nina laughed, "This I've got to see!"

With Nina observing, Bessie and Alex sat before the computer monitor. Now adorned with the trinkets, the staff stood unmentioned against the wall. Their headbands donned and visors tipped up, Bessie began, "You guys have watched me during the virtual battle games, but when doing them it's..."

Excitedly, impatiently, Alex asked, "It's what!"

She finished, "It's very different!"

He asked drily, "OK, Space Queen, how's that?"

"First for both of you, I'm still new with this so we need to rehearse. Alex, I'll be coaching you from start to finish. And Neen, for the whole time, maybe fifteen minutes max, you can—"

Interrupting, Nina held up her phone. "I'll be filming you guys."

"Right. So Alex soon as we get there I'll help *you* to take a soil sample, and I'll have zip-lock bags for that. Now here's the important part!" She gave him a meaningful look. "I'm still not sure my bubble will co-operate with this but let's assume that it does. When you reach down to sample surface material like sand or rocks, I'll be practically draped over your back."

Again Nina interrupted, this time grinning, "I've wondered when you two would get around to that."

Making a face at her, Bessie went on, "We need to be fast and in unison for you to grab that sample. And Alex, I do mean fast! I'm too new with shifting the bubble to hold that position very long."

Serious now he nodded. "I've got it, but first you've got to get us there."

"I know that. I just want all three of us knowing what to do when we are there. Neen, you'll see us looking around and gawking at Mars, and grabbing samples. You'll also hear what we say to each other and to you. When talking to us, though, you'll need to say it loud." Getting more excited about this as she went on, she wrapped it up. "I really can't think of anything else you guys. Oh, but Neen, will you be able to make this film, um, professionally scientific?"

Nina was more than ready to play her part in what was about to unfold. "Girl, as your director I'll have this docudrama collecting an Oscar! You guys just get rolling and don't worry about me!"

As best as Bessie could figure, all had been said. Feeling the thrill of anticipation, all this week she'd been dying to take Alex along on a virtual trip. Winding up with someone else, especially Nina, witnessing it was even better. Turning to the monitor, she said to Alex, "Are you ready?"

"Yep!"

"Nervous by any chance?"

"Another yep!"

"I always am. Lower your visor." Lowering hers, she began the NASA DVD of Rover Explorer's mission on Mars.

Watching, Nina spoke the date and starting time into her phone. Though she couldn't even imagine jaunting off to a crazy place like Mars, seeing her friends setting off to do just that was already shaping up as a movie script. Shaking this off, she focused on what Bessie had explained, that soon as the DVD showed the Martian landscape on the monitor, the three of them at first would see the same scene. But once Bessie and Alex shifted to their virtual phase, what they saw then would be far different from what Nina still followed on the monitor.

As Bessie and Alex set off, she knew his first impressions could throw him off track. She thought, I hope he's a quick study with this! Fully aware of him on her left, she felt him jerk as all around them abruptly went black. As the freeze frames appeared, he exclaimed, "Whoa! What are those!"

She told him, "Just let them go by, they'll disappear any second!" When they did so, she was able to quickly teach him to create his own glow line. Where hers was solid, his however was flickering and segmented its whole length. Straining to make it solidify, he muttered, "Sorry, mine's not so hot!"

Feeling the strain for both of them, she told him crisply, "You're not focused enough! Do that!"

He did so and then, "That's better, right?"

She grinned beneath her visor, "Just fine...for such a rookie!" She was loving it, too, teaching *him* for once to put quantum physics to work. She added without turning around, "Neen, can you hear us? Be sure to speak up!"

She heard faintly, "I hear you perfectly!"

Excitedly, Alex asked, "OK, what's next?"

Excited herself, she said, "Now we'll aim these beams down at Mars!"

The gigantic sphere lay directly below in contrasting tan, orange, and red. Seeing his line sliding around, she told him, "Steady it!" When he did, she said, "Drop lower...a little more...right there! And Hold!" Then arranging hers alongside his, she said, "Now I'll join us."

Still a bit confused, he began, "You want me to–?"

Muttering, "No, I'll get it," she right away had their single glow line slanted down toward the Red Planet's equator. Next she ordered, "Voice command!"

After the GPS woman's voice answered, Alex began, "Huh? What's...?"

She nudged him, "Shush!" Within seconds, using the given GPS, she had their destination targeted below with a bright solid line. All that remained was riding it down together to the planet's surface. Heart racing, she told him, "Lean forward, it helps!" And then, "Hang on, here we go!"

What Nina saw a few feet in front of her was Alex digging in his heels while exclaiming, "Hey, we're heading down too fast!" She heard Bessie tell him, "Don't panic, I'm slowing us!" And next, very excitedly, "See? We're here!"

Chapter 32

They had landed in a region fairly free of the dust storms. Overall, the vast reddish expanse of Mars spread out before them beneath the golden yellow sky with the small moon of Phobos hanging above the far horizon. Jaw dropping while gripping his chair arms, Alex had all he could to just take it all in.

Thrilled beyond words to have someone else, especially him, along with her, she grasped his forearm, "Don't you just love it!? Oh! And look at that dust devil out there!" The length of a football field to their right, a towering one whirled off in that direction.

He pointed toward the rim of a large crater to their left. "Look at the size of that thing! You could fit in half our town!"

Nina next heard them excitedly trading remarks about the likely compositions of nearby rock formations. Shaking her head, she laughed, "OMG, you two, get a life!" Then hearing them discuss picking up rock samples, she quickly switched her phone's movie camera to wide angle close-ups. Luckily she caught Alex, apparently following Bessie's instructions, bend lower to reach his left hand down beside his left sneaker.

Her chair against his chair, and left arm over his shoulder for support, Bessie called out, "Neen, are you filming this!"

She yelled back, "Of course I am! Keep going with the action!" Then she saw Bessie reaching her hand down to cover his. Next she heard Bessie say, "I can't reach from here! Back your chair up a little and use your right hand instead!" Hearing, "OK!" from him, Nina saw Alex reach down his left hand and Bessie cover it with hers.

Ignoring the DVD's Mars Rover photos and the attending narration and now totally focused on filming this action scene, Nina's own heart was beating faster, As they stayed poised in this position Nina heard them count down in unison, "One! And two! And..." At "Three!" Alex's hand, with Bessie's on top, lunged lower to grab at something Nina could not see. Then she did see, for a fraction of a second, their joined hands shimmer and become indistinct. As if momentarily immersed into wavelets of water reflecting sun light.

Nina blinked. Camera tightly focused upon their every move, like any movie director she wondered, That happened so fast! Doubting there'd be any second takes, she spoke into her phone about whatever she *thought* she'd seen. The two were already sitting straight up again. Nina saw Alex hold out his right hand palm up for Bessie. And in it were...

Jerked straight up, her hand rigidly gripping the phone still filming, Nina gasped, "No-no-no, am I really seeing this?!" In Alex's hand were several tan-colored pebbles and a bit of reddish sand! His face was visor-covered from the bridge of his nose on up. The bottom part split with a huge grin, Nina heard him say, "Martian rocks! These are unbelievable!"

She saw Bessie grin back. "Am I ever glad we did this! Genius Boy, you have made my day!" She added over her shoulder, "Neen, did you get this?"

Nina replied loud enough for both to hear. "I got it all!" While thinking, I hope! And then, "When are you guys coming back?"

"In a flash!" Bessie answered.

Within a few minutes they had returned. After their headbands came off, Bessie quickly got the three of them out in the kitchen. She told Alex, I'll put down a paper towel on the counter and you can spread your sample on it." She smiled over at Nina, "Then our director here can faithfully record that too!" Her voice fairly shook with excitement.

When they'd finished with all of this Bessie said, "Thanks, you guys! Neen, I'll download your photos to my log! Alex, can you analyze these rocks?"

The consummate scientist, he nodded eagerly. "I'll cut and polish one of them. Scanning it with my microscope, I'll snap photo micro-graphs for you to download." Staring at the Mars rocks, he shook his head, "I'm still hardly grasping it, me on Mars! But Bean, you've converted me! I'm in all the way from now on!"

Shaking her own head, Nina grinned, "Me, too, and think of it! If we do this right we'll all be up there in lights!" Clutching her phone, she was literally spinning in tight circles.

Bessie tapped her shoulder. "Hey, girl!?"

Stopping, Nina asked, "What!?"

Bessie returned a level look. "Later for those lights, girl. For now the only others I want in on this are Lucy and Ravi. OK, and my brother, but nobody else!"

"Oh come on!" Nina countered. "This is huge! Like when...what's his name walked on the moon!"

"Neil Armstrong!" both Bessie and Alex said at once.

"Right, him! And later, stepping out in front of every TV camera on the planet, we're talking fame, girl! For all of us!" She realized, however, that Bessie, staying silent, was shaking her head. "You're not buying it."

"Neen, spending my time in celebrity freak shows is the last thing I need."

Knowing her really well, Nina also knew when to back off. She laughed, "You're right, we'll set this...pilot show aside. for now. But meantime!" Pinching a loose lock of Bessie's har and doing the same with the sleeve of her

Green Bay sweatshirt, she sighed. "We do need to get you into make-up and costuming!"

After they all laughed at that, Alex told Bessie, "Actually it's too late to dodge your fame. As of today the Center and my mom and others know at least something about what you can do. I'd say our secret is out."

She shrugged. "True, but as scientific researchers they won't announce it to the world. Not until writing it up and publishing it, and that could take years."

Nina said, "But with this no publicity thing, what if it *does* get out? I'm no rocket scientist like you two, But even I know what instantly zipping off to other places is. I mean, teleportation would be the biggest thing that's ever happened!"

Bessie said, "I know, you guys, and I've thought about it a lot. The thing is, I'm not going to have my whole life turned toward a direction I won't like. If I go on to do my own research with it, that's different. For now I'll keep on enjoying my virtual trips...with you guys in on them too. Oh. And Lucy, Ravi, and Butt Brain."

Alex said, "Wait, didn't you say a guy from the U.S. Defense Department was also there?"

"Yes, a Major Meacham, but he seemed like someone else I can trust. He'll file his reports but I'm sure neither he nor his superior will shout it out. With anything really new I've heard these military people sit on it for ages."

Alex shook his head. "From my own time at the Center I know the military won't sit on something like this for very long. There's also those Ultra characters. From what I know of that Moorland guy he's no problem, and neither is that medical guy, Dr. ..."

"Myers!" Bessie finished.

"Right, but Moorland's other half, Dr. Manley, will go wild over this teleportation thing! You saw how intense she is, right?"

Glowering at him, Bessie held that look, until Alex stepped back. "Hey, what's that for!"

Relaxing the stare, she smiled, "That's what she did with me. Like I told your mom, that gave me the creeps, and it's why I'm not going back there again."

"Oh? Mom was looking forward to you being there more than once, I know. So what did she say to that?"

"I filled her in when she drove me home, and she understood perfectly. She even admitted she's concerned about Ultra Tech, and mainly with Manley."

Alex knew all about Veronica Manley's bitterness over being usurped by his mom's assistant directorship. "There's no love lost between her and Manley. And yeah, Manley is super intrusive about the Center's ongoing research. I personally know what a pushy pain she is. It's tough for Mom to complain with U-T providing so much of the funding for the Center's big addition."

Nina said, "Enough with that, you two, we have a five day weekend coming up!" She held up her phone. "Let's download this and start planning for that!"

Chapter 33

Driving the van today and circling them through Howard neighborhood, Trainer asked Girardi, "After the Howard girl and her friends went inside you came up with zilch, right?"

Trying not to doze off, he yawned, then answered, "Same as that other time, a few power surges and nothing else."

Nearing the Howard's, he said, "I'm pulling in across the street."

Adjusting his headphone, Girardi nodded, "Kay!"

Once parked they unlimbered the listening device, the night vision 'scope, and their spy camera, this upgraded ability to gather whatever small amount of light was available. The recorder and computer systems were mounted in the van's instrument panel along with the GPS system.

Tracking Bessie and her friends during their most active time from mid-morning through 8 PM, they were backed up by two other teams. After reluctant approval by Moorland, Manley intended these others to cover tonight's graveyard shift, the stretch with the least activity. She'd also made it expressly known, however, they were not to engage in any rough handling of those they tracked.

Leaning back, Trainer also let out a yawn. "Won't be dark for awhile. Once it is, this van won't be so noticeable."

Girardi laughed. "Not to worry. Does anyone ever notice us repair guys? In any case, we're in for another really slow night."

Flicking his forefinger at the top sheet of Meacham's

report, Hensley growled, "These science people, have they got any security?"

Seated across from him, Meacham admitted, "From what I've seen and from additional info I found through this evening it's little or none. On entering the research area none of us pass through any metal detectors. Back during my first visit I only filled out a standard visitors form. Everyone else came and went wherever and whenever they liked."

The general shook his head. "Same old story and I've said it a hundred times. Whenever these research types are on to something big, they never keep it to themselves. Not even when it concerns us."

Meacham nodded. "They view the benefit of full disclosure. If everyone on the planet is told on a day to day basis about the progress made with anything there'd be no mad scramble with constantly outdoing the other guy. They honestly believe this would eliminate arms races to develop high-tech cybernetic weaponry."

Hensley went on, "You've also highlighted this info about Moorland and Manley. Do we need to step it up with watching them too?"

Having developed a gut feeling about those two while watching them trying to corral Bessie Howard, he said, "Yes, and starting right now. As important as what I saw over there today is, I'd say we have no other choice."

Chapter 34

Living two blocks north of the Howard's, late this afternoon Sierra was cleaning up the leaves out back. Finishing the last pile, she dropped the leaf blower and after it went her gloves. Top ranked in the Covington High martial arts class, she took a T-stance.

Right leg whirling around..."Yee-ah!"...her heel shot out just shy of the large oak trunk.

Straightening, she glared up at the leaves still clinging to the branches. "For two cents I'd torch all of you and the tree you live on!"

Covington allowed no leaf burning. After clinging to branches during the mild autumn they were finally falling all over town. The dozen or so bags she'd stuffed full still had to be hauled out to the curb for pick up. Muttering to herself, she pulled her phone from a jeans pocket and punched Mimi's number.

Mimi Jarret, was a first team medalist in gymnastics. Though getting a bit tall for the sport, her motto, "Use what you've got while you've got it!" made her one of Sierra's best friends.

Answering instantly, she whispered, "Sierra, I told you I can't talk! They've already jumped on me for calling you while I'm cleaning out this garage. They catch me doing it again, they'll chain me down out here!"

Sierra also kept quiet. "The same here. Finally, the first stretch in months with time off from work and I'm dealing with all these leaves!"

More loudly Mimi replied, "Stop the melt down, girl, you're not shoveling cow pies out of a barn. We both...just got yelled at again, gotta go!" She clicked off.

As Sierra stared at her phone, stepmom Melissa called out from the back stoop. "Your friends can wait, young lady! Finish up with those leaves!"

For Sierra's part, at age ten when her mom died, she'd become caretaker for Daddy Jack, fixing his meals, cleaning up after him, chiding and then helping him to buy better clothes, along with countless other things. She also became his protector from women trying to *console* her so-called lonely widower dad.

When Sierra was fourteen, her dad met and soon married Melissa, older sister of Connie Howard. From then on her stepmom's sincere attempts with being understanding and getting along had helped Sierra in recent times to begin to reciprocate. While at other times, no way, not yet!

In turn, compliant for too long and no longer caving in with Sierra's stubbornly willful ways, Melissa also allied with Daddy Jack to help reign her in. And so, cop that he was, he too had told her, "We've let you get away with murder too long! So either clean up these leaves or I'll cuff you to this leaf blower till you do!"

Busy again and soon finished, she cleaned up and joined her parents for dinner. As hungry as she was, her earlier upsets out back made her give the meal only a perfunctory taste. That is, until excusing herself to use the washroom, where she actually worked in privacy a learned mental exercise.

This past summer, Mr. Watanabe, her main martial arts instructor, had taken her aside. "Sierra, you're the very best I've got in this class!" She had liked that. He'd gone on, "What I try to instill in you young people, besides your skills is confidence. In tandem with this, at least some of you will gain inner serenity. You've nailed the confidence part with the skills but, more importantly, you need to practice gaining control over *runaway* emotions. Otherwise, on any given day *they'll* run over whatever you try to do!"

Equally helpful had been the adjunct instructor, Lieutenant Joyce Cary. Assisting from the U.S. Army Intelligence section in Madison, and a black belt, she, too, had taken Sierra aside after a sparring bout to caution her in no uncertain terms, "I don't want you flaring up out there on the mat on and crippling someone!" She'd been reached by Lt. Cary, who'd gone on to thoughtfully advise an on the spot self-help method to use anywhere and at any time.

Practicing this was hard at first, but the quick relief and getting back on track had quickly engrained in her the value of doing it more and more often. When back to the table, in fact, she cleaned her plate with second helpings added in.

Heading out the door, she saw it would soon be dark. With Mimi also without wheels, Sierra texted her to meet at the corner. Hurrying along the walk with head up and a long steady stride, Sierra even looked like who she truly was these days, a willful young woman, if also brash and outspoken, purposely striding her chosen path in life. And also unabashedly proud of herself for doing that.

The night was nearly dark enough for the parked van to not be conspicuous. In the same vein, as with yesterday, they wore nondescript work clothes.

In the drivers seat, Trainer spoke quietly to the dashboard mike, "In position two doors south and across the street from the Howard residence. It is seventeen-fifty hours." He glanced at his watch.

Moments later, they both noted the good-looking blonde girl walking up behind them on the other side of the street. Using her phone, she turned left at the Howard's driveway and went out of side in back.

Girardi said, "I've seen her before, a friend of the Howard girl. She gave us a look before disappearing."

Trainer shook his head. "With her on the phone I doubt it registered we were even here. In any case, if she and the

Howard girl go anywhere we'll trail them."

Almost to her own place, Nina texted Bessie, whats u*p?*

Bessie answered instantly, *done raking leaves /U?*

Nina punched in the sign for "evil grin", *<g>* and then, no leaves 4 me/just back fr mall.

Bessie came back, there's no justice/come over!

Sending, nearly there, Nina noticed the white van. With darkness setting in she barely made out the two figures in front. She did see the van's dish on top and that it pointed at the Howard's place. Recalling that Sierra had said something about this, she laughingly dismissed her next thought, that these people could be staking out Bessie.

She caught both Bessie and Ben busily bagging up the last of the leaves in the back yard. Finishing the draw-tight on her bag, Bessie greeted Nina with a grin. "That's it, I'm done!"

Ben tossed Nina a wave. "We've bagged a billion of these things! Now I'm out of here for some gaming!" With that he sauntered off to the back door.

Bessie shook her head with a laugh,, "Getting out of doing leaves for your folks and going to the Mall! How do you do it, Neen?"

Doing a modeling turn, Nina gave her an over the shoulder, "I simply charm them, my dear!" She laughed ruefully, "I got away with it today but tomorrow they'll have *me* working." Seriously, she added, "For what it's worth, that white van I've been seeing lately is parked across the street. Also, girl friend, the dish on top is pointed right here."

Bessie frowned. "I wonder if that's the one I saw at the Center this morning."

"Ah. If so, that's not good, the Center's putting a tail on you"

"No, it's definitely not the Center. Did you see Ultra

Com on the side?"

"Come to think of it I did. And so?"

"I found online that Ultra Com and Ultra Tech are one and the same, Tech being the bigger parent company."

"Uh-huh, so maybe *we* need to keep an eye on *them*."

"We?" Bessie grinned.

"Of course, we!" Nina grinned back. "You don't think I'd let you do that by yourself, right?"

Walking south toward the Mall, Sierra and Mimi texted their other girl pal, Caitlin, to meet them there. Dressed in shorts and light sleeveless blouses, they were just a pair of pretty girls enjoying the summer-like evening air. Or at least Caitlin was.

Still fuming, Sierra did a little hop, then "Yee-ahh!" and shot out her fist.

Stopped, Mimi stared. "OMG! What are you doing?"

Sierra laughed, "Karate-chopping my oak trees!"

Knowing her friend as well as anyone, Mimi merely nodded, "Oh. OK."

Girardi shifted himself on the seat for what could be a long, dull evening. Raising his night-vision binoculars, he scoped two figures approaching. "Here come two more girls. It's Girl's Night Out around here!"

Trainer nodded, "It's a warm one. There'll be lots of people out and around."

"Oops, now they've stopped."

"To do what?"

"They've both got out their phones." Setting aside the binocs, he held up the pistol-handled camera-mike. "Should I aim it at 'em? They're in range."

"No, but keep it handy. If they live near here they might be friends with the Howard girl."

Halting, Sierra grabbed Mimi's arm to stop her. "Don't stare at it," she whispered, "A white van with a dish on top is parked across from Bessie's." As Mimi automatically began turning toward it, Again Sierra hissed, "Don't look, I said, and keep your voice down!"

Trying not to peek, Mimi whispered back, "Why? What's wrong?"

"Trust me, that's a surveillance vehicle. My dad showed me theirs at the police station. Let's take out our phones, then do as I say!"

Mutely obeying, Mimi muttered, "What *are* we doing?"

Tapping out a message, Sierra held her display for Mimi to read, don't even whisper/ they can hear/pretend we're making calls.

On her own screen Mimi asked, what are they doing.

Sierra answered, a stakeout on Bessie I think/follow my lead.

Girardi lowered the field-glasses. "Here they come again. What do we do?"

Trainer handed over his clipboard. "Ignore them. If they're nosy and ask what we're doing, flash this at them." Covering Trainer's notes, the top sheet read in boldface type **Ultra Com Field Service Form**.

Chapter 35

Drawing nearer to the van, Sierra and Mimi kept up the act of laughing and chatting with one another. When they reached the van's passenger window, Sierra gave her friend the prearranged nudge. Stopping, both turned to face the man looking back at them from the passenger side.

Flashing her sweetest, most innocent smile, Sierra sang out, "Why hi there! What are you guys up to tonight?" As he gave a little start, she thought, My-my, aren't we jumpy tonight!

Girardi stammered, "I, er, we're doing some, uh, routine field work here."

Any *routine* field work, Sierra knew, would've since been done for the day. Still smiling, she tipped her head, "Working late, so sad! Whatever are you so busy with? Seeing the driver lean toward him, she heard, "Show her your clipboard!"

Holding it up for Sierra to see, Girardi pointed to the Ultra Com heading. "See that? We're a big outfit and always busy! I bet you've heard of us, right?"

Sierra's smile tightened, "Uh-huh, but busy doing field service at night? That sounds really odd to me!" She turned to Mimi. "Doesn't it to you?"

Mimi nodded. "Very odd!" Also staring at Girardi, her own smile vanished. "Like lying, I'd say!"

Through playing games, especially with these phony characters, Sierra snapped at Girardi, "She's right, field guys don't sit around doing diddly squat like you two!" She jabbed a finger at the pistol-gripped mike-and-camera unit on the seat. "They don't use those, either! What are you *really* up to!?"

Shocked by the abrupt turnabout, Girardi's jaw dropped. Shaking his head to collect himself, he barked, "Now hold it, take a look at this clipboard!" To emphasize the official heading, he held it out further.

Sierra's hand shot out and snatched it away.

"Hey!" he yelled, reaching for it.

Backed up from his flailing hand, she cursorily glanced at the blank top sheet. Flipping it over, she saw the next page covered with notes. With an intake of breath she saw Bessie Howard written above the scribbled jottings. Keeping her cousin's name to herself, she sneered, "All that you're busy at is snooping out our neighborhood! Here, you can take this back!" She hurled the clipboard at him.

Grabbing for it, he missed, and it clattered off the curb. Angrily jerking open the door, Girardi began clambering out, and Trainer did the same.

Sierra said to Mimi. "It's time we split!" Striding briskly away, they heard Girardi yelling. Glancing back, Sierra saw the clipboard in one hand and him shaking a fist, "Snotty kids, you better watch out!" She saw, too, the other guy staying silent but giving them a look heated enough to burn her leaf piles.

Unable to resist, Sierra yelled back, "Hey creep, my dad's the police chief here and *he* might come looking for *you!*"

Hurrying away even faster, they stopped after a couple of blocks to look back along the dark street. Sierra said, "We've lost them for now, but they'll stay after us." With a short laugh she added, "I think we've got them annoyed!"

Mimi replied, "Annoyed! We're lucky they didn't shoot us or something!"

"No, they weren't even armed."

"Oh? How do you know?"

"My dad taught me to look for that. Which is why I also know they're staking out Bessie, and now we'll tell her! If these creeps think they can come in and just roll over us, they've made a big mistake!" Then catching herself heating up and heading off track, she took several deep breaths to calm back down.

Mimi was still looking down the street. "Fine but some place other than here." She pointed to the park across from them. "Let's cut to the next street over and warn her from there!"

"All right and then to the Mall! That's as good a place as any for a meeting!"

As they hurried across, Mimi asked, "What kind of meeting?"

Staring back from where they came, Sierra wore a determined little smile. "To figure a way to teach those clowns a lesson they won't forget!"

Pulling away from the curb, Trainer said, "You pretty much blew it, good buddy, and good luck with explaining this to Manley!"

Girardi raised his hands, "Sorry, those snotty girls caught me completely off guard! So now what?"

"With nothing going on here with the Howard girl, we're going after them!"

"OK, and if we do catch those two, then what'll we do?" Girardi added a rueful laugh, "Call their parents? Or spank 'em?"

Eyes moving from side to side, Trainer laughed back, "Somebody should! But no, we'll just throw a good scare into them!"

Girardi returned a worried look. "I shouldn't have left our notes about the Howard girl on my clipboard. Miss Smart Stuff caught a good look at it. Worse, the way these kids talk, they'll spread it all around in a New York minute. I don't like that her dad's the police chief, either."

Trainer shrugged. "We work for Ultra Tech, remember?

We've got her and her friends heavily out gunned. This includes her dad, so stop worrying."

"OK, but are we reporting this to Moorland and Manley? He might not care, but she won't like this blow-up I had with the girl."

Slowing at another corner, Trainer shook his head. "No need mentioning your shouting match with her. They're only interested in what's what with this Howard girl."

Visibly relieved, Girardi ventured, "Have you found out who Moorland and Manley report to?"

Trainer shook his head. "Uh-uh, we're not supposed to even ask that."

"Knowing you, you probably did, though, right?"

Stopped at a stop sign, Trainer gave Girardi a serious look. "Now listen, OK? I do know people who have ways of finding things out. What I've heard so far, the one calling the shots is above the M&Ms, and I've also heard they'll stop at nothing to get control of this Howard girl. And Charlie, they've got plenty of power and money to do it, so from now on don't ask. I don't want to even think of what could happen to us if we wind up knowing too much!"

Girardi caught the barely concealed apprehension in Trainer's tone. As they slowly drove **o x?** through the next street he quickly changed the subject. "I bet we'll be watching these other kids besides Bessie Howard. You might have to call in more help."

Eyes searching left to right in the darkness, he nodded. "I've already got some others in mind. Meantime, I'll have one of Ultra's carriers get us one of their new cell tracers, and by tomorrow morning we'll put it to work.

Chapter 36

Criss-crossing streets to shake pursuit, the two girls drew nearer to the Mall. Sierra said impatiently, "Meems, Bessie's phone must be off and my call index doesn't include...what's her face, who's always with her. But yours does, right?"

"OMG, you two are something else!" she exclaimed, "but sure, watch for those creeps and I'll call Nina to clue Bessie in! Give me a second!" Keying her phone, her thumb fairly flew – *sierra & I caught ultra creeps staking out bessie/ tell her turn on phone!* Muttering, "Come on, come on," she too kept looking back down the darkened street.

Nina looked at Bessie worriedly. "You know, I've heard you say those Ultra observers at the Center are totally intense."

"Too true" Bessie nodded, "with Dr. Manley, anyway."

"Then you should watch out for... !" Her phone chimed and then the caller ID surprised her. "Well for...it's Mimi Jarrett! She says she and," a pause, "Pizza Girl saw that van out front, and it's staking you out! And to turn on your phone!"

Taking hers out and thumbing ON, Bessie frowned, "You're right, Neen, that van means I do need to watch out." She sent back – *I'm here too/ standing by.*

A moment later Bessie's phone chimed, and then – *hi cuz/ ducking hiding/ you know who R van creeps?*

Bessie replied – *fr ultra tech/ veryBIG/ Uwatch out!*

Sierra sent – *will do/back soon* – Then her texts stopped and stayed stopped.

To get her back Bessie kept hitting – *RUthere?*

Abruptly, she was – *saw creeps car lights & hid!*

Relieved, Bessie began once more – *lostU/UOK?*

Sierra instantly came back – *fine but all need to meet/where?*

Watching over Bessie's shoulder, Nina said, "The Mall. Tell her that."

Nodding, Bessie sent – *meet@mall/you me others make plan.*

Sierra came back – *sending that not smart/but2late/ CUthere.*

Reading this, Nina asked, "What's wrong with what you sent? I don't get it!"

"Sierra says these Ultra are tracking our messages," Bessie said. She started off to the front sidewalk. "Come on, let's go to the Mall and take it from there."

Breathing in the mild evening air, Nina grinned, "We couldn't have picked a better night! And me going right back to my favorite–"

Bessie cut in, "Them stalking me like this, I feel...betrayed!"

Nina instantly refocused, "You said they hung all over you at the Center. If they saw what I've seen you do, of course they're after you!"

Generally believing others, Bessie no longer knew whom to believe. "Like I said, Moorland and Manley were a pain right from the start, but during the testing I forgot they were there. Afterward they were all smiles, or Moorland at least. He even said I could consider them colleagues!"

"Really? For sure, he is a jerk!"

Bessie wanted to do something about these people. But what? This meeting was a start. Was there anyone else they could bring in?

Nina snatched that from her head. "What about telling

your parents? They'd report these stake-out creeps to the cops."

Bessie nodded. "They would, until I also told them why they're doing it" She added a mirthless laugh, "Because of seeing me alter the cyber soccer games/'"

Nina dryly laughed back, "They'd think you were mental!"

"Uh-huh, exactly like you guys, remember?"

Crossing the mall parking, they heard someone shout, "Bessie! Nina! Wait up!" It was Caitlin Parks, another of Sierra's best friends. Joining them, she said, "From what Sierra and Mimi sent me, they were pretty excited. What's up?" The school paper's star reporter, she definitely had a nose for the latest news.

As Bessie and Nina filled her in, they all joined Sierra and Mimi waiting at the main entrance. Already parked in the lot, Ben came in with Alex, Ravi, and Lucy. Everyone had caught the urgency in the texts they received.

Irrepressible as always, Ravi grinned, "Well, people, now that someone intelligent has arrived, we'll go after those Ultra guys!" That pretty much matched the mood of every-one present.

Warily glancing at headlights circling the Mall ring road. Sierra pointed to the entrance. "We're too exposed out here! Let's go in!"

Once inside, they were jostled by others drawn out by another unusually mild evening. From all sides came the crowd noise and loud speakers blaring about bargain sales. They next needed a suitable meeting place amid the busy, noisy hubbub. With stores closed lots of people were strolling the Mall corridors. Secluded places along these, however, were nil. Lucy pointed to the still open and fairly crowded food court. "In there we'd be invisible in this crowd!"

Next to her also as always, Ravi grinned, "I like it,

hiding in plain sight!"

Mini looked at him doubtfully. "I don't know, Wiz, you didn't see those guys up close! They're scary!"

Ben saw two security guards chatting across from them on the thoroughfare, "Mimi, if they do show up and spot you two, they won't pull any rough stuff. Not with all these pe-ople around and security right over there!"

With tables full up, others carrying food trays were searching for someplace to sit. Luckily two tables in front of Bessie's group abruptly emptied out. Quickly seated they began devising a plan to get back at Ultra.

For openers, Sierra reminded them, "We need to watch it with phoning and texting. My dad showed me how his people patch in on this, which means so can Ultra. They can also pick up over quite a distance what we say. If you spot any suspicious characters nearby and vehicles too, then watch your mouth!"

By unspoken agreement Nina became the organizer. Ravi instantly volunteered to start hacking Ultra's cyber-systems. Lucy, said she'd lend her expert hand to identify and describe the working extent of their latest cybernetic designs. Their next major problem was traveling long distances in a hurry when they had to. Everyone had either driving permits or licenses, but only a few had access to a car. Sierra wasn't currently allowed to even drive. The lone car owner, Ben elected himself their main driver.

For most present, however, something else still needed clearing up. Looking around at all of them, Bessie said, "I see some of you shaking your heads. Except for Nina and Alex, you're not buying it yet, that I've actually made these VR trips through time and space, am I right?"

Sierra raised her hands. "Cuz, we all know you never lie about anything." All present nodded. "Other than Alex and Miss Hollywood here, the rest of us have never seen you go off on your trips! What I do know is that a company the size of Ultra wouldn't spend two seconds tracking you unless you had something they really, really want! So I'd like to see what you've got that has them so worked up!" Stopping, she looked around for anyone acting suspiciously.

Mimi nudged her. "I doubt those creepos would come after us in here."

Getting a grip, Sierra agreed. "No, a surveillance team couldn't sneak around in this food court."

Finally Caitlin put in, "Bessie, you know I'm a reporter for our school newspaper. It's a seeing-is-believing thing for me and this includes your virtual trips." A reporter for the Covington High Gazette, along with its managing editor, she also interned for the Covington Daily Journal. Known by both for relentlessly tracking down the facts and nothing but the facts, they held her in high regard..

As they all went quiet, Alex dug out several tan-colored pebbles from a pants pocket and placed them on the table. One was cut in half and polished. Holding it up, he too looked around, "Anyone guess where this is from?"

Bessie was impatient with guessing games. "They're from a crater on Mars! I took him there two days ago!"

"She did," he said, "and then I hustled to my home lab where I cut and polished this one. I also made a couple of thin sections for my microscope."

Lucy asked, "What is it?"

"It's andesite, a common mineral right here, and so much for proving I went to Mars. Even so, pass it around." He handed it to Ben.

As it continued past him, he told them, "They showed it to me later when I got home. So look, I know my sis really is nuts with her outer space stuff but Alex isn't, so I'm behind her all the way!"

She smiled tightly, "Thanks, that's nice for a change." She turned to the rest. "Tomorrow mom and dad will be in Madison most of the day. They're leaving at eight, so come over afterward and I'll prove to you what I've been doing. Who can show up?"

Most could and the rest said they'd try. Sierra added, "After tonight's fun and games with our creeps, I'd like to see you do this stuff. What's in store for us, cuz?"

"I want to take one of you with me on a trip," Bessie raised an eyebrow. "By any chance would you volunteer?"

"Well sure, why not? But where would we go?"

Thinking a moment, Bessie replied, "For you, just out to the back yard wouldn't work, would it!" Sierra pretended a wide yawn "The same with tripping over to Madison, right?" Seeing this rate only a head shake, she smiled, "In that case, are you up to meeting some dinosaurs?"

Chapter 37

Passing a slower vehicle on the beltway, Trainer said to his dashboard app, "That's right, put me through to Dr. Man-ley. I'll wait." He said to Girardi, "The receptionist said she's working late." And then, "Dr. Manley, its Trainer and we're coming in. We only got a little with our client but we'll do more tomorrow." They spoke euphemistic drivel when phoning and texting higher-ups. Though confident about its communications security, Ultra's corporate mindset said, One never knew! He went on, "We also had an incident that...Well, you know how difficult our clients are at times. We'll fill you in shortly." When off the phone he told Girardi, "She wants to hear all about it. We'll be ushered right in."

Seated at her office desk on the top floor of Ultra Tech's office building, Manley was no sooner off her phone when it chimed again. The caller only kept her on for a moment. Punctuated by vigorous nods, Manley replied with short utterances..."Yes, we certainly will!...Of course!...As soon as we can!" and finished with, "I understand perfectly!" Mo-tionless for a moment after the call, she gave a start as her desk speaker spoke, "Dr. Manley, Carl Trainer and his part-ner just came in. As you instructed, I've sent them up."

Shortly, she poked a finger at Trainer. "Tell me about this mishap of yours, the whole thing!"

Telling about their confrontation with the two girls, Train-er went on, "Then they took off. With nothing happening at the Howard's we drove after them. We saw them again a couple of blocks away but they spotted us and ran into somebody's backyard. We lost 'em and that was..." He glanced at his watch. "...forty-five minutes ago."

"And so?"

"In the first place, Dr. Manley, Charley and I have kids nearly the age of those girls. So we know these two will right away spread the word to their pals. Worse, when the smart-mouthed one grabbed Charlie's clipboard, she got a good look at it. There's no doubt she saw the Howard girl's name on it."

Manley slapped her desktop. "Oh, fine! So now she knows you were staking her out?"

"Ms. Smart Mouth made us, all right. This means if you want us to also cover her, we'll need a few things."

For Manley her own purposes for surveilling Bessie How-ard were still not well defined. This wasn't the case with her mysterious, more highly placed caller. Not to also mention whether this was even right, having her ordering these two to tail a fifteen year-old. She replied shortly, "Like what!"

He passed his hand over his white coveralls. "We lose these uniforms and also the van. Everyday clothes and a regular vehicle gives us a fighting chance to stay undetected. Also, along with Ms. Howard we'll be watching her family and friends, including Ms. Smart Mouth, To put twenty-four hour coverage on all of these I need at least two more teams."

Manley returned a quick nod. "I'll see to that and you'll have them no later than tomorrow. By then I'll have arranged for all your teams to also have our latest long range monitoring devices." Turning away, she looked out the window at the city lights as if considering something else. She faced him again. "We'll also need a...special kind of team. For that I have to first run it past Roger Moorland."

Trainer saw her looking worried. "Is there a problem, Dr. Manley?"

"Not with Moorland, no. You see, Mr. Trainer, some-one..." She raised her eyes to the ceiling. "...at the highest level spoke to me before you came in. I was told in no uncertain terms that we must now keep an even closer eye on this Howard girl. And I do mean much closer!"

Chapter 38

Sierra and Mimi showed up at Bessie's house at just past 8 AM. Alex had arrived shortly before, and Ben had chosen to stick around until heading for school later to suit up for the varsity football game. Via their texts in prearranged codes, the rest were on their way.

Next to arrive were Lucy and Ravi on his scooter. First through the front door, Lucy told Bessie, "When almost here we saw Ultra's guys circling the block."

Behind her with his lap-top, Ravi laughed, "What else is new!" And then, "Last night and again this morning I tried burglarizing Ultra's files in Madison. But nope, getting past their blocks is still tough."

By 8:30, nine of them, Bessie, Nina, and Lucy, along with Alex, Ravi, and Ben, and finally Sierra, Mimi, and Caitlin were in the computer room. Bessie took the time to tell everyone about her by now practiced routines for making her VR trips. She looked around at them. "That's basically how I do these. Any questions?"

Wearing their headbands, backs toward the console, she and Sierra faced the others.

Worriedly eyeing Sierra, Mimi asked, "While you guys are back there in...the Triassic, is it?" At Bessie's nod she continued, "You won't get eaten by any of those god-awful dinosaurs, right?"

Wagging her finger as an all knowing professor, Bessie deepened her voice. "Now class, in the Triassic those won't even exist for millions of years yet!" Act falling apart, she smiled, "We'll be safe, Mimi. Whatever does exist can't pass through our quantum bubble." She raised an eyebrow toward Alex, "And neither can anything else, right?"

He nodded. "I've been on a trip with her, you guys, and no problem. Nothing can get through, no dinosaurs, no birds or lizards, or anything!"

Nervously bouncing a knee, Sierra turned to Bessie. "Let's get rolling, OK?"

"Let's do it."

The two girls turned their chairs to the monitor.

Pressing PLAY for the DVD's prehistoric Triassic epoch, Bessie instructed, "Now we drop our visors."

Circling the block, Trainer and Girardi drove a common light gray-colored passenger car. Another two person team stayed in contact from farther out. Girardi studied his lap top. "Earlier the other team caught part of a text from some kid tagged Wizard. Apparently he told those at the Howard place that he and somebody called..." Pausing, he laughed, "Beauty Bot were on their way. That's it."

"OK, they're doing this in code. Tell the other team to record all these texts. Piecing 'em together later could have something important show up."

Having coached Sierra with the fundamentals, Bessie knew it wouldn't hurt to repeat them. Keeping it simple, she said, "Sierra, don't look at me when I talk. Stay focused on the screen." Her travel companion simply nodded.

As seen from outer space during the early Triassic, Earth had only one major continent, Pangea, everywhere else was covered with blue seas. Those watching from behind the girls would see this and whatever else the DVD showed.

Bessie went on, "Now like I told you before, image up a glowing line pointing down at it from where we're sitting."

Struggling, Sierra replied, "I've got the line but I'm having trouble steadying it! It keeps flickering! Argh! There it goes again!"

"Fix it in your mind, and I mean really focus on it. Got

it?"

Abruptly Sierra's voice was high, excited. "I've got it!"

Bessie kept her voice calm and steady, "Stick with it. I'll join mine with yours and then give it a boost."

Unable to see any of this, the watchers could hear their words. Whereas, the travelers saw their glow lines pointing in parallel toward Earth. Along Sierra's line were little gaps, compared to Bessie's solid one. Stepping up her own concentration, Bessie's flared briefly before joining Sierra's. The instant their glow lines fused into one, all went black and freeze-framed images rose all around.

As the images sailed past, Sierra exclaimed, "That's a picture of me! And that's Dad! And there's our school! What's happening?"

Bessie said quickly, "They'll go away in a few seconds! When that happens, no more talking, just do what I say!"

Obeying orders never quite Sierra's style, though, she did this time. Freeze frames abruptly vanishing, the Earth reappeared targeted dead center with their glow line. This at least drew a short "Ah!" from her.

In turn all business, Bessie said, "Next we'll point our line where we want to go! Then we'll ride it down on my signal! And again, *don't say anything*!" She swung their line to the edge of the land mass, there bounded by the deep blue sea. "Now, Sierra, let's ride it!"

Following it down, they saw the globe quickly expand to a horizon-filling balloon. The super continent became vast green and brown areas rushing up.

Ignoring instructions, Sierra gripped her chair arms, "Better slow down or we'll crash!"

"No, no, think it with me, slower-slower-slower!" As they did so, the now gradually closer land area formed into verdant greenery.

Again tossing instructions, Sierra said, "I can feel it around us too, that bubble of yours!"

Bessie patted her forearm. "Yes, and remember we're safe inside it!"

Smart phone screen swung out and aimed at the time travelers, Caitlin spoke to the phone in clipped tones, "Going virtual, Bessie Howard and Sierra Hutchins are traveling back in time to," She turned to Alex. "What age is it?"

Forgetting the travelers wouldn't hear, he stage whispered, "Early Triassic."

She whispered back, "Alex, I want to make sure of this. Jurassic Park showed T-Rex, but he wasn't in the Triassic?"

"Nope, there was nothing as large as those, I think. Not on land, anyway."

"Got it, thanks!"

From her other side Nina said, "Caitlin, I tried keeping a record of this but you're better at it. This could be hugely important."

Knowing Nina little more than the one girl Sierra liked the least, Caitlin returned a surprised smile. "I appreciate that. Mind if I plug in something about you as I go?"

Nina grinned, "Are you kidding? I'll take all the publicity I can get!"

Both flinched as Sierra yelled, "I can't believe this, girl! We're really here!"

With the bubble grounded on a beach of reddish sand, they saw the surf swirl past stand alone rock formations. Bordering the beach stood a forest amid giant ferns swaying in the breeze. To their right near shore the sea was emerald under the mid-morning sun. Farther out a boiling, black cloud mass crackling with lightning was coming on fast.

Bessie said, "Nuts! That means we won't be here for long!' Humorlessly she laughed, "No kidding, on all of these trips I've hit nothing but storms!"

"It's not here yet!" Sierra pointed up. "What's that, a pterodactyl?"

"No, they don't even exist yet. Smaller than those, it's a pterosaur, an early ancestor. When I came here alone, one was on the sand right next to me."

Sierra reached out to the inside of their bubble. "This bubble gives but when I push harder it's solid. What is it again?"

"Our quantum energy field. It gives a little, but if a freight train fell on us, it wouldn't even twitch."

Though knowing they wouldn't, from Bessie having said so, Sierra almost wished a T-Rex or a two-story tall brontosaur would burst out of the trees. Turning to the sea, she saw that the oncoming storm clouds would cover it any minute, Lower she spotted very large grayish humps rising and falling in the waves. "Are those whales?" she asked automatically.

Bessie began, "No, they didn't exist back here either. Those might be..."

Abruptly one of the humps became mostly a monstrously gaping tooth-lined mouth, leaping way, way up and falling back down with a tremendous splash!

"Mosasaurs!" Bessie finished with a gulp.

"OMG!" Sierra exclaimed, "That thing could swallow a whale!" Then she saw Bessie press her hand to the back of her head. "What is it, cuz? One of those headaches you've mentioned?"

Bessie muttered, "It's starting up but I brought my aspirin. I always do with these time trips." Digging the bottle from her shorts, she shook out only one tablet. "The last one! I should've brought that full bottle!"

Sierra frowned, "Should we go back? I don't want you getting a killer migraine on my account."

"I'll be fine." She motioned toward the storm, "With that almost here we need to hurry with what else we do." She waggled the phone, "I'll snap you with the trees behind you. Then you shoot me with the sea at my back."

"These will prove that we've been here, right?"

"No, they'll look like those copied from a DVD or a book about this time period. I take them just to know that I *was* here. Now let's do this!"

Watching them take turns with the photos, Caitlin said, "If I was there, I'd take lots of shots. They'd be amazing additions to an article."

Ben laughed, "Yeah, for a science fiction one!"

Storm clouds nearly on top of them, Sierra said. "We'll be rained out. First can I bring back a souvenir to look at?" Seeing Bessie hesitate, she said, "Listen, I know what you said about bringing things back, but a bit of sand from millions years ago? What kind of a problem would that cause a problem in the present?"

"From what Alex and I know, maybe none!" Inside, she added, I hope.

"So how do I get the sand? The bubble won't let me reach through it."

"Like with Alex and his Mars rocks we'll do it together and lightning fast!"

"I'm good but first!" It occurred to Sierra their friends were looking on. She called out. "Can you guys hear and see what we're doing?"

She heard Nina's voice, though faintly, "No need to yell, we hear you perfectly. We also see your every move."

Alex said, "Bean, I heard something about your head! How's it feel!"

Still aching somewhat after the single aspirin, it bothered her less than the idiotic nickname. "I'm fine and stop calling me that! Are you taking your notes?"

"I am and Caitlin's recording everything. You guys will

be up there getting the Nobel someday with me!"

With storm clouds directly overhead Bessie knew they had to hurry. "Let's get out of our chairs and kneel side by side. Then we'll reach down to your left."

When on the carpet, Sierra laughed, "I love it, so totally insane! What next?"

"Reach down to the edge of the carpeting. Yes, like that. Now I'll lay my hand on top of yours like so."

Sierra was even more excited. And impatient. "OK, OK, and now?"

Fingertips touching the carpet's edge, the red-colored sand was only inches beyond. "Now listen closely! Tune out everything but our hands! On one, two, three, go, grab some sand and yank it back! My hand will follow yours!"

"Got it!"

Staring at their hands, Bessie intensified her concentration. She said through tightened lips, "We've got to be fast! I mean really fast! Ready?"

Also intensely focused, Sierra said, "Ready!"

"OK! One! Two! Three! GO!"

Chapter 39

For those behind Bessie and Sierra the DVD by now showed Triassic creatures simply living their daily lives. To prehistorically appropriate background music the narrator described their activities. So far this had played for ten minutes.

Mimi returned from keeping watch over the Ultra surveil-lance drive-by teams . Taking a seat behind Nina, she saw Bessie and Sierra rise from their knees and sit down. "What are they doing?" she asked,

Nina replied, "They're on an ancient beach and just now grabbed some sand to bring back."

Mimi shook her head, "What are you talking about? What sand?"

Alex chimed in, "We can't see it but...virtually they can!"

Caitlin added, "They also said there's a storm moving in."

Ben finished, "So they'll be back from this crazy stuff any minute now."

Then they all heard...

"All right, let's image up our glow line," Bessie said.

Sierra answered, "Got it! There it is! It looks more solid than when I first tried it!"

"It does, but...*shushhh*! We both have to focus more."

They saw the two girls then stay motionless. They noticed too that Sierra's right hand was clutching something. After another pause they saw both straighten up and look around through their visors.

Sierra began removing her headband. Still reorienting, Bessie grabbed her wrist. "No, no, no, we leave these on for a minute!"

Shortly, Sierra said, "Ah, the computer room! All right, I'm good!"

"Me too! Now they come off!"

Minus her headband, Sierra whirled around in her chair to face the others. "I'm telling you, what a crazy, beautiful trip!" Opening her right hand palm up, she grinned, "Check this out! From over two hundred million years ago!"

Behind her on the screen the DVD still played. but no one paid it any attention. All leaned forward to better see what she showed them.

Mimi still couldn't believe what she was seeing. "Girlfriend, you're putting us on, right? It looks like ordinary sand."

Ben laughed. "Yeah? She didn't have it when they started!"

Amid the ensuing chatter Bessie winced, "Ouch!" Pressing a hand behind her head, she wondered, Are these headaches worse the farther back I go?

Nina asked, "Where do you keep your aspirin?"

Ben beat Nina in rising from his chair. "I'll get it!"

As he headed for the door, Sierra called after him, "While you're at it, bring me a zip-lock bag for my sand, all right?" She turned to Bessie again, "Want me to get a cold towel or something?"

Exiting behind Ben, Nina said, "I'll get that!"

After two more aspirin and the cold towel behind her head, Bessie told them, "I'm probably getting used to these aches. It does feel better." She looked around. "So what did all of you see during our trip?"

As they all started talking at once, Nina waved a hand. "Hold it, one at a time! Alex, you first!"

He said to Bessie. "Look, taking someone besides me on

a time trip is great and all that, but like we talked about," he switched to Sierra. "Bringing back that sand sample is bad news!"

Sierra narrowed her eyes at him. "You and Bessie have told me about those... whatever, those time ripples and I agree! But with a handful of sand? Get real!"

Unlike others with Sierra, Alex held his ground. "Look, bringing back anything *might* have a ripple effect. And no, chances are slim to none your sand would do that. Still, you don't want to risk even the slightest *might!*"

Bessie agreed, "He's right but we did and that's that." She held up her phone. "Our photos are perfectly OK, I think. If any of you are still doubters, we'll show you these."

Sardined into the computer room long enough, Nina said, "Let's stop all the talking! It's time we came up with a plan for Ultra!"

Sierra sided with her for the first time ever. "She's right, let's do that right now."

Surprised at seeing these two agree about anything, the others echoed their own agreement while filing out of the room.

Mimi pointed out the living room window. "I saw a couple of cars keep circling several times real slowly. They're definitely watching us."

Lucy said, "They'll soon see Ravi too. He'll show up any time now."

With all seated around the dining room table, Bessie had a blank page in her note pad turned up. Marking it, she muttered, "Can't think unless I'm doodling. Give me a minute." Then she pointed her pen at the first X she'd drawn. "This is us right here. This little circle around it are those Ultra people outside." She tapped her pen on two nearby X's. "The closest X is the Center, but I didn't bother to circle it."

"Why not?" someone asked.

"I know for sure that they're harmless. As for the Ultra observers, it looks like they're breathing down my neck wherever I am."

Nina asked Alex. "You still intern there, right?"

"Only parttime and lately hardly at all." He looked at Bessie, "Now that you've been there, Mom says they're interested in having only you come back." When she returned a vigorous headshake, he simply nodded.

Lucy said, "Bessie, you've marked Madison for the farthest X and you've circled all of it. What does that mean?"

Without waiting for her answer, Nina said, "I get it. That X is Ultra's building complex."

From Bessie's other side, Sierra smiled, "And that circle is us, right?"

Bessie smiled back. "That's *us* watching *them*. As for this biggest circle around my whole page, it's the entire Midwest. Ultra really is that big, you know."

Ben swept his hand to include all of this. "We're too small a team to cover that much. Our playing field is strictly in Madison and right here. With mostly me as our driver, that's all the game we can handle."

Lucy said, "With the Madison X, Ravi and I can get into their files, I think."

They all stopped on hearing someone at the front door. Without waiting for anyone to answer it, Ravi walked in seconds later. He told Bessie, "Sorry I'm late! Oh, and one of those tracker cars saw me coming up your walk!" Grabbing a spare chair, he squeezed it in next to Lucy, then shrugged, "They probably paid no attention to me. Or if they did, so what? Counting me, they've got..." he counted around the table, "all nine of us marked by now. So what's up?"

Lucy clued him in. "I just told everyone you and I could

hack into Ultra's Madison files and grab whatever we want. At least you could with me helping."

Rumpling his long black hair, Ravi said seriously to everyone, "Normally my cyber soulmate here would be right. But not this time, which is why I dashed over here. I couldn't break into Ultra's files, not hardly!"

Ravi's hacking abilities practically legendary, Alex was surprised, "Jeez, did you manage to get anything?"

His grin came back, "You had to ask? Their blocks for files marked "Most Confidential" actually were impenetrable. Almost. Their code breaker program had a greater range working with new Cee-Vee Two (light-velocity squared) computers. Like I said, this *almost* stopped me."

Nina's fingertips drummed the tabletop. "Come on, Wiz, what *did* you get?"

"Coming to that! First, so all of you know, Ultra's detection system is incredibly high speed. I barely began acquiring even their less secret info, when the detectors were on me like a shot! Only my uncanny brilliance let me snatch a few important items. Then I split as fast as I could!"

Again Nina asked, "Would you just tell us what you do have?"

"Ah! I wrote it down." Rummaging through a pants pocket, he pulled out a crumpled piece of paper. When he spread it out on the table they saw that it was a torn open envelope. "These are door codes for entering certain departments. There are also some log-ins and passwords for their computers." On the side printed with his parents' address he had scrawled sets of numbers and letters. Cramped for space, one password looped up and over his parents' address.

Lucy smiled sweetly, "Want me to buy you a notebook?"

He smiled back. "Offer accepted," he said and flipped over the envelope. On it was a schematic he'd drawn of the main building's floor plan. "Sorry, it's torn and wrinkled, but I was in a hurry to get over here. Can we use this?"

He drew applause, along with "Nice work!" from Bessie. Then she frowned, "We still lack hard data about what they're up to with me."

Nina said, "Without that we can't do much. Any ideas?" The table stayed quiet until she asked Bessie. "What's to stop you from paying a night time virtual visit to their files over there?"

Mimi squashed that notion. "Doing it unobserved won't happen. My Aunt Polly, who works on the next floor down, says they work 24/7 upstairs."

Bessie said, "I've already thought of that. Even with no one up there at night I'd first need a photo of that area to focus on." Anticipating Ravi's question, she told him. "And no, your floor plan won't work for me either."

After being pursued halfway across town the night before, Sierra felt a real urge to get back at who'd done the chasing. Eyes fastened on the offending X on Bessie's pad, she said, "In other words to get inside we're talking undercover."

Nina nodded thoughtfully, "We might get away with that," pausing, she looked at Alex, "with one of us who looks old enough."

Catching her look, he shook his head, "With me, forget it, Manley and Moorland would recognize me from the Center."

Ben laughingly admitted, "Even in suit and tie I'd still look too young and dumb to pass as an upper level type. You'd have to look and act like a higher-up to access what we   need."

Ravi said, "Forget me! Even dressed up, I look twelve! With any of us, in fact, we'd be busted in a heartbeat!"

Mimi spoke up. "Even with makeup I'd still look too young."

Lucy said, "I'd never pass."

Caitlin said, "If made up just so I might get by. but once up in Ultra's R&D area I'd have to be very sharp with cybernetics and with VR units too. I'm not!"

The mention of makeup setting Nina's mental wheels to turning, she spent a long moment sizing up Sierra.

Sierra shot back, "What!"

Already mouthing fashion tips to herself, Nina arose. "Mind getting up for me? I'd like to look you over."

Grinning, "Ah! To be your 007?" Sierra stood. "I'm all yours!"

After looking her up and down, Nina said, "Listen, we've both had parts in our high school plays, so I know you can act. And you're good!" She added to the others, "Not as much as me, of course, but close."

Sierra smiled wryly, "That good? Do tell me more!"

"Glad to! My quickie make over would make you look the part." She held up a lock of Sierra's short-cut blonde hair. "The color and the punk rocker style, I can hide all that. It's the acting that's key."

Sierra actually had been praised for her roles in the plays. Her other plusses included consistently holding high grades in school, keeping up to date with current events, and being highly competent with using cyber systems. Adding in her yen for a successful professional career, she realized that fitting the part Nina had in mind was doable. She asked, "So who do I need to become?"

Again looking her up and down, Nina was all business, "First we lose your style of attire, hairstyle, and how you apply your makeup, All these have to go."

Equally all business Sierra nodded, "I can toss them. What then?"

"No offense, but I need to teach you," Nina paused, "some class." Then more quickly past any interruptions, "Overnight my make-over with your walk, your talk, and the whole package will give you that! Can you handle it?"

Sierra's reply was Sahara-dry. "Uh-huh, so you'll change me to someone," her turn to pause. "*better* than me?"

Nina laughed. "No, no, no, not at all, Sierra dear! That's too far a reach even for me." She turned to Bessie, "Can she and I meet here tomorrow? Early?"

"Wait, wait, wait!" Sierra broke in. "How early!"

Bessie said, "My folks will be gone by eight, all right?"

Nina turned back to Sierra. "This'll be time enough to polish up rest of your act." Ignoring Sierra narrowing her eyes at that, Nina circled her some more to do what she did best, a fashion critique. "OK, some fairly shapely legs. And no, your butt's not too wide. Ah, and that narrow waist will do." She frowned at Sierra's chest. "Hmm, a bit large but overall not bad."

Sierra wore a sideways smile. "I passed the audition?"

Missing none of the sarcasm, Nina too caught up in her make-over to care. "Don't mention it, but now for the hard part." She asked Bessie. "Didn't you say this Moorland guy is a girl chaser?"

"With the best looking ones, sure. But I've never seen him get anywhere."

Nina smiled craftily, "Ah! We can work with that!" Raising her hands, she framed the taller girl's face. Which made Sierra flinch. No longer having any more nonsense, Nina narrowed her own eyes. "Could we stop all this stuff between you and me? We'll be way too busy for that, all right?"

Surprising herself, Sierra simply nodded, "You're right, so go ahead."

Again framing her face, Nina went on, "Excellent basics here. When done I'll have him hitting on you non-stop. Part of your role of course is distracting him."

Sierra laughed, "You mean...pretending to seduce him?"

Ignoring her, Nina went on, "Clothes aren't a problem.

For your business attire we'll outfit you with a white, long sleeved blouse," Another glance at Sierra's chest. "Buttoned to the neck. You'll also need a dark colored knee length skirt that's close fitting, and a matching blazer. Tiny pearl earrings are good, too." She looked at Sierra's face. "Nuts!"

That took Sierra off guard. "What! What's wrong with my face!"

Nina waved her hand dismissively. "It's too pretty, that's what."

Sierra switched to pleased agreement. "So?"

"We've got to make you look older. What are you now, eighteen?" Sierra was seventeen and a half. But, not waiting for an answer, Nina traced imaginary lines on her subject's face. "Working wonders with make-up, I'll raise you to...oh, the mid twenties. You'll have the college years with cyber-netics and a few more with that later on with management. The only thing that worries me...." She drew back for a more thoughtful pause.

By now everyone else was fascinated at seeing these two, once nearly arch enemies, now getting along. One of them laughed, "Don't stop now! Tell her!"

Sierra said, "Please do."

Knowing her well enough by now to not overstep, Nina said carefully, "Now don't jump all over me for this, because you are one of the girls the others look up to. But," And next very fast, "You really are totally lacking in sophistication." And faster yet, "And with my coaching you'll be over-flowing with it. With you as Eliza Doolittle and me as Professor Henry Higgins, I'll teach you to be polished! How's this sound?" Following all this, she let out partially held breath.

As the others primed for Sierra's reaction, she surprised them, and Nina too, with, "So when do we start?"

Nina said, "How about right now!" Realizing she wasn't

alone in this, she looked at the others. "What do you guys think?"

Caitlin was first to ask, "If we do this, what about our folks? Do we let them in on...er...our plot here? They'll know pretty quick we're up to something."

Sierra vehemently shook her head. "And then they'll screw everything up. Besides, these Ultra creeps are mostly ours and Bessie's affair."

Bessie added. "It's already complicated enough without letting our folks in on it." Assenting nods made it all the way around the table.

Alex ended with his own. "We've got our double-oh seven. I know Sierra needs an Ultra employee I.D. just to get into the place and to also pass through their high security doors. Any ideas? With this I'm totally blank."

"My Aunt Polly works on the third floor and hand-carries high-security memos to the fourth floor," Mimi said. "She's home this week. If I do a quick visit, get her ID somehow, and we copied it, I'd have to return it right away!" She thought for a minute. "I'll leave something behind over there. When I return for it, I'll slip the I.D. back where I got it! It'd be a scramble, but only a few blocks away, I could jog there from here!"

"I can copy it," Ravi said. "But Sierra, I'd first have to attach your photo and add your...007 name, birth date, and whatever else. Next I'd plasticize the ID but the only plasticizer I know of is at our school's office. The thing is, staff people are working there today. I'd also need someone to drive me to and from."

Pulling out her school I.D., Sierra made a face at her photo before handing it to Ravi. "Not looking my best but here it is. Oh, wait! Nina, what color is my hair going to be? I'm blond in my photo."

"I want you a brunette to look more business like. Ravi, can you use the copier to darken her photo hair? You're the

Wizard here with electronic...thingies."

"Forging is my middle name, I'll come up with something!"

Ben checked his watch. "We'll use my car but I'll have to double back to the school afterward for football practice. We've got to be really quick with all this!"

"We need the I.D. first!" Nina said. "If you run Mimi to her aunt's, you guys can hurry to the school office. Except, can you think of an excuse to use it?"

"I'll go with!" Caitlin said. "I always use it for our weekly newspaper!"

Seeing Ben, Mimi, and Ravi already going out the door, Nina was delighted to see her Ultra plot springing to life. She told Caitlin, "Super! Let's go for it!"

Seconds later, Ravi's head popped back in. "Hey, 007! I'll make up your birth date and where you were born, but I need your name and official title!"

"For my cover name?" Sierra replied. " I can't think of one!"

Bessie said, "This morning I almost took you to the Devonian Period! Let's make your first name Devonia!"

Sierra laughed. "That's not too weird! And my last name?"

"Churchill, naturally. Besides, Devonia Churchill sounds official." She told Ravi, "But don't make her a Ph.D.! Because Veronica Manley is the only one over there, she'd be really annoyed. Let's award our Ms. Churchill a Master's degree!"

"I'm on it!" Ravi said.

As soon as he left, Lucy put in, "Sierra, while you mingle with Moorland and Manley, being clueless about Ultra's cyber systems is a no-no. Ravi gave me his data about some of that, so I'll hard copy this for you to memorize. Opening her laptop, she began.

Bessie said, "You've got to be stronger too with math

and physics. Alex, let's do what Lucy's doing."

"OK, Bean, let's do it!" As they marched off to the computer room, the others heard Bessie say, "Fine. And knock it off with calling me Bean!"

Sierra told Nina, "I'm too restless to stand around. Can we start with me?"

Nina felt the same. "Let's get over to my place. Then we'll dye your hair and a few other things. Come on!" They left.

A little over an hour later everyone but Nina and Sierra were back. Running late, Ben hurried back to the school. Looking hurried himself, Ravi exclaimed, "I'm telling you, people, what a rat race! We first took Mimi to her aunt's!"

Mimi broke in, "While getting Aunt Polly to bring me a glass of water, I swiped the ID from her purse. When she was back I said that...oops, there was something I'd forgotten to do. Then I charged out the door!"

Ravi went on, "When she joined us, Ben broke the speed limits to the office! There were people working there, but...! I'm out of breath! You're next, Caitlin!"

"Always scrambling to make deadlines, I told the staff I had Ravi with me if I needed his help with...well, not the plasticizer., but the copier. Then I decoyed them away while Ravi forged the ID. And then...We raced back to my aunt's before the ID was missed!"

Just then, Nina and Sierra walked in. Presenting her, Nina wore a self-satisfied grin. "Not bad if I say so myself."

The collective "Wows!" and admiring grins and nods from guys and girls alike said it better. No longer a blonde, Sierra's sleek black hair swept smoothly back from bronze-tinted Foster Grants. These plus Nina's judicial touches of make-up, showed her admiring audience not only a young executive career woman, but a strikingly attractive one at that.

Meantime Bessie, Alex and Lucy had their research printouts in hand. With so much to memorize let alone begin to understand, Bessie asked Sierra, "Really, cuz, how are you with cramming?"

Taking the printouts, Sierra glanced at the material. "Whew! Better than usual, I hope." She posed the bigger question to Nina. "So when do we pull this off, our undercover bit?"

Lucy also asked, "What about it, Neen? We've all got classes next week!"

All their scurrying around had allowed them to easily stall on the *When* question. Now getting down to it, their edginess was setting in, even with Sierra.

After a silence, Nina told Sierra, "I've thought about that. First, a weekend day at Ultra would have fewer of their people around for you to worry about."

Secretly relieved this would still be two days from now, she eyed Nina, "Isn't that the best time?"

"No, I think all their busy-busy stuff on a regular work day would have you less noticed." She eyed Sierra back. "How does first thing in the morning sound?"

Chapter 40

Rob had headed off to work and Connie was ready to leave, She saw Bessie and Ben in the middle of discussing something. She asked, "So what are you two up to today?"

Ben said, "Later it's football practice. For now…" He gave Bessie a disgusted look. "…I'm stuck with giving her some driving lessons."

"And I'm stuck with you!" Bessie said. She turned to Connie. "Anyway, Mom, that's about it! See you later!"

Truth was, they'd been in the middle of going over the plan again with getting Sierra inside Ultra.

The minute Connie left, Bessie and Ben also went outside. Ben's red Chevy was parked in the driveway. As they walked toward it, he called out, "Come on out spies, let's hit the road!"

The rest of the group started out from around the side of the house. Bessie waved to them, "Quick, you guys, before those trackers drive by again!"

Holding up her hand, "Give us a second!" Nina told Sierra, "Walk to the car like I told you!"

The blond hair, hoop earrings, and spandex shorts were gone. Wearing a self-satisfied smile, with head up with back straight, what strolled confidently toward Bessie and Ben was the very picture of today's glam-chic business woman. Now in her twenties Sierra's black hair swept smartly across her forehead and back. Strikingly light gray eyes hidden behind amber Foster Grants, she wore a close fitting charcoal gray skirt and matching blazer, with black high heels added in.

All this and more made Ben gasp, "Wow! Who is that!"

From behind her, Nina grinned back, "Some of my very

best work!"

Pinned to Sierra's left lapel was her Ultra Tech ID: Ms. Devonia Churchill; Research Analyst. Beneath was her photo to which Ravi had added his own touches to make her look older. Working like the very devil, he'd transposed the photo onto a rectangular card and plastic-sized it. Proudly handing it to Sierra, he'd promised, "It should pass through their scanners perfectly."

Nina gave it a pat. "That's for good luck, Devonia."

Sierra made a rude noise. "Not the catchiest name, do you think?"

In fact, Sierra had stayed attentive to Nina's instructions. She'd said, "When addressed, just give them *that look* over the top of your glasses, that you take no nonsense from anyone. Remember an up and coming exec like you doesn't have to!" With practice, practice, practice, she had finally seen her creation walk away as coached, as if heading for an important meeting. After a short count Nina had called out, "Hey there, miss!"

Stopping, Sierra had archly looked back over the top of her glasses. Edged with annoyance she'd replied sharply, "Whatever it is, I simply haven't the time!"

Next to the car Alex looked up and down the street. "Hurry it up, everyone, while the coast is clear!" Mimi and Caitlyn were each posted a block away in each direction. Only a moment before, his text from Caitlyn south of here had said – *go, go/geese migrating south!*

Motioning that way, Alex told Ben, "That's our tail, so we go north! Fast!"

Nina would ride in front between Ben and Sierra. Before climbing in, she reverted to her former ways by giving Sierra a heated look over who got to sit next to Ben. Then suddenly they both laughed.

Sierra said, "Go on get in! Besides, I'm the one who's being dropped off."

Relieved to see them finally getting along, Bessie jumped in back, followed by Alex. With the door barely shut, Ben took off with squealing tires to the north.

On the way to Madison, Nina called a cab company and arranged for them to pick up Sierra at an intersection a mile or so away from the Ultra complex. It would never do, of course, to be dropped off by Ben's red Chevy directly in front of the place. Meantime driving around Madison, but near to the complex. Later if Sierra got into a jam, she'd call the cab to scoop her up out front.

They were counting on lots of people being at Ultra's main building for their regular workday. This, they hoped, would make it easier for Sierra to blend in both on the ground floor and at the upper level research area – *if* she made it that far.

Ben said, "Here comes our intersection! OK, and the cab's waiting!"

As he came to a stop next to it, Bessie told Sierra, "Listen, you'll do fine! If you do need us, we're only minutes away!"

Doing her best to stay calm, Sierra said simply, "OK and good to know!"

As she got out, Nina told her, "Remember! No ducking and hiding like some timid little mouse! Act like you own the place!"

As they drove away, Sierra was motioned by the cabbie to get in. After doing so, she began, "Just get me to...!"

He finished, "I know, lady, to that Ultra place!" and then, "We're off!"

To avoid undue notice she had him drop her off a little way from the buildings main entrance. Exhaling a deep breath, she thought, Okay, let's do this! Briefcase gripped like a vise, she strode toward the entrance.

As she mounted the steps, two thirty-something men in business suits were talking animatedly while coming down.

Drawing closer, their conversation stopped the instant they saw her. With appreciative nods and wide smiles they both said "Hi!" Barely turning her head in passing, she returned a short nod and the briefest of smiles. Continuing up, she suspected they'd turn for a second look. Thinking, Oh, why not? She added more sway to her hips.

Feeling more self assured inside the lobby, Sierra walked briskly to the lobby's main desk. Several others ahead of her had just left. The receptionist, an attractive smartly dressed middle aged woman wished her, "Good morning!" Glancing at Sierra's I.D. she smiled pleasantly and pointed to the entry log. "Would you sign in, please?"

Nodding, Sierra picked up the stylus attached to the log. Feeling her heart rate jump up a notch, she started to sign her name...and went blank. Leaned forward frozen in place, she stared down at the log – OMG, what IS my name!

Feeling as if drowning, she heard the receptionist ask, "Is something wrong, Ms. Churchill?"

Clutching it like a life preserver, *Yes-yes-yes-Churchill!,* Sierra entered it as an illegible scrawl. Switching to the Destination box, she made this entry more readable. Looking up, she said as calmly as she could, "Not at all. I'm visiting the fourth level unannounced, so the R & D directors aren't expecting me." Soon as she said it she wasn't sure she should have.

Surprised, Sierra saw the receptionist's own smile widen. "They're both up there. You say you're paying them a surprise visit?" Before Sierra could dream up a response, the receptionist's voice hardened, "Just between you and me, Ms. Churchill, they surprised me too by calling me in to work from now through the weekend, which I'd made sure to have off!"

Sierra managed, "Oh, really?"

She frowned. "Yes, really, with me needing a break from this place."

Coming from someone usually so calmly, professionally put together, the remark caught Sierra by surprise. Yet she suddenly sensed a possible ally here. Sympathetically, she nodded. "If you're stuck here, that makes two of us. I also had the rest taken of this week off."

Instantly commiserating, the receptionist smiled wryly, "Life in the big city, I guess. So how can I help you?"

Winging it, Sierra smiled back, "All right, for starters I'm at a disadvantage with never having met either the director of his assistant. If you'd describe them to me, I'd at least be a step up on them."

Both now sharing conspiratorial smiles, her new ally nodded, "More than happy to! Director Moorland is middle-aged and average height. With silvery white hair and always smiling, you can't miss him. He's quite the charmer too, especially with you younger women." She looked Sierra up and down. "And believe me, he'll be very charming with you! His assistant, Dr. Manley, is a trim-looking brunette almost your height. Unable to miss her, either, *she's* the one who *never* smiles! Is that helpful enough, Ms. Churchill?"

It was, and Sierra temporarily ditched her aloof pose on behalf of her new found friend. "Just call me Devon, okay, and you've been a big help. Which of those elevators behind you should I take?"

"And I'm Bonnie. Devon, don't fool with the public ones. Take the one marked *For Employees Only*. Incidentally, security, as you probably know, is very tight on the fourth floor. Soon as you're up there, they'll immediately call me to confirm that you didn't sneak in as a spy or something." They both laughed at that. Bonnie added, "But no problem, I'll back you up!"

Next in front of the elevator marked For Employees Only, Sierra knew she'd be strictly on her own up at the fourth floor. First Ravi's stolen entry codes had to get her up there. After sliding her ID card through the sensor slot, she punched the five digit password he'd also given her. With a heart thud she saw the display light up bright yellow, reading "Password Unidentifiable! Please Re-enter!"

Looking to see no one watching, she tried again, muttering, "Come on, come on!" This time glowing orange, it read "Password Unrecognizable! Entry Denied!" Imagining, dreading what might be next – a wailing siren? – she began sliding the card once more, or tied to. Fumbling, "Argh!" she dropped it. Snatching it up, she stabbed Cancel and quickly walked away.

Completely unfamiliar with the area, Sierra strode aimlessly into the large exhibition hall at the far side of the lobby. Half hiding herself on the other side of the entry arch, her mind raced, What do I do now? Just leave? Made of tougher stuff she wasn't feeling a full blown panic attack. She knew, though, that trying to stick it out in this kind of shape would blow the whole operation. She had to stand still someplace and calm down.

Spotting an exhibit where other visitors were gathered, she walked over and joined them. Now merely another Ultra Tech employee casually taking in the exhibit, she saw atop the platform a hologram. This convincingly displayed several people conducting a practical application of Ultra's most recently developed Augmented Reality unit. Seated a few feet away from a bionic cybernetic prosthesis was a young man missing his right arm. He wore an AR helmet with trailing cables and fitted with a wrap around visor. A woman's voice narrated to the onlookers about the AR exercises being performed.

Watching quietly and hearing the woman's pleasantly modulated tones, Sierra felt her keyed-up apprehensions melting away. Relaxed and clear headed again, she critically noted the bulkiness of the AR unit and the somewhat slow reaction time in which the bionic arm responded to the young man's commands. She mused, Ultras are a bit behind what we can do!

Around her were several of her fellow UT employees. On seeing her badge, they greeted her with congenial smiles. Ally Bonnie having done the same, Sierra wondered for a moment if Ultra Tech really was the mega-corporate menace that she and her fellow plotters were making it out to be. Were they be making fools of themselves with this cloak and dagger routine? When the original stake-out at Bessie's sprang back to mind, Sierra's original resolve was greatly restored.

Marching back to the elevator, Sierra reasoned that Ravi's emulsion job might have been too heavy. So slide it through the slot more slowly? Lifting her card, while taking a deep breath, she did so...and the display message glowed green *Enter the elevator! Watch your step!* Quickly stepping inside, she punched the button for the fourth floor. Anxiously tapping a foot while waiting for the door to close, she hissed, "Come on, you idiot thing!" and the door slid shut.

Chapter 41

Sierra stepped out of the elevator on the fourth floor. Glancing both ways, she saw no one. This being an especially secure area, the people up here were probably discouraged from doing casual inter-departmental visiting. Having memorized the schematic, she turned right and headed up the corridor toward the R&D area. Here, according to what little Ravi had found, were contained Ultra's latest files pertaining to research and development, cost and accounting, and de-tails about current security and surveillance operations. The third of these was the most important. To get to it she had only to turn left at the end of this hall.

Smiling, she thought this had actually been pretty easy so far.

Rounding the far corner, Carl Trainer and Charley Girardi walked directly toward her. Their light blue jackets had Security stenciled in front. Sierra stifled a groan – OMG, it's all over! Made of sterner stuff, however, she spontaneously stayed centered in the corridor...to bluff *them* into stepping aside.

As Trainer held a muted exchange on his phone, Girardi to his left was first to see her striding purposefully toward them, Automatically shifting right made Trainer do the same. Chin up and eyes straight ahead, Sierra pointedly ignored them in passing. But her clicking heels in the silent corridor rang in her ears like gunshots.

From behind her came Girardi's voice, "Say Miss? Excuse me?" Heart racing for the umpteenth time in the past twenty minutes, she kept walking. This time louder and more insistently came, "Hey lady, if you don't mind!"

Coming to a stop, her heart sank at knowing she'd been caught! Resigned to her fate, she figured, What's the worst they can do, toss me out? Another part of her knew that in a high security place like this it could come to much more. Then Nina's coaching sprang to mind – act like you own the place and they'll back off!

Half turned, she peered back at them over the top of her glasses, Sierra's brittle tone said it all. "You're speaking to me, I presume?" Eyes level with her questioner, she arched an eyebrow. "I'm extremely busy! What do you want?"

Not menacing at all, Girardi's demeanor was merely apol-ogetic. "Sorry to bother you, ma'am, but it's our business to know everyone up here and you look new to me." Squinting at her, he added, "Problem is, I'd almost swear we've met before. Have we?" Still on his phone, Trainer threw her only a perfunctory glance. Seemingly agitated, his only interest was his phone conversation.

Girardi watched her expectantly, hoping Sierra might refresh his memory. Staying coldly silent, she let him stew. Yet, her instincts screamed for her to take off running out of sight before his recognition bell went off. Instead, she somehow replied frostily, "I doubt it! I *never* mingle with...*security* staff!"

Smile instantly gone, he growled sarcastically, "No, way up at your level I don't suppose you would. Sorry, I must've been mistaken." Exaggeratedly tipping her an imaginary hat, he turned and the two of them walked away.

As she looked after them, Girardi stopped and faced her again.

Starting to ask her something, he muttered, "Nah!" and hurried after Trainer.

Hurrying in the other direction, Sierra resisted the urge to look back. If he did the same and caught her doing that, this could be her final blunder in a morning already too full of them. Just get around that corner! she thought. When she did, as with Ravi's schematics, there was the open floor research area and office cubicles.

Trainer's office was at the opposite side of the building from Moorland's and Manley's. Paying little attention to the young woman exec they'd just met, he was upset because one of his new surveillance teams was phoning in they'd lost track of Bessie Howard and half the kids in her crowd. Frowning over it while entering their office, he had Girardi hard on his heels.

They stood across from each other at their planning table, this affording the room to spread out data charts, street maps, and various printouts. One of the bulletin boards on three of the four walls displayed 8X10 photos of Bessie Howard and some of her crowd so far. Both the Manchester and Chen girls were up there, along with the Howard girl's brother. Also were the photos Charley had hurriedly snapped of the two girls from the other night. There would be more photos later from this morning's team who counted nine of these kids at the Howard place. Trainer figured that he, Charley, and the others would be at least another few days gathering information about all nine. Manley's latest orders were to use whomever and whatever he needed and to be quick about it. To her mind this Howard project was that important and never mind the expense.

Girardi broke into his thoughts, "Carl, did that young woman exec we just met remind you of anyone?"

Trainer nodded, "Sort of. It'll come to me after a bit. Anyway, one of our teams told me they lost sight of the Howard girl and half the kids who were there."

"Aw, with two teams how'd they manage that?"

"While driving past the Howards'. one team saw the Howard boy's red Chevy in the driveway and some of that bunch with him. When our guys came back the Chevy was gone. They drove around looking for it but no dice!"

Charley said, "Yeah, when we trailed that kid he was hard to keep up with. What else?"

"The other team mainly watched the Howard's place. I told both teams to stay there until we relieve them."

"Carl, what do you think all those kids were doing? So many this early on a no school morning sounds fishy."

"Charley my friend, it wouldn't surprise me a bit if they were having a planning session. As for what?" He barked a short laugh, "It's probably about us!"

"If so, they don't know who they're foolin' with!" He returned to what mainly nagged at him. "Back to that woman in the hallway, I didn't get a good look at her I.D."

"And I was on the phone. What I did notice was something familiar about her voice and the high-handed way she acted. At the same time, there wasn't anything suspicious there, nothing that I could see."

Partnered with him all these years, Girardi knew Trainer was razor sharp with remembering people's faces, the clothes they wore, and what they said after first meeting them, which was why he headed this department and Girardi did not. "That's pretty unusual for you, though. You never forget a face."

Trainer tapped the side of his head. "It'll come to me sooner or later. It always does."

Chapter 42

Standing in the R&D entryway, Sierra saw people bustling to and fro out on the expansive floor area. Others worked within cubicles, and to the right of these were rows of computer stations, most being used. Still further right was the walled off research area with two sets of Entry-Exit doors. Ravi's layout showed the large glass-partitioned offices at the far wall that belonged to the directors.

Brief as Bonnie's description was, Sierra easily picked out Dr. Veronica Manley. Across the room with two men in white lab coats, she was of average height. Pale complexioned, with black hair tied back and wearing large frame glasses, Though thinking the Morticia-meanness tag by Bessie and Alex a bit much, Sierra could not miss Manley so angrily jabbing a finger at the two men. Not a happy camper, obviously.

Nearer to Sierra was a lean thirty-ish man of average height in a tan business suit and red tie, with startlingly white hair. Bent closely over a young and pretty computer operator, he was laughing about something...practically in her ear. As she pointedly stared straight ahead at her monitor. Sierra realized this self-styled Don Juan must be Roger Moorland.

Discouraged by her refusal of his intentions, Moorland turned away...and spied Sierra. Staring for a moment, he straightened *way* up. Giving his tie a perfunctory tug, he flashed Sierra a huge grin and quickly approached. Behind him the abandoned young woman turned and stuck out her tongue at his back. When her eyes met Sierra's, she passed on a sisterly wink and turned back to the monitor.

Stopped before Sierra, Moorland was close enough to

wrap his arms around her. A bit shorter, he straightened up, she bemusedly noted, to be taller.

Positively beaming, he smoothly greeted her, "Hello, I'm Roger Moorland, the director! Can I help you with something, Ms. ...?" Dropping his eyes to her lapel I.D., he took overly long to read it. Looking up, he finished, "Ms. Churchill, I see. I'm not familiar with the name. Are you a new addition to our team or just visiting?" As he spoke, his eyes again darted down at her chest.

Flaunting her assets to keep him off balance was one of the things she and Nina had talked about, Initial stage fright now gone, she smiled to herself – When you've got 'em, flaunt 'em! - and pulled back her shoulders. Also realizing her aloofness was lost on this guy, she openly grinned back, "Actually, Director Moorland, I certainly am on your team. You see, our group wants me to report what you are accomplishing here and at the UW Center. So far, I'd say this is very impressive!"

On cue with her emphasized flattery his smile spread wider. "Thanks for your kudos, Ms. Churchill, and yes, *my* team has had it's successes! Oh, and no point in standing on formality, so call me Roger. He added with a little laugh.

Sierra's own smile widened. "Why, how refreshing of you...Roger! And you can call me..." Pausing, she again had to recall her name. "...Devonia! Or no, make it...Devon." She had sense enough, however, to not overdo laying on the charm. She recalled Alex telling her what his mom had grudgingly admitted, that Don Juan here was also a top flight departmental manager not to be too trifled with.

And yes, dropping his own act, he became all business, if also a touch apologetic. "Devon, I'm sure your credentials are in order, otherwise you wouldn't be here. Since I'm personally unfamiliar with you, and we are high security here, do you mind if I call the main desk? Strictly a formality, of course, a but we do this with everyone." He beckoned the security guard patrolling this floor. "John, call down to tell them Ms. Churchill is up here...and so forth!"

Trained to keep a close eye on new arrivals, the security guard, Sierra saw with a heart leap, first took a long, very good look at her. Nodding to Moorland, he got on his phone. She knew that "and so forth" was her background check. Ready for this too, Ravi had downloaded into Devonia Churchill's purposely accessible file her bogus scholastic record and later research work. Handing her a hard copy, he'd grinned, "This says you're the best they've ever worked with!"

Half listening to Moorland's convivial chit chat, she nervously watched the guard. Abruptly nodding at his phone, he gave Moorland a thumbs up...and she was in! Better yet, with him back to all smiles and looking her up and down again, this 007 bit might work pretty well after all.

Driving just off one of Madison's main streets, Ben was staying within a mile or so of Ultra's complex. With Bessie and Alex in back, Nina was scrunched up against the passenger side window in front. No flirting with Ben today, she asked him instead, "What time is it? Mi-god, she's been over there forever!"

Ben said, "Three minutes later than the last time you asked. Settle down."

"Well, I can't help it!" Turning, she looked in back. "I've really been having second thoughts with all this!"

"Why?" Bessie asked.

For all her apparent self-confidence, Nina was also a self-admitted control freak, whose confidence was seldom apparent without everything neatly tied together. Having controlled nothing since dropping Sierra off, she'd projected trouble ever since. "For one thing," she retorted, "what we're doing is *illegal*, you know! And what if she's caught using a fake I.D.? Especially in Ultra's max security area she could be arrested! And we could too for putting her up to it!"

With his forefinger Alex tapped the top of her head. "We're illegal? What do you call what they're doing with Bean here and all the rest of us? I bet it amounts to undue harassment of the underaged or some such!"

"They're as illegal as we are, Neen, and Sierra knows it," Bessie said. "On our way here she talked to me about it. She told me if she does get busted and they threaten her or whatever, she could have them arrested!"

Nina nodded. "Okay, I hear that and you're right! Ben, what time is it?"

With help from Bonnie, no doubt, Sierra knew her Don Juan had just learned her background was fine. She was fairly sure, too, of already having him hooked...on her. Now more confident in her role, she began reeling him in. "Roger, our group needs to create a special document about the work you're doing. Then we'll refer to it with both current and future studies. We'll first submit it to you for *your* approval of course." Giving Moorland the final say so over her work had him smiling and nodding at that.

Having rehearsed this part with Nina and Bessie, Sierra thought this had gone OK and now? Winging it with the next part, she added more spice for him to savor. Giving him a knowing wink and placing a finger to her lips, she stage-whispered, "We'll keep the vital parts of your work our own little secret. Can we do that?"

That had him draping an arm over her shoulders. "We sure can! For starters, how about I show you around, would you like that?"

Again her dazzling smile, "Why thank you, Rodger, I'd like nothing better!" while dropping her shoulders from under his arm. Briefcase in one hand, she pulled out her phone and smiled winningly. "For my day to day recording I'm never without this. It's practically part of my body." Soon as she said it, she could've bitten her lip.

He chortled. "Ha, but not the best part I'd say!" Oblivious to her wince, he then led her off on a tour. Talking nonstop about his departmental functions, Sierra made supposedly interested sounds, "Mm-hm!...Ah yes!" and several times, "Oh my!"

Finished with winding them through the outer office cubicles he came to his own sizable one at the far side. Arm swept out, he said, "From my nerve center here I pretty much direct and manage all of our projects. But Devon..." He threw up his hands. "...keeping up with so many is really a struggle!"

She saw the truth of that through the glass partition, the two baskets of heaped folders on his deck, one of the stacks spilled on the desktop. Paperwork odds and ends also littered his computer console. The glass partition for the adjoining office was lettered "Dr. V. M. Manley – Assistant Director." Showing no untidiness at all, her polished desktop was free of all but a monitor and keyboard, her entire work space arranged neat as a pin.

For all his managerial abilities, Roger's office disarray marked him as what he said, unable to keep up and, thus, hurriedly careless with leaving Ultra's high security items out in plain sight. In glaring contrast Manley's office displayed her to be always on-task with the utmost efficiency. Including, most likely, watching over her copies of secret items like a hawk.

Inviting her into his office, he asked, "You already know about what we also do at UW's Cyber Research Center, right?"

Beside his desk she stood directly over his stacks of folders. Sneaking a sideways peak to look them over, she diverted him with small talk...or started to, "Well, Roger, we're just now..." Eyes riveted to the folder titled *R. Moorland & V. Manley ONLY!* and beneath this, *Re: Ms. Bessie Howard.* Sierra, drew a short intake of breath. Covering it with a cough, she fell back on another of Nina's teachings, that unexpected surprises on-stage would leave you tossing the script and ad libbing it. "As I was saying, we're especially interested in your results with a young person you've observed...a certain Ms. Bessie Howard?"

"That's right, just the other day, and she struck me as pretty amazing!"

His willingness to talk ceued her to draw him out, "Oh? Amazing how?"

As he described Bessie's incredible talents, Sierra suddenly realized she was running out of time. Getting into their files from here was a no go with Moorland or Manley or both hovering over her the whole time. No, she had to somehow copy this Bessie file staring her right in the face. But how! And a more unsettling thought, what if those two surveillance guys walked in? Any minute now, the one she'd tangled with last Friday could recall where he'd seen her. Then all of them, and especially Bessie, would be in deep trouble. As Moorland went on, Sierra felt for her pocketed phone. Reassured it was handy she hoped her fellow plotters were close and standing by.

Chapter 43

Tensely keeping within her lane, Bessie swerved then straightened out. Eyes fixed directly ahead, she didn't dare glance at Ben next to her. "Oops, my bad! I'll watch it!"

Her newness had Ben coaching her on a quieter side street. Poised to grab the wheel and to kick the brake pedal, he saw a stop sign approaching. His usual coolness long gone, he said, "No problem, Bean, but come to a complete stop at *this* sign!"

From Alex in back, "Do that, OK? You drifted right through the last one!"

"All right, all right you two!" she retorted, "I guess my mind was on Sierra."

From Nina, also in back and calmer by now, "Ours are too, but let's not crack up, OK? She'll call if she needs us."

Again throwing an arm over Sierra's shoulders, Moorland said, "You know, Devon, why don't we get some coffee and we can discuss this in detail?"

Again sliding out from under his arm, Sierra thought, *In your dreams, Roger dear!* Originally amused and even flattered by him coming on, she'd had enough by now. Worse, she was still racking her brain with how to get hold of that file. She pasted on a smile, "Can we take a rain check on that?"

Disappointed, he started to reply, when Manley stuck her head in the door. Completely ignoring Sierra, she asked, "Roger, could you come out here? We have a situation with one of our virtual users." Now looking at Sierra, she said frostily, "If you don't mind?"

In turn, Moorland told her, "As for that rain check, I'll

be back in a minute!" Hurrying out, his right hand brushed one of the folder stacks and knocked the top ones, including Bessie's, to the floor. "Ah, nuts!" he said and doubled back to gather them up.

Suddenly knelt down to them, Sierra held up a hand. "No, no, Roger, you go ahead with..." Pausing to catch Manley's eye, her own reply even chillier, "...the good doctor and I'll get these!"

As they went out on the floor she restacked the folders except for Bessie's. Its cover opened and her phone aimed down, she copied page one. Its typed comments and observations were interspersed with red-penned remarks, and the remaining pages were the same. Looking up, She saw Moorland and Manley already apparently wrapping it up with two others. Quickly copying the final page, she replaced the folder atop the stack. While hoping he'd not seen her do that. If he had, never mind the silly flirting, he was smart enough to instantly put it together why she was really here!

Entering, he simply said, "Sorry about that. With me, no matter how busy, there's always something they need me to do! Now where were we?"

Wanting to just get out of here, Sierra changed the subject. "Roger, you've been an enormous help today and I'll be thinking of some way to thank you. But for now I'm needed someplace else, and so..."

Again looking disappointed, Moorland said, "Oh? Well, Devon, I'm sorry you're leaving." He added a smile oozing with charm, "Can I by any chance give you a lift somewhere?"

Thinking, I'll give you credit, Roger, you never stop trying, she smiled back, "No, a cab will be picking me up. Thanks for offering, though."

After Moorland made his fond farewells, Sierra hurried down the hallway toward the elevator. Desperately praying not to bump into those two security guys again, she waited for what seemed a lifetime for the elevator door to open. Her disguise had worked once with them but she doubted it would a second time.

Stepping into the elevator, she sent a text to Nina – *send cab quick!* Next exiting through the lobby, she traded waves with Bonnie.

With no one else around, Bonnie called out. "How was your surprise visit to Lover Boy?"

Wishing they could swap Roger tales, there wasn't time. "Better than I hoped!" she called back. "Remind me to tell you about it next time!" Going out the front entrance, Sierra was exultant, while also thanking her lucky stars to be free and clear of the place. Once down the front steps, she let out a huge sigh of relief at seeing the cab coming toward her.

Chapter 44

Standing at the intersection, Sierra saw Ben driving toward her. She made a sweeping motion signaling to pick her up on the fly. Slowing way down, Ben jerked his thumb for her to jump in. Now in back, Nina already had the door open.

Tossing in her briefcase and piling in beside Nina, Sierra said, "Go, Ben! Get us out of here!" As he sped up, she threw back her head, "Woo-hoo! We did it!"

Dying to hear about it, they all fired questions at her. Waving a hand, Sierra laughed, "Give me a second to wind down! I've had a morning you won't believe!"

They let her be until out of the lot and headed toward the beltway. Then Nina was all over her. "Our Devonia act must've really worked, right? You were in there for an hour and a half!"

Removing the wig, Sierra ruffled her short blond hair. "At first it was like...a *week* and a half, but then it flew!" Handing the wig to Nina, she grinned, "Your coaching worked like a charm! And get this, Moorland even asked me out!"

Passing back her folded clothes, Nina laughed delightedly, "Told you! So here's your other things. We don't want Ms. Churchill seen riding with us."

Bessie persisted, "Whatever with that, tell us what happened!"

"Let me change first! You guys up there, eyes front!" Mo-ments later in running shoes, spandex shorts, and tank top Sierra was back to looking herself. Quickly filling them in, she dwelt on one part. "Like I said, I had a moment there with those two security guys. Other than that, it went really well."

Bessie asked, "OK, super spy, so what did you get?"

Proudly Sierra replied, "Their file on you, mainly." She added a wry smile, "So now I'll cram for my math exam on Monday!" This drew a laugh all around.

Neither Trainer nor Carney had taken a vacation since either could recall. Today with these youngsters eluding the other teams, they had to scotch any notion of taking time off. Disgruntled as they were, professionalism made them determined to catch up with and cover these kids.

With Trainer behind the wheel and approaching the Howard neighborhood, Girardi answered his cell. "Yeah, team two, what's up? Oh? OK, hold on!" He turned to his partner. "They just now spotted the Howard boy's vehicle. Al says there's a car load and they're nearing the Howard place.

"You want our team to turn around and follow them?"

"No, we'll be there shortly. Tell them to back off but to stay close."

After Girardi passed this on, Trainer continued, "When we do catch up with these kids, let's watch for awhile. If nothing else happens, we'll have our guys come back and cover for us."

Surprised, Girardi asked, "Why? Are we going someplace else?"

Trainer nodded. "We'll tell Al that so long as they don't screw up and lose 'em again, he and the other team can give us a break."

"For how long?"

"At least an hour. Or no, make it a couple."

Brightening, Girardi nodded. "With Frank's Sports Bar near here we could find out what the Packer's are planning for this week's game. What do you say?"

Trainer agreed. "I'm for that. But Charlie, we've also got

to have a talk about what all we've been doing with this Howard girl."

After a quick exchange of stories with those who'd stayed behind, Ben said, "OK, all you spies, you need me for any-thing else? Otherwise, I'm headed for football practice."

Tremendously relieved their undercover operation had gone so well, Nina felt relaxed enough to flirt with him again. "Thank you, Ben *dear*, lots and lots! We couldn't have pulled this off without you! Now we're through being driven around today." She turned to the others. "And also spying I'd say!" She smiled at Ben again. "There is one place you could take me. Would you mind dropping me off at the Mall?"

Bessie waved him off. "No-no-no, brother dear, she needs my help to finish her essay for Modern U.S. History! You go do football!"

Standing there smiling, Sierra couldn't help being pleased about Bessie declaring a strike-out for Nina with Ben. At the same time she was beginning to like the girl. With no desire to cut her legs out from under her when it came to Ben, it was enough to know she probably could if she wanted to. Although, after a morning spent being pursued by Moorland, there'd be no more pursuing today by or for anyone. No, because maintaining a grade point for a college of her choice meant finishing a research paper and turning it in next week. She practically laughed out loud at her next thought – that here they were, a jumble of high school juniors and sophomores having to take a break from combating one of the state's biggest corporations. After final thoughts were shared, they all agreed to meet up tomorrow. Saying their farewells, Sierra and Mimi headed north up the sidewalk.

Chapter 45

They were in the southbound lane and the Howard place was a block ahead on the right. From behind the wheel Trainer said, "Don't look now, but here comes your pal, Miss Smart Stuff and *her* pal!"

Looking up from his lap top, Carney saw Sierra and Mimi walking toward them. Letting out a little groan, he sank lower in the seat. He needn't have, the two girls so busily gabbing, it seemed they never gave the car so much as a glance.

Without turning to look behind them, Mimi asked Sierra low key, "Did you notice that car that went by?"

Making a rude noise, Sierra grinned. "Of course! They've done it so much lately, I'd miss them if they didn't go by."

Girardi let out a low whistle. "I've got it again, Carl, that feeling!"

"Like what?"

"We just now passed Miss Smart Mouth, I know who she reminds me of!"

"Ah. So, who is it?"

"Remember that young woman exec we bumped into this morning?"

"That... Ms. Churchill? Sure I do."

"OK, you give Miss Smart Mouth a wig, some shades, and a blazer, she'd look a lot like her!"

"Nah, in some ways Madison's not that big a town. For all we know, this Churchill woman's her aunt." Trainer wasn't sure he believed that as he said it.

Girardi laughed. "She looked too young to be anyone's aunt! But then, even if disguised our snotty blond chick could *never* pass for an Ultra exec."

His partner's remarks sinking in, Trainer was suddenly not so sure about that. "You know, Charley, we are talking a talented little group here."

"I agree, but do you think they're also feisty enough to try putting one of their own inside our work place? That would be a bit much."

As they rounded a corner, Trainer shrugged, "Don't put it past them. I bet they've already tried hacking our Ultra files. They could do that, you know. Some of these kids have been known to break into files at the Pentagon!"

Carney nodded. "My own son kidded me about pulling a stunt like that. In checking today's texts, these kids have gotten real quiet. With nothing going on for a change, nothing that I can see, you want to call it quits for the day?"

"Tell you what, call the other teams and tell them to come back here. I want them to spend the rest of the day intercepting texts that do show up. Let's head for Frank's Sports Bar over on Main Street. You buying?"

"Yep, head on over while I get back to our guys."

Once seated in a booth over a couple of beers, they only cursorily took in the sports events shown on TVs scattered throughout the place.

Again Girardi switched from the closest TV to Trainer. "You're not watching this stuff any more than me. You still stuck on this Howard-girl thing?"

Trainer pushed aside the stein he'd barely sipped. "We've been tracking her for what, a week now?"

"Yeah, it's been at least that."

"Well, Charley, it's what Manley told us before we left the building today, her plan about taking it up yet another notch."

"We're all over the Howard kid and her friends as it is.

What's she want us to do next, kidnap her?"

Trainer scowled, "I've got a bad feeling it might come to that."

"If it does, then count me out. We're getting' paid pretty well to keep a surveillance on her, but I'll have no part of any rough stuff with these kids, including Miss Smart Stuff. I've got a kid almost their age and so do you, old buddy. I hope you're not buying into any of that from our M&Ms!"

Trainer shook his head. "Moorland's not much for any of this surveillance stuff. No, it's Manley who's so intense with it and I have a hunch..." He paused. "Strangely enough, as tough as she seems, I don't think her heart's all that in it either. Which leads to my other hunch."

"Which is?"

"That someone higher up has ordered Manley to push these kids even harder, and now she's pushing us even more. Charley, this could raise the game to a much higher level and I don't like it."

Throwing up his hands, Girardi leaned back with a sigh. "OK, so what is it you think we should do?"

Trainer gave him a tight little smile. "It's time for you and me to meet Manley face to face with all this, OK?"

"Okay, Carl."

An hour later they sat before Manley at her desk. She said to Trainer, "All right, let's have it, what's obviously troubling you two!"

He said, "First off, let's talk straight, OK?"

Rather than showing them her usual sharply rigid persona, she replied slowly, hesitantly, "I see...no problem with that, It...could help us, er, to be on a better working basis."

Trainer thought this was odd, Manley suddenly seeking his support. "You say you're adding a fourth team. Why is that? And who are they?"

Finding it hard to meet his gaze, she turned away to

clear her throat, but the look she returned was unsteady. "First of all, I've been ordered to by someone higher up."

"You mean Moorland?"

Manley brusquely waved him off. "No, no, much higher than him. As for who, I...er...I really don't know. This person has spoken to me only over the phone with a voice-distortion unit." She quickly finished, "Secondly, the pair in this extra team aren't our own. All I was told is that they are with an agency that's...specially trained."

Knowing the likes of these specially trained types, Trainer narrowed his eyes. He leaned forward, "There'll be no harming any of these kids, not if I have anything to say about it!" Uninterrupted he continued, "Now you'll have four of us teams operating and using who knows how much special equipment. I'd really like to know what is so all fired important about this girl!"

Manley looked out the window for a long moment before turning back to him. "You're right in wanting to know, I'll grant you that. But please listen very closely! I can tell you only a little and you've got to keep it to yourself!" Pausing, she looked at Girardi, "And you too, er...?"

He replied, "It's Girardi, ma'am...but just call me Charley!"

Chapter 46

Edmund and Martha Wells, Ultra-Tech's owner's and majority stockholders, were still healthy and vigorous in their seventies. A U.S. Army communications officer in Vietnam prior to military withdrawal in '74, he'd come to despise everything about warfare. Later in college on the GI Bill he emerged with an electrical engineering degree. Soon caught up with the newly developing cybernetics, Wells became a man on a mission, not only building his technological business but devoting it toward entirely unwarlike uses.

Wife, Martha, from a wealthy family and of like mind with this, had been more than willing to help invest in his budding Ultra-Tech business. Busier than ever, Putting off having children, they had their only one in the mid-1990s.

Despite the wealth and success, Ed and Martha were basically down to earth. Generous with their employees, they extended not only money but a good deal of personal time to helping others. Meantime U-T had grown too vast to per-sonally manage. To exercise even a semblance of managerial control, they'd delegated overseeing responsibilities to di-visional heads and hoped for the best. In fact, Ultra Com, was second in size only to their parent corporation. Some-what out of touch anymore with U-Com's daily workings, Ed and Martha found this vexing because their only off-spring had recently taken over its management.

In the kitchen with head cook, Monica, Martha was help-ing to prep for this afternoon's meal beneath the enormous pavilion out back. Appearing at the outside entry, Ed called to his wife, "Sorry to interrupt, but you got a minute?"

Hands to her head and giving it a shake, she laughed. "Ye-gods, honey, can it wait? We're right in the middle of prepping this buffet!"

Monica patted Martha on the forearm. "We can handle it! Go see what he wants!"

A minute later the two of them were outside and well away from anyone else. Waving off one small group seeking to come over and join them, Ed told them genially but firmly, "We're having a secret powwow! You folks go have yourselves some hors' d'oeuvres or something, all right?"

There was plenty of room for others to go roaming off someplace else. Stretching away in three directions from their rambling estate were acres of lush lawn, gardens, and great shading oaks. Bounding the east side of their property was a mile-and-a-half shoreline of sand dunes and beach. Beyond lay the wide expanse of Lake Michigan.

She looked up at him with a worried smile. "Is everything all right, dear? You've been edgy about something this whole last week."

Brushing his hand over his bald pate, he squinted down at her through his old-fashioned spectacles. "Ha! I could tell it better if I could see you!" Removing the glasses, he reached down and pulled out a blue bandana he kept wadded into his pocket. "Give me a second to clean these things!" Muttering, he began rubbing at the lenses with the cloth.

Snatching the glasses away and holding them up to her eyes, she laughed. "What were you doing with that horrible rag of yours? Changing the oil in one of our cars?" Reaching into the right-side pocket of her ever present apron, she withdrew a clean tissue from the endless fund of things she stored there. Taking out a tiny bottle of eyeglass-cleaning fluid from the left pocket, she spent a moment cleaning the glasses. Holding them up again, she gave a satisfied nod and handed them back. "Honestly, you old codger, what would you do without me?"

Slipping them back on, he grinned, "You're right, I'd be lost." Then he got serious. "Listen, when was the last time you spoke to Tommy?"

She sighed. "It's been weeks since Tommy and I talked person to person. Since then I've left messages but all I get back are more messages...Sorry, I'm conferring in Milwaukee!...or...No time to chat, I'm closing a deal in Madison! I've received quite a few lately from there, by the way."

"And so?"

She held up her hands, But more and more it seems. In the latest message our daughter even mentioned doing some personal micro-managing."

He held up his own hands, "It's time for us to rein that kid in! I don't like this secret scurrying around. Who's minding the store?"

She patted his shoulder. "Tommy's surrounded by others who can. We made sure of that, remember? Now, back to our guests, we have three CEO's, two House representatives, and quite a few cyberspace engineers, plus, all their kids. Counting in neighbors here on the shore, there are forty of us. So, go mingle with our guests, while Monica and I get the meal ready. Would you do that for me? Be a dear."

"You're the chief. Once all of this is over and done, I want us to pay a visit to Madison. I'd like nothing better to visit Brice Hensley too."

"Fine with me, we're overdue for seeing him anyway."

Chapter 47

Thursday dawned sunny and warm. After dodging and plotting and escaping being caught, Bessie and her whole group were ready for a break. Including spending at least part of these next four free days to catch up on more normal activities. First agreeing to meet, they chose the park just south of the school.

Sierra, Caitlyn, and Mimi were plunked down in the grass next to a giant oak. Mimi lowered her voice, "Look, here comes that guy In my history class! Is he hot or what!"

Walking between his pals, all three played first string on the varsity football team, Going over their plays for Saturday's away game. they gave the girls eyeing them not even a passing glance.

"These guys," Mimi groused, "nothing but football and more football, and we don't matter!"

Looking after them, Caitlyn laughed and nodded her agreement. Turning to Sierra, she held up her phone, "Anyway, girl, I have an article about Ultra in mind for the Covington Journal. In case we need it, all right?"

"Good idea," Sierra said, "We probably will. Your audio is on?"

"It is," Caitlyn replied, "and so...tell us, Ms. Hutchins, did yesterday's undercover operation at Madison's Ultra Tech accomplish anything worthwhile?"

"Oh, yes, including what we were mostly after, a copy of their whole file on my cousin, Ms. Bessie Howard. And who, by the way, is still only 15!"

Caitlin spoke into her phone, "Very interesting. So why would a corporation that size have a file on someone that young in the first place?"

After another stretch of questioning and answering, Caitlyn did her wrap up. "I must say, Ms. Hutchins, you've provided us with a most astonishing expose'. Can you tell us anything else that will interest our readers?"

In all seriousness, Sierra replied, "Actually there was something else that I found pretty interesting."

Caitlyn held her phone closer to her interviewee, "Such as?"

Sierra laughed. "That Ultra's R&D director...asked me out on a date!"

Formed in a semi-circle they saw Alex, Ben, and Ravi ambling toward them across the lawn. Ravi shouted, "Ho-ho, the plotters are having a meeting!"

Following behind them were Bessie, Nina, and Lucy. Nina waved a hand, "Shush, Wiz, the whole world can hear you!"

Alex jerked his head toward the street. "Our Ultra guys already have! Anyone notice that slow moving car coming up the street? It's the second time in the last ten minutes." All heads turning to look through the chain-link fence, they saw the car approaching on the opposite side of the street.

Ben said, "Jeez, don't' stare! You're as good as telling 'em – Hey, we know you're watching us!"

Sierra smiled tightly, "Trust me, I'd say they already know that we know."

As the car passed the fence, the guy on the passenger's side was doing his best to conceal a tracking device aimed directly at them.

Looking back at them and holding high her middle finger, Sierra called out, "Have a nice day, you creeps!"

As the car suddenly sped away, everyone burst out laughing. After they settled back down, Mimi said, "Well, there goes our secret plotting. They'll be onto us more than ever."

Ben shrugged. "It would've all come out in the open

pretty soon anyway. Besides, we're better off since Sierra's spy mission yesterday. That was a huge game changer and you all know what kind I like! We're finally on offense!"

Mimi ventured, "But they're ahead with equipment, like audio receivers and zoom-in mini-cams. We can't even send texts without them tuning in."

"We were okay just now, though," Lucy said. "They couldn't have heard us very clearly." She pointed at the chain link fence and the large oaks lining the city sidewalk. "Their sonic detectors are partly blocked by the trees and the metal fence. We'll watch what we say when out in the open. We also text in code, remember?"

"Hey, here comes another of those tracker cars," Alex said.

Ravi laughed. "One right after the other? Man, they're busy today!"

Behind the wheel Trainer asked Girardi, "Did our other team catch anything from our merry little band in the park? Besides being flipped the bird?"

Girardi shook his head. "Not enough to count for anything. Their first time around they heard nothing. During the next drive-by they caught something about the whole world can hear, but that was it."

"Uh-huh, and them flipping us the bird means they've made us, which makes our job a lot tougher. I just hope Manley will appreciate that."

Over a secure phone line shortly before, Manley was told by the person she now called X that another tracker team was being added to those she already had. The strangely distorted metallic voice ended the call by telling her to keep Trainer as team-leader overall, due to the experience he already had with tracking Ms. Howard and company. Starting today, Manley would merely channel through the directives from X to this newest team. These would override her own and any that Trainer issued. Knowing he and his partner were due any minute, she washed down two Excedrin tablets with her bottle of Evian.

The call from X had badly shaken her. Disturbing enough was the electronically disguised voice giving no hint of gender, age, or emotions. Worse was being told in no uncertain terms that time was up and that, whatever it took, the Howard girl had to be put under total control of Ultra Tech,

Manley's immediate objections to this were so adamant that, to her surprise, the mysterious X had instantly backed down, reiterating that this latest plan would go into effect only should the need arise. When Manley objected just as much to this operation being considered in the first place, X again relented to assure that its purpose was merely to protect the girl.

Wondering what 'protect' meant, she was startled by her intercom. "Dr. Manley, Trainer and Girardi are here. Do you want them sent straight up?"

"Yes, right now," she replied.

Finished with his daily report, Trainer said pointedly, "That's it, Doctor. So now I'm asking you, just what is it that you want from us? I've already said we're not pulling any rough stuff with our surveillance. These are just kids, you know."

"I'm fully aware of that, but I can't help wondering if you know how vitally important it is to stay on top of them! And especially this Howard girl."

Trainer raised up his hands. "OK, I know we're just a couple of security guys you've got keeping such close tabs on her. It would help to at least tell us why." In saying this, his training had him noting Manley's appearance. Usually fastidious, her lipstick was smudged, a loose portion of pulled back hair hung down over her cheek, and her normally pale complexion was flushed.

"All right, I owe it to you to tell you a little, but you must keep this absolutely to yourselves! Am I perfectly clear?"

He nodded. "We don't carry tales, Doctor."

"All right then. This girl has special abilities that no one else has. I won't go into it at length because it would take too long. From what we do know so far, these abilities allow her to literally travel across time and space!"

With a smile of disbelief he started to say something, but she cut him off. "No, no, you wanted me to explain, so let me do it! First, I've heard all this from reliable sources..." Leaving out she'd heard it from Carmen Ricci, she went on, "and I've witnessed this myself when this girl uses a VR unit.!" As Trainer again began to interrupt, she waved him off. "No, let me finish! I...er...! Where was I?"

He shrugged. "You lost me back with...crossing time and space."

Unable to help himself, Girardi guffawed. "Go on, you see that on the Sci-Fy Channel! I'm no rocket scientist, but even I know that nobody can do that!"

Trainer added, "If they could, they'd wind up ruling the whole planet!"

She gave him a level look. "Precisely, and thank heavens the Howard girl seems totally disinclined to take it that far. My point is, gentlemen, and I'm sure you'll agree, there are those out there who definitely would!"

Though neither was sold on her traveling though space and time remark, they both knew about those types. Trainer said, "In other words we're protecting her from those you're talking about?"

She let out a weary sigh. "That's exactly right, along with the business world to consider. If our competitors somehow grabbed up Ms. Howard and used her for their own purposes, they'd dominate the world market! In any case, I think…" she struggled for the right words. "Rather, I'm sure this is what the one who's directing me thinks."

To Trainer she looked not sure at all about this. He decided to call her on it. "What if your someone also happens to be some power crazy nut? I don't mean only with business but with everything?"

Refusing to meet his eyes, Manley replied almost inaudibly, "God, let's hope not." Then more clearly, "For now it's best to assume we're just making sure that Ultra stays on top. And we'll try not to be," she forced a smile, "Evil dictators ruling the planet. Lastly, you and I," She glanced at Girardi. "And you too. with everyone else involved, stand to make an awful lot of money if we succeed. Now go do your job".

As both men rose, Trainer said, "Okay, we'll be on our way. We'll check in with you first thing in the morning."

Once they were out the door Girardi asked, "About those other two that Manley just put on, have you met 'em yet?"

"No, but from what little Manley told me, this guy and his woman partner were not brought in from around here or even from our own country."

Chapter 48

As the two girls walked home, Nina swept her phone at the clear blue sky. "Can you believe this? My weather display says it's seventy!"

Bessie was also delighted. "It's so nice, I'm ready to take you to the Mall!"

Nina beamed, "OMG, yes! I'll grab a bite and then we'll go! I mean, no lie, you want to shop instead of heading off to outer space?"

"Neen, I have a whole long weekend for that. I'm planning on it, in fact."

"Ah! Where will you be off to this time?"

"I'll tell you later. Right now I just want to get home and eat whatever I can find for lunch. I am freaking starved!"

"Me too for once. See you in a bit! Be ready to shop!"

As Nina headed up her front walk, Bessie's mental radar gave her a tug. Looking back from where they came, a car slowly approached. She thought, Uh-huh, and what else is new! To her surprise it pulled to a stop just across from her.

Seeing two men in the car, she tensed to take off running. As they just sat there looking back at her, something made her wait to see what they wanted.

Leaning across the driver, the passenger called out, "Sorry to bother you, Ms. Howard! Can you spare us few minutes?" His tone of voice and open expression held not the slightest hint of a threat.

Still tense, her reply was curt. "I've given you a week's worth already!"

He nodded. "You're right, but we've got to talk – right here out in the open!"

After a hesitation she pointed to the sidewalk bench

between her house and Nina's. "I'll wait for you over there, but stay in your car!"

Trainer waved. "That'll work! Be over there in a few!"

As the car drove up the street to turn around, Bessie glanced toward Nina's front windows to see if she was watching. Unable to tell, she walked to the bench and stood behind it to wait. Oddly, she felt no inclination to bolt for her own front door. Odder yet, she realized she wanted to see and even hear these people close up for once. Until now these two and the rest were just nameless, faceless watchers from within the dark interiors of their vehicles.

The car pulled up to the curb. Grip tightened on the back of the bench, she was greeted through the open window by the man on the passenger side. "Ms. Howard, I'm Carl Trainer and this guy next to me is my partner, Charley Girardi. We're the ones who began tracking you last week."

Still thinking it best to keep the bench between them, she said slowly, "I know that, Mr. Trainer, and who you work for. So what do you want?"

"Cutting to the chase, Ms. Howard, we're both fed up with shadowing you, snooping out texts between you and your pals, and chasing after you, the whole routine!" Girardi nodded in agreement. "I can imagine how you feel about this. So first, I apologize." He looked over at his partner. "Right Charley?"

Girardi nodded, "He's right, it is!"

Trainer asked her, "How am I doing so far, Ms. Howard?"

"Fine, you've said you're sorry," she replied, "Is there anything else?"

He nodded. "There sure is. You see, I'm in charge of all the other teams, and they all answer to me. Got me, so far?"

Her own curiosity and his openness here in broad daylight made Bessie feel far less cautious than before. "Yes, go ahead."

As he started to, there came a shout, "Hey, girlfriend, are you OK?"

She turned to see Nina hurrying toward them across her lawn. "I'm fine! Come join us!" She smiled at Trainer, "Do you mind?"

He shrugged. "Why not, with you two joined at the hip!"

Now beside Bessie, Nina gave him her over the shoulder look. "We are that, Mr. Trainer! So, what are we talking about today? Oh, and call me Nina, okay?"

He frowned, "And I'm Carl, but how do you know my last name? You doing surveillance on us?"

She grinned. "My spies always watch you, Carl!"

This drew a short laugh from Trainer. Then he got serious. "For now I've sent all of mine someplace else, but they'll be back, so listen up." As both girls nodded, he went on, "First, if what I tell you gets back to my boss I'm finished, understand?" Again they nodded. "Good, so listen close! Along with my other two teams, another one was just added, or maybe even two."

Bessie asked, "Maybe? Don't you really know?"

"Not yet, but I do know these others are not under my control. With their orders coming from above my own, I've got nothing to say about them."

Still cocky about her undercover op against Ultra, Nina began, "Don't worry, Carl dear, I'll get my own teams after them and then we'll...mph!"

Hand clamped over Nina's mouth, Bessie asked, "How bad is this for us?"

"Being mostly out of my hands, it's not good at all for you and your friends! I've heard, too, that the operatives in these other teams play very nasty at times." Seeing them watching him more closely, he made his point. "Bessie, I strongly advise you to not...I repeat, not go wandering around alone! Nina, this goes for you and your other pals too! If you've got to go anywhere at all, travel in pairs and only in public places. Finally, be extra careful with phoning and your texts, they're all being tracked."

Just then, Girardi answered his phone. After a terse reply he looked at Trainer. "We need to get out of here. All our other teams are checking in."

Trainer ended with a final look at the girls. "Be careful! Charley and I and our original teams will help however we can! Fair enough?"

Bessie answered earnestly, "More than fair and thanks."

"Glad to do it! Can you think of anything else?"

Bessie started. "No, there's nothing that...No, wait!" She held up her phone. "What if those others you spoke of do suddenly show up and then I'm in trouble?" She glanced toward Nina. "And also my friends. Do you have an emergency number where we can reach you?"

Trainer held up his phone. "These others I mentioned don't have it, but Charley and I and my other teams have our own quick response signal. If I give it to you, you've got to promise never to use it, not *ever*, except for worst case emergencies, OK?"

"I won't," Bessie said. "Can Nina here and the others have it too?"

He shook his head. "While helping you the best we can, we can only do so much. So, no, this signal is only for you." At her nod, he quickly showed her on her phone his app, a six figure code beginning with E for Emergency. As she entered it, he muttered as if to himself, "Of course, what'll keep 'er from giving it to her friend...when we're gone?"

Girardi interrupted, "C'mon, we gotta go!"

As they drove away, Bessie nodded, "We just made a couple of much needed friends here!" Holding out her phone to share Trainer's E-code, she saw Nina still watching their car drive away. Bessie tapped her shoulder. "Hey there!"

Nina faced her. "Huh? What?"

Bessie held out her phone. "Get yours out for his E-code." Seeing Nina's distracted look, she asked, "OMG, did you hear any of what he said about this?"

Raising her own phone, Nina grinned, "Of course, every bit of it. And did you notice that Trainer guy's shirt? A Pierre Cardin and he looked cute in it!"

As Girardi pointed the car toward Madison, he laughed ruefully, "Well, all those kids have to do now is leak out what we just did, and then we can kiss our jobs goodbye! You think we should start making out new resumes?"

Trainer returned the laugh. "I am, soon as we're back!" For the moment, though, he felt pretty good for a change.

Chapter 49

By the next day, Friday's mid-morning was sunny and warm. Wanting to spend it anywhere but here at his desk, Hensley frowned irritably at Meacham. "Now wait a second, Tom, you think whatever's happening in Covington is really that important for you to go over there today?"

Stopped halfway to the door Meacham nodded. "Not only me but my other sources have noticed it too, that something big is about to happen."

"Such as?"

Meacham held up two fingers. "It's the other two teams Ultra added to cover Bessie Howard. So far we've gotten bits and pieces of messages sent to them."

"By whom?"

"Not only Dr. Manley but some *unknown* person has stepped up their messaging a lot more. And especially this morning."

Hensley frowned. "So you figure to do what?"

"To go to Covington along with one of our other people as a back up."

"OK, but who for instance. Like Lieutenant, um, what's his name down the hall? Johnson?"

"No, I mean the one right out here at the desk, Lieutenant Cary."

Hensley guffawed, "And when you are over there she'll do what? Type notes or answer your phone?"

Meacham smiled back, "Actually, Lt. Johnson can do that for you right here. Meantime I'd prefer Lt. Cary covering my back."

"Her? Really?"

"Absolutely! In her free time she assists as a martial arts

instructor at Covington High. I've also seen her rank Expert over at our shooting range."

"Well, I thought I knew everything about everyone around here. By all means, bring her along." As Meacham again started to the door, Hensley added forcefully, "For both of you, though, there better not be any shooting! Under-stand?"

With two more teams added to the other two that Trainer already had, he'd heard from Al Maynard, his back-up leader in Covington, that nothing much was happening this morning with their coverage of Bessie Howard.

Trainer's instant gut reaction was, "If that's the case, how come Manley suddenly has so many of us over there?"

He told Maynard to stay put and that he and Charley would join up shortly. Kept in the dark about the two latest teams, all he'd been told by Manley was that they answered mostly to a certain Hans Gruber and partner Rovis Franc.

Finally heading to Covington with Girardi, Trainer called all four of the other teams to meet at the Mall parking lot. Arriving, he found Al Maynard and the others out of their cars.

He asked Maynard, "So where's the rest of them?"

Maynard shrugged. "After I told Gruber and that other team to meet us here, I lost contact. At first anyway."

"OK, and?" Trainer asked.

"When he did get back, he said he was trying to catch up with the other guys in their van. Said that being new to this area they kept getting lost."

Trainer scowled, "Gruber said that? Sounds pretty fishy, Al."

"And to me too. But Carl, that guy and his bunch really are on a separate page from the rest of us. To tell the truth, I don't much like any of them."

"There's no love lost between me and them either. I'll

try reaching Gruber."

Slowly circling the neighborhood where Bessie Howard lived, Gruber's dark SUV was in the lead. Three others in a white Ultra Com van were following half a block behind. Hunched over the wheel, Gruber flicked his eyes from side to side to spot their quarry. If Bessie Howard did appear outside and alone, he'd signal the van to close in. And then? He knew from past experience the five of them were more than enough to do what they'd been ordered to.

Equally watchful from the passenger side, Franc suddenly answered her phone. Listening for a moment, she replied, "Just a second!" Phone to her chest to block out the caller, she said, "This time it's Trainer. He said to meet him at the Mall. Right now!"

Gruber said, "Tell him..." or started to. Suddenly they saw the young blond woman just ahead on their right and walking south. As they drew closer, she looked back at them over her shoulder. Immediately faced forward again she simply kept walking.

When past her Franc exclaimed, "From our photos! Isn't she one of them?"

Gruber rasped, "That's her! We'll see if she's meeting any others."

A block ahead they saw three other girls in front of the Howard's house. Franc said, "Aha! That tall one is our target, the Howard girl!"

Gruber cursed, "Ach! Too many others! We'll circle around to see if they've split up. Tell the others behind us."

This lovely day was cause for high spirits with most. Bessie's were mixed, with yesterday's scary warning from Trainer so at odds with his promised support. Added to her confusion was Nina's text only a moment before – *Lu meeting us 4 Mall time!*

The thought of spending another minute holed up and hiding out inside made Bessie text – *I'm in!* Still out back she saw her staff leaning against the big oak. Minus the trinkets, these still in her day pack, it was what it was before, just a six foot bare branch. Last night she'd wondered about just tossing it or what? Hefting the staff's solid oaken weight, she thought it a shame to cut it up and stuff the pieces into a yard bag. Still carrying it, she went out front to meet Nina.

Not only Nina but Lucy was there too. Nina ignored Bes-sie's sneakers, shorts, and old T-shirt, but not the staff. "Uh-uh, for the Mall that won't work."

Only half kidding, Bessie laughed, "It might...for protection! Remember what Trainer said?"

Nina sighed. "You're right, but while shopping, no way!" Looking over at Bessie's place, she saw that Ben's car was gone. "Speaking of protection, where are the guys today?"

Luci held up her phone. "Ravi said Ben is taking him and Alex to a car lot. To check out some wheels for Alex."

Bessie said, "He needs some," and then, "Nuts! I left my phone inside. I'll get it."

"We'll wait," both girls said.

Bessie waved them off. "No, you start and I'll catch up." As they turned to cross the street, Bessie saw them wait for an SUV to pass by. After they crossed, a white van marked Ultra Com drove by. Frozen stock still, she relaxed as both vehicles kept going. Thinking, well, what do you know, real workers for once, she saw Nina and Lucy, now a ways off, motioning for her to hurry up. Laying her staff on the grass, Bessie rushed in for her phone. When back outside she saw Nina and Lucy already half a block south. Looking the other way, she saw Sierra coming toward her at a dead run.

Throwing a glance back from where she came, she reached Bessie and grabbed her arm, "Come on, we're getting you off the street! Before they're back!"

Pulled off balance, Bessie dug in her heels. "Wait a second! Before who's back? You mean?"

"None other! Not just one carfull of creeps but two of them!"

Bessie looked back over Sierra's shoulder. "I don't see them now."

"If they saw me spot them they must've turned off."

Then Bessie recalled the SUV and the van. "Argh! They went by while Nina and Lucy were out here with me!"

"So where are those two? They picked a bad time to leave you!"

"They didn't exactly. They're probably... " Stopping, Bessie saw approaching once again, but more slowly this time, the black SUV and behind that the white van. Snatching up her staff, she said, "Run for it!" while then thumbing her phone.

Chapter 50

As Girardi and the other four men waited, Trainer finally caught a short call from Gruber and Franc, and then they were gone again. He told the rest, "Rovis Franc said something about waiting for...*their* other team and then we were cut off."

Girardi groaned, "At this rate we'll be here till dinner time!"

Suddenly Trainer's phone set off its E-code. He barked, "No we won't! We're all heading over there right now!"

Pulling them out of the lot, Girardi growled, "Should we alert Manley over this? I'll bet anything it's those other characters she put on."

"Later, Charlie! Just get over to the Howard's to keep those kids safe!"

As he neared the Howard neighborhood, Meacham eyed Lt. Cary, "Glad you dressed for the occasion."

She returned a tight smile. "For a field exercise I knew my dress shoes and uniform skirt wouldn't work."

"No, but let's hope whatever is going on doesn't amount to much."

"Don't worry, Major, if it does I'm ready."

Bessie saw Sierra key her phone. "Calling for help?"

"It's a GPS my dad set up in case I'm in trouble! He'll be on his way, I hope!"

Making his weekly circuit of the town, Chief Hutchins said to patrolman Morris, "Jed, take a swing through my neighborhood, and then we'll head back."

"Gotcha, chief,' Morris said.

Just then Hutchins's phone sounded off. Yanking it from a shirt pocket and thumbing the app, he saw the GPS marking the spot by his daughter. "Right where we're headed! Step on it and I'll get us a back up!"

After passing on their left, the dark SUV had pulled over to the curb just ahead. Blocked that way, Bessie and Sierra also saw the van parked behind them.

Ben approached his neighborhood. Alex spoke up, "Sorry for cutting this short, guys. Normally I'd spend all day at the car lot, but now, uh-uh!"

Ben said, "No problem, man, neither could I!"

From Ravi in back, "My leaving Lucy by herself was stupid!"

As Ben slowed to make a turn, they saw Caitlin and Mimi walking in the same direction, but fast at nearly a jogging pace. His window down, Ravi called out, "Hey, where are you lovely ladies headed?"

Stopping, Mimi yelled back, "Sierra texted to come a running! To Bessie's!"

Caitlyn added her yell, "Give us a ride, guys, it sounds like big trouble!"

Doubled back to see what was keeping Bessie and if she was all right, what Nina and Lucy saw up ahead stopped them in their tracks. Closer to them a black SUV was parked. Several houses further on, a white van was also parked. Then seeing what was happening in between, the girls broke into a sprint.

Stepping away from their SUV, Gruber and Franc advanced slowly, like lions stalking their prey. Moving in from the other direction, four men wearing camouflage gear formed a barrier allowing no escape that way.

Side by side with Sierra between them, Bessie felt the menace from the man and woman coming inexorably toward them. Heart in her throat, while gripping her staff, having Sierra directly on her right helped a little.

Until she said, "And four more behind us, that's a problem!" As Bessie began turning to look, Sierra gripped her arm, "Just these two, they're closer!" With no time to switch, she dropped into a t-stance facing the woman. "She's mine, he's yours! Use your staff!"

Too scared to think of anything else, Bessie simply replied, like being asked to pass the butter, "Okay."

About her height but much heavier, and within arms reach, the man leered, "Come along quietly, Miss Bessie, and you won't get hurt!"

As car doors slammed nearby, Bessie heard the voices of the guys and girls in her crowd ringing out. To her right Sierra was closing with the woman attacker. Dimly aware of any of this, Bessie pointed her staff butt first at the man coming for her. When he reached for it – "Give me that!" – she yanked it back. Hand missing the grab, he stumbled off balance.

Bessie's fright vanished! Gripping the staff two-handedly she snapped, "Here it is, creep!" and punched the butt end into his nose!

"Aii!" he cried, covering it with both hands. Giving Bessie the time to bring the staff around full swing... Crack!...across the shins!

As Gruber fell yelling in pain, Franc already lay on her face. On top and applying an arm lock, Sierra snapped, "Don't want it broken? Hold still!"

Above her a woman's voice said, "Very nice take down! Top of the class as always!"

Looking up, Sierra saw Lt. Cary, her assistant martial arts instructor, smiling down at her. Sierra grinned back,

"Glad to hear that! Coming from you!"

Struggling to no avail, Rovis Franc gasped, "Whoever you are, get her off me!"

As Sierra got up, Cary told her, "I've got this." Staring cold-eyed at Franc, now sitting up, she flashed her I.D. "U.S. Army Intelligence! And you stay put!"

Groaning with one hand to his face and the other rubbing his shins, Gruber was hunched over. Through blurred teary eyes he beheld Bessie, her auburn hair in disarray and blue eyes blazing. Gripping her staff like a baseball bat, she smiled humorlessly, "So, ready for more!?"

He threw up both hands. "No, no! No more!"

That broke Bessie's spell. Staff lowered, she realized Major Meacham stood next to her. Taking in Gruber and Franc, he laughed, "I'd say these two needed our protection more than you did!"

Seeing the happenings farther away, she smiled wryly, "You know, Major, I'd say the same for the other four!"

Having obviously been gang tackled, one was stretched out face down in the grass. Straddling him and bending up an arm in back, Nina was explaining to him what a jerk he was. Knees pinning down his other arm and hands keeping his head still, Lucy nodded in agreement. Face up on his back with Mimi and Caitlin on top, and Ravi above him with fist drawn back, this second guy had also given up. Flattened by Ben, standing over him, a third one was still down and clearing his head. The last one, after making a run for it back to the van, was slung over the shoulder of Alex, now carrying him back to rejoin his pals.

Two squad cars with lights flashing were also parked, as Chief Hutchins and three other cops were already sorting out the attackers. Having just arrived ahead of their other two teams, Trainer and Girardi got out of their car and quickly joined the sizable crowd on the lawn.

Chapter 51

During the next few days, Bessie, Ben and the others explained to their parents about all of this. Or most of it, Sierra's undercover work with Ultra and the hacking of their files by Ravi, everyone agreed, were secrets to be kept. Meantime, Hans Gruber and Rovis Franc remained in the custody of the U.S. Army's intelligence section in Madison. The little that Meacham was allowed to pass on to Bessie was that neither had been informed about the purpose for their mission. Further questioning revealed they knew even less about the mysterious someone behind all of this. When questioned about directing her stakeouts of Bessie in the first place. Dr. Veronica Manley openly disclosed she had assumed "X" to be an upper level U-T executive wishing to remain anonymous.

Also according to Meacham, the use of vans belonging to the subsidiary, Ultra Com, made the trail lead up to the corporation's owners, Ed and Martha Wells. This included their daughter, Thomasina Wells (or Tommy), who headed Ultra Com. Beyond this, General Hensley, a close friend of the Wells family, would say no more.

Searching for evidence, reporter Caitlin had finished what she gleefully called her expose' article. To Bessie and her crowd this amounted to reaching an impasse or truce. By Friday, however, this last had her wanting *nothing else* but getting back to her virtual space travels.

Out in front of her place that evening, Bessie said goodbye to Nina. They'd not reconnect until she finished tomorrow's modeling stint in Madison. Both Lucy and Ravi would be busy with cyber activities, and Ben would be playing tomorrow's out of town game. Also leaving early, her folks were off to Green Bay a day early to meet with friends. Then they'd all be at Lambeau Field on Sunday for the noonday game. The anticipation of having the house to herself, increased her excitement about her virtual trip. Nothing would stop her from tomorrow's virtual trip!

Starting inside, she saw Alex hurrying toward her and waving. Having just sent him a text saying where she was going tomorrow, she braced herself for what was coming next.

A moment later he stared at her. "Come on, Bean, Pluto is too far!"

Bessie didn't want to hear any of this. "No, you come on! Besides, you've been to Mars, and so what"

Looking away, he scratched his head, then turned back. "It's closer and we're already *on* Mars too. Ok, with Rovers and all, but we are there!"

"And so what? You know as well as me with quantum physics, that three and a half billion miles versus forty million means...nothing!" Then she smirked, "No, wait, you're worried I'll get hurt?" Taking a cue from Nina, she gushed, "I'm so glad you care!"

He sighed, "I do! And you *are* so nuts! Just sayin'."

Smile tightening, she wagged a finger. "Uh-huh, so now I'm crazy?"

Turning away, he muttered, "You wag that finger just like your mom."

At this stage in her life that finally did it! After scrambling her hair, "Argh!", she grabbed his arm. "You look at me!"

Facing her, he gulped, "Whoa!"

Red hair in wild disarray and blue eyes flashing, she looked like Sheena; Warrior Queen of the Death Star in his favorite video game. Though dearly loving her mom, she grated, "I'm nothing like her!" Catching herself jabbing the finger, she quick made a fist.

He answered lamely, "Sorry I said it."

"And stop calling me crazy! That really hurts!"

"Jeez, I never meant it."

"You thought it, which is worse!" Then his hangdog look made her quickly relent, "You're forgiven." Then she reiterated, "I've told you I *am* going to the stars! And trust me, the distance to Pluto is nothing compared to how far those are. But it's a good start, and next I'm going to..."

Apology forgotten he cut her off. "No you won't! Without traveling faster than light, you'll never..."

Hands on hips she interrupted right back, "No, no, no, you and I have already done FTL! It took us only seconds to reach Mars, so your speed limit with light is...Poof! Gone! And after my folks leave tomorrow I will too, for Pluto!"

Knowing the battle was lost and turning toward home, he gave her an over the shoulder laugh, "You do that, Bean old girl! When back in town give this Earthling a call, hey?"

Chapter 52

Watching her parents about to leave, Bessie impatiently bounced a knee. Seeing Connie beckon from the SUV, she groaned, OMG, now what!

Connie called out, "Honey, the replacement mat is still in the box! Before going online, put it down to keep the chair from poking holes in my new carpet, OK? Love you! Bye-bye!"

Bessie forced a smile, "Love you too, Mom!"

About to get in behind the wheel, Rob yelled, "Last chance, Bess! With the Pack playing the Bears tomorrow it's their biggest game yet!"

"Love to, Dad, but this astronomy project is my biggest yet!" Thinking, True enough, she made a thumbs up, " Have fun, go Pack!"

As they pulled away, she dashed inside. Heading to the bedroom and pulling off the T-shirt. On entering she kicked off the sneakers and shorts. Within minutes she wore her ski jacket over a heavy sweater, Spandex pants were tucked into her hiking boots, and ski gloves were stuffed into the jacket pockets. Looking ready to hit the slopes, Wisconsin's hottest November on record allowed none of that.

Her reflection in the mirror returned a wry smile. Instead of all this, I'd be just as safe in a string bikini! The smile faded when, again, her virtual destination sprung to mind. Of all the stats she had gathered about...Pluto, the scariest was its average surface temperature, a minus-375 degrees F.! Though protecting her perfectly on the other trips, if her quantum bubble failed on this one, she'd be a flash frozen popsicle no matter what she wore. An inner voice cautioned, Maybe just forget it? A louder one over ruled, Don't talk yourself out of it! Do it!

Snatching up her box of special items, she hustled to the computer room and placed it on the console. Next she rolled in the castor chair from the hall. Seating herself, she pulled the items from the box and laid them within easy reach on the console, her LED flashlight, dad's claw hammer, mom's metal container with snap-on lid, and the thermometer borrowed from the patio. Seeing the staff, with trinkets attached. leaning against the wall, she told it smilingly, "We're sticking together from now on!"

Scooting the chair closer to the console, she pulled her hair back and slipped on Maxwell. Next she inserted into the player NASA's DVD of New Horizon's 2015 fly-by of Pluto. Suddenly remembering the mat she had left in the hall, she saw a perfect square of prints in the new carpet. Well nuts, she thought, I'll need to brush them out later.

The DVD intro made her wait for Pluto to appear. Drumming fingertips on the console, she recalled last night's parting remark from Alex. Still fuming about it, she thought, Call you? Count on it, smart guy!

To lighten up she clicked an old favorite song on her phone and laid it on the console. With Eleanor Molina's "You Rev Me Up" doing nicely, Bessie dropped the visor. Instantly, she felt the oddly pleasant sensation of the quantum-flux energy bubble forming around her. When the parade of freeze frames disappeared a moment later, Pluto's cratered surface rushed straight at her! Slowing the descent and soon hovering over the surface, she looked past her boots at the landing spot. Satisfied, she touched down.

Gripping the chair, Bessie gasped, "Oh-my-god!" From directly in front of her a vast ice field of muted yellows and grays stretched off to the flanks of a large crater. Beyond towered a row of narrow peaks like monstrous jagged teeth. A few feet to her to her right lay a low rock outcrop. Above her the mighty Orion Spur of the Milky Way swept its majestic arch of countless brilliant points across the jet black sky. The brightest one, low on the horizon was the Sun.

To Bessie the stark desolation all around beneath the vastness of starry sky looked utterly beautiful and terrifying. A chill running through her, she reflexively hugged herself. An instant thermometer check showed it steady at 70 degrees, With it confirmed the temperature and the air she breathed were those of the computer room, she relaxed to take it all in.

Then it struck her that something was odd. Out here so far from the Sun why wasn't it almost total darkness? She blinked, Its light enough to read by! Her flashlight staying where it was, she wondered, "What's causing this brightness?" Swiveling the chair around, she found herself being moon-bathed by Pluto's largest satellite, Charon. Though a third the size of Earth's Moon, but only 12,000 miles away, it covered sixty-four times as much sky!

Eyes wide, she sang out, "It has rings!" Their great ellipse rose to a sharp apex above Charon and plunged from sight at the far side. While nowhere the size of Saturn's she thought them wondrous all the same. Abruptly she realized, My camera! Gloves dropped in her lap, she photographed everything she saw.

Purely delighted, she leaned back to ask herself for the umpteenth time, How am I doing this? Here, Mars, and wherever else I want! I'm so amazing!

Feeling unstoppable, Bessie was ready to collect a sample. She saw plenty of ice within arm's reach. Spectroscopic analysis by NASA's fly-by indicated that the largest percentage of Pluto's frozen surface was nitrogen, a highly stable gas.

She frowned, "What if it's frozen methane?" Once inside her 70-degree bubble it could quickly sublimate into something like sewer gas. Her chemistry class taught this wasn't all it might do. Tremendously volatile, a static spark could make it explode, the very last thing she wanted inside this bubble. Whereas, super cold, bare rock was harmless. She hoped.

Still deciding, she found herself swaying in time to her music. Picturing Nina and the others seeing her out here, billions of miles from nowhere, and moving to music only she could hear, Bessie broke out laughing.

While enjoying the moment, her science-based discipline reminded, Are you getting that sample or what! Slapping her chair arms, she said, "Let's do this!" Gloves back on she asked the outcrop with more cheery confidence than she felt, "Like to come home with me?" It seemed simple, grab the sample and seconds later be home free.

Hammer in her right hand and open container in the left she pushed the chair forward and leaned down to strike the rock. Conforming to her shape, the bubble's top lowered toward her back but pushed its bottom past the carpeting...into Pluto's surface. The terrible deep cold instantly penetrated her waffled soles!

"My god!" she cried and kicked backward. The bubble obediently regained its original shape.

Stunned, she dropped the hammer and container, tore off her gloves, and fumbled with icy fingers to undo her boots. Rubbing her chilled hands and stocking feet, she knew they'd soon be warmed by the temperature of the computer room. Drawing no comfort whatever from that, her self confidence of only a moment ago vanished. She'd have all she could do to snatch this sample and split!

After tugging the gloves and boots back on, she took a deep breath and looked down, Okay, rock, ready or not! Eyes locked on it she pushed forward and swung the hammer as fast and hard as she could. A chip bounced off the container to land near her boot. Afraid to grab it even while gloved she gasped, "Argh!" and kicked backward.

With one of Sierra's martial arts screams, "Yee-ahhh!" she lunged again and struck! A piece arced into the container, *klink!* Cheeks, feet, and hands going numb, she shot out her heels and pushed back. Unfeeling fingers all but useless she chinned the container's lid shut and let it fall. Making mewing sounds like a stepped-on cat, she ripped the gloves off with her teeth. Unlacing her boots being hopeless she left them on.

Still stubbornly sticking it out before heading home, she gasped out white puffs, with hands clamped beneath armpits and stamping her feet. Thawing began stinging like needles, making her teary-eyed. Brushing them away, she looked down at the container and scolded through chattering teeth, "You're mean but I gotcha!" Next seeing her thermometer plummeted to its lowest at sixty below, came her last thought, Get out of here!

Unthinkingly, uncaringly, Bessie flung her headband and sprang up. Nearly tripping over the chair, she grabbed the backrest. Steadying herself, while gulping in the room's blessedly warm air, she pressed hands to her head to keep it from spinning. Through blurred vision and only half comprehending, she saw upside down on the carpet the container covered with ice crystals and a vaporous cloud curling up from the lid.

Her jacket hit the floor and a moment of struggling with her boots left them there too. Somehow remembering her phone, she grabbed it from the console and jammed it into her waistband. Stumbling into the kitchen and her whole body shivering, she saw the wall thermometer registering its usual 70 degrees. This made her shiver even more. Scrunching her toes and rubbing goose bumps on her arms, she paced in circles as her first clear thought took hold, that the temperature differential between where she'd just been and this cozy kitchen was 450 degrees!

Blowing warm breath on her hands, she heard her inner

voice half-heartedly try praising her for the heroic venture. A newly wiser one sneered, Idiot, you nearly killed yourself!

Startled by her phone's chime she yanked it out. The Caller ID said it was Alex. Bursting to tell him what she'd been through, all her tightened throat allowed was "Awwk!"

He asked, "Bean? Is that you?"

Too shaken to care about the Bean thing she tried again but only squawked.

He laughed, "You okay? You sound like the duck in that commercial!"

After coughing to clear her throat, her words rolled out like spilled marbles. "Alex, I nearly froze to death! Pluto was so terribly cold that…!"

"Whoa! Start over!"

Hand to her forehead she tried again. "I couldn't believe it! While chipping this rock my fingers and toes nearly froze solid! I…!"

Without the jocularity this time he cut in, "Jeez, Bessie, were you hurt?"

"No! I mean, yes! God, I don't know what I mean!" She took another breath. "Are you free?"

"After what you said last night I was coming over anyway to see if you were okay. You feel like going for a walk or something?"

This sounded like the best idea in the world. Better, the sound of his voice was literally bringing her back to Earth. "Give me a few minutes and I'll meet you out front!"

"Okay, Bessie, I'll be out the door pretty quick!"

After clicking off her next thought was too familiar. Because of not coming with on this trip would he even get it? What a nightmare it was? No matter, she wanted to go somewhere, anywhere with him right now and pour it out! Set to charge out the door she saw herself in the hallway mirror. Any of her hair not tumbled around her shoulders stuck out in all directions. Looking down, she wore only one sock half off. Holding out a handful of bedraggled hair, she grimaced, No way can I meet him like this!

Leaving her winter clothes where she climbed out of them, she pulled on her shorts. Wiggling bare feet into sneakers, she did a quick hair brushing. Even so, the dresser mirror said she still looked a wreck. But, no time to waste!

Ducking into the computer room for the rock sample, she saw the container's ice crystals were melted. Gloved, she gingerly lifted it while poised to pitch it if need be. There wasn't. Container held in front of her, she went out the front door.

An "Ahhh!" escaped while feeling on bare arms and face the wonderful warmth of the sun so near and so large again. Going down the steps, she saw Alex coming toward her. She felt another kind of warmth as it occurred to her, He called me Bessie for once!

Chapter 53

They sat on a park bench, the container between them and her rock thawed enough to hold bare handed. Having ex-amined it with his hand lens, Alex had just finished looking at the photos on her phone's screen.

Bessie expectantly raised an eyebrow. "I know they're dark but the close-ups are way more detailed than from NASA's flyby." Jabbing a finger, she added, "Mine prove I was there so don't go thinking I'm crazy, all right?"

He laughed. "I stopped doing that after your first two trips!" Then he waggled the phone, "You won't like what I say about these. Just don't go yelling at me, OK?"

"I won't, I promise! Say it!"

"Well, NASA can enhance their photos to look just as close. People could say you ripped these off from theirs."

She yelled at him, "You jerk! I'd never do that!"

Alex held up his hands. "Whoa, Bean, I know that!" He missed her growl at the nickname.

Dismissing the stab of irritation, she brushed away a stray lock. "So forget the photos, what about my rock?"

Unwilling to face any more glares he first quickly made a longer inspection of it. Lowering the lens, he shrugged, "The dark patches mean it's carbonaceous." Next the grin, "I'm also brilliant with mineralogy, you know."

Not quite ready to banter as always, she said dryly, "I'm sure you'll get the Nobel." She made an impatient beckoning motion. "Come on, what else? After traveling three billion miles to get it, I'd really like to know!"

"There's some green, probably olivine like you'd find near a volcano."

"No, on Pluto I didn't see those where I was."

"And none are erupting in Wisconsin so it's not from here. My little home lab wouldn't prove it's from Pluto and neither would the school's."

Bessie threw up her hands. "Whether with photos or even samples I can't prove any of this!" Slumped down, she muttered, "It's no use."

Ignoring her poor little me act, Alex said, "You know what really bugs me about your virtual trips?"

She said testily, "What?"

"None of us can do them like you, not even with the same kind of headset. It's like you're some kind of mutant." Seeing her eyes narrow, he held up a hand. "Hold it! What about when you hit your head and they scanned it at the hospital? You said they found what…besides empty space?"

Sitting here safe and warm beneath the noonday sun, she found it impossible to stay angry with him. Her own sense of humor on the rebound, she leaned toward him and said straight-faced, "You're right, it was empty. Or…no wait, they did find…" letting him hang for a second, she finished, "Old Star Wars DVDs!"

They both laughed. Then he began, "Seriously, Bean! You said they found…" Seeing her flinch, he shook his head, "You don't like it when I call you that."

"I hate it. Anyway, Dr. Myers said I had only a mild concussion. But he did say my brain structure was different from that of anyone else."

Alex waited for her to go on. She shook her head. "I'll say more someday, but this one's too beautiful to talk about…my brain."

"Fine, because that's not your problem."

"What is?"

"It shows when talking about your trips. It's that none of us come with. OK, except for me and Sierra, only once each is all."

She nodded. "I have felt pretty lonely with that."

"So why not take me along some more?"

Her deep blue eyes regarded him thoughtfully. After several long breaths he began to fidget. She clapped her hands and he jumped!

"Gotcha!" she grinned. "We both know that you *are* a believer, right?"

"Correct!"

"Good, then you can come along again."

"Fantastic! When?"

"Not today, but we will though, next chance."

For Bessie, no longer alone with all this, with someone she liked very much in on it with her felt...just lovely. No longer the least unhinged over Pluto, she asked, "Let's do something, you want to?"

He nodded. "OK but forget space travel. With the Badger game ready to start let's watch it!" Hardly anyone followed the Pack or the Badgers as avidly as he did. The shy guy thing set aside for the moment, he added a lecherous grin, "So, baby, your place or mine?"

As they stood she whacked his arm. "In your dreams, *baby*, I'm under orders! But let's meet at your's, all right?"

"OK, and if mom makes her killer dip, we'll have us a Badgers party!"

"Sounds good!" She reached for the rock he still held. "I'll take that." Dropping it into the container, she snapped shut the lid. "And that's that!"

Seeing her disappointment, he said, "Look, you did go there! And also to Mars, which I oughta know! And don't forget, you went on the time travels!"

As they started off she nodded, "All right but you know what?"

"No, what?"

Bessie laughed. "I still haven't a shred of evidence to prove...I went *anywhere!*"

Epilogue

On a world beneath the starry blackness billions of miles away lay a panorama of rounded hills strewn with craters. An ice field swept up to the flanks of a larger one and out in the plain where the ice began was a low rock outcrop. In a layer of dust at the base of the outcrop were distinct waffle-sole heel marks and a set of a chair's castor imprints arranged in perfect squares.

ABOUT THE AUTHOR

Gratefully retired from the normal workaday world of earning a living, Gib Check, with the totally essential guidance from wife Ruthie, is a full-time (and even lower paid) freelance writer. Living on a lake in central Wisconsin, Gib and Ruthie fill their days hiking, biking, kayaking, and with inviting themselves to visit (sometimes unannounced) family members from coast to coast.

Made in the USA
Monee, IL
19 February 2021